THE HAUNTING LIFE OF HUNTLIEGH PARRISH

A STANDALONE

THE GHOST HUNTER CHRONICLES

STEPHANIE ANNE

Spellbound
Publications

TO THOSE HAUNTED BY THEIR OWN GHOSTS

AND TO MY SISTER, EMILY. THANK YOU FOR BEING ONE OF THE FIRST READERS OF THIS BOOK.

TO KLAUS, YOUR SUPPORT MEANT SO MUCH. I WISH I GOT TO SAY GOODBYE.

1

GHOST SERIAL KILLERS

"IT'S NO BIG DEAL," I SAY, CLIMBING over the creaking chain-link fence that separates the road from the national forest. "How hard can it be?"

On the other end of the phone, my aunt, Josephine, makes a clicking sound of disapproval, but her tone is less *disapproving parent* and more *I did this to myself* when she speaks.

"*It's a school night,*" she says, which is a lie. It's a Tuesday and still summer break.

I roll my eyes and lower my backpack to the ground. The old highway—which has been closed since a string of random murders basically destroyed the town—is pitch black. The full moon is hidden by a thick layer of clouds that glare down at me, threatening rain, rain, and hell, probably more rain.

I just have to beat it before it beats me.

Or, you know, before the spirits find me.

A shiver of anticipation—and maybe a little fear—crawls over me. I pull a flashlight from my bag and flick it on. The beam of light does fuck-all against the looming darkness of Bradford National Forest, where ghostly-murderers like to hide and lure unsuspecting victims. Too bad for them; I'm neither unsuspecting nor a victim.

I'm the resident ghost Hunter just trying to do her job.

When nothing jumps out and scares me, I lower the flashlight and shoulder my bag once more. The car is probably ten feet from me, but a chain link fence and some police tape block the way. I might be agile, but Aunt J and I do *not* spend enough time at the gym to be *that* good at jumping obstacles...or running fast.

Which means I need to outsmart the spirits.

My breath fogs in front of me as I wander down the overgrown patch of grass beside the road, my back hunched and hands shoved into the pockets of my oversized jacket. In my ear, Aunt J murmurs random facts about the spirit we hunt—even though we know all but nothing about them.

"Hitchhiker...suicide...murder..."

I clear my throat and cast a wary glance into the darkness of the forest. "Anything you wanna tell me?" I ask. There are no other cars for miles and no other souls out here other than me. Plus, it's probably cold enough to freeze the balls of the devil, so I'm not too worried about the living.

"Hmm?" Aunt Josephine laughs to herself, and I hear the fluttering of paper over the Bluetooth earpiece. *"Oh, it's nothing."*

"What's nothing?" I ask. In my pockets, my hands tremble slightly.

When we moved to this town, there hadn't been any talk of hunting or solving a big bad mystery. But our first day here, there was a murder, and two local kids went missing definitely made for a fun little exercise and training experience.

Authorities haven't been able to figure it out; the local

gossipers like to whisper about a witch living in the national forest, picking off any who cross her path. Aunt J and I know the truth: it's a ghost who thrives off pain and is probably stuck in a loop, returning to what they did when they were alive. In this case, it probably means they were a killer before, and they're enjoying the freedom of doing it when dead. Only problem is Aunt Josephine and I can't *find* anything about a local killer. Not even a troubled person taking their life or being murdered themselves on this stretch of road. Violent deaths are notorious for creating violent spirits; it wasn't a stretch to assume the spirit had been born out of death itself.

I release a heavy breath and run a hand through my now tangled, damp hair. In my ear, Aunt J also sighs. *"I still have nothing, Hunt. No sudden deaths, no suicides, no murders."*

I groan softly and come to a stop by the car. "Then we might be looking in the wrong direction."

"I thought the same thing," Aunt J says, tapping on her keyboard. *"So, I looked into missing persons..."*

"Anyone who might fit the bill?" I ask, preparing to climb the chain link fence between me and the promise of warmth. Aunt J remains quiet for a few moments, silence buzzing across the earpiece. "Aunt Josephine?" I prompt.

"Hmm? Oh, sorry!" she laughs again, and I roll my eyes. In the distance, something catches my eye: a white streak against the black night. The hairs on the back of my neck stand, and the little voice in my head starts screaming that *something isn't right*.

Finally, Aunt J continues, *"Yes, there are two that date back to a year before these haunting's first appeared. It was twenty years ago, but..."* The line goes silent for a moment.

I swallow thickly, eyes trained on the place I saw the white streak. "And?"

"And... The dates fit. Looks like neither of these fellows are really what they look like."

"Aunt Josephine, could you please hurry? I think something's here." Out of the corner of my eye, I notice another blur of white speed past me. My chest tightens as my heart thunders erratically. "I think it's here."

"Okay, okay." Aunt J flicks through more pages loudly; probably the files she'd snatched from the local library. *"A year before these disappearances started happening, there were similar occurrences in the next county over. People wound up missing along a stretch of road out by the highway and their bodies were later found mauled in a cabin in the national forest by that same road. Although they managed to find the bodies, they were never able to convict someone of the murders.*

"They did, however, have two suspects under observation. Howard Kenley and Brock Lester. Neither were charged, but police and detectives were sure one of them was the killer."

"What happened to them?" I back up towards the car as she continues to flick through the pages, humming to herself as she does.

"Well, both Howard Kenley and Brock Lester up and disappeared. To this day, authorities have no idea what happened to them, except for the fact that witnesses claim to have seen both men cross the county line. But they're most likely dead, which is why we're seeing a repeat of their crimes here."

And if it is them, then I can expect a whole lot of bodies. Maybe more spirits waiting to come through but are too afraid because of the negative energy Howard Kenley and Brock Lester are conjuring—and consuming.

The blur of white passes me again, this time along the line of the forest. As a sensitive—or Empath—I can feel the energy of spirits, their emotions when they died, and unlike any normal person, I can see and hear them, too. Which makes my job so much easier.

Both my parents and Aunt J have the ability, though Aunt J

goes one step further and has visions: past, present, and future. She's like a psychic medium and that alone takes a toll on her mental health.

"Any chance they were working together?" I ask, if only to break the silence.

Aunt Josephine clears her throat. *"It's plausible, but police never put two and two together apparently. Turns out, Mr. Kenley was Brock's teacher. Extracurricular activities?"*

I groan. "That's just creepy. Who takes their student on a killing spree?"

"The Hannibal Lecturer?" Aunt J laughs at her own joke, but I remain quiet. *"Anything?"*

"I—" Trees rustle to my left, and I come to a complete stand still, fear pulsing through my veins. *Toughen up,* I chide myself, *you've done this a thousand times before. Go in. Exterminate the threat. Get out.*

"Time to get out of there." Aunt J's voice changes, a hint of fear entering the bright and cheery tone I love. *"I'm getting a bad feeling, and you shouldn't be out there alone."*

"Look, I'm already here," I say, turning in a slow circle. "I might as well finish the job."

"Huntliegh Megan Parrish," Aunt J says through static, *"when I tell you—"*

The phone cuts off, leaving a buzz in my ear. Swearing, I end the call and keep an eye out for anything floating or about to kill me.

Ghosts (or spirits, if you want to be technical; Aunt J used to call them Lost Souls) can't be seen by just anyone. It comes with either a gift or a curse, depending on your viewpoint on such paranormal occurrences. Sometimes you *are* cursed with it though—but I don't know how that happens, and when it does, it's rare. Like, seeing the devil rare.

The flashlight flickers in my hand, a warning from the spirit. I look down just as another flash of white passes me, this time closer. The trauma of death—sour and foggy with decay—washes over me. The voice in the back of my head tells me to run, that maybe I'm not ready for what I'm about to face.

Swallowing back that fear, I turn to face the forest. From where I stand in the darkness, illuminated only by the soft glow of the moon, I see only shadowy shapes. But there, hidden amongst the copses of trees, hiding behind an overgrown shrub, are eyes. I meet the stare evenly, though my breath hitches in my throat. The pair of eyes blink away a moment later, but he's here, and he's been watching me.

I try dialling Aunt J again. It takes a moment, but the call connects.

"*Oh, thank goodness,*" she breathes. "*Are you alright?*"

"Yeah, I'm fine. I think they're playing with the connection, so I have to be quick." The lull in activity makes my stomach churn. "Is there a photograph of the guys?" I take a step back towards the main road and check it twice—no lurking white figure, no eyes. The feeling in my gut tells me that these aren't coincidences, or a trick of the eye.

I bet Aunt J would know straight away.

I'm nowhere near as powerful as Aunt J. I have inklings, dreams, and I can see what others can't. But Aunt Josephine…there is more to her power than even she lets on. It led us here, whether she likes to admit it or not.

"*No,*" she replies, and I hear the frustration in her voice as she huffs and falls back in her squeaky chair. "*No photos were ever released.*"

"Did you look online?" I ask as the flash of white passes me, even closer. Now they're toying with me.

Bastards.

I hear her grumble under her breath. Her long nails click across the keyboard of her laptop. "*Nope. Well, there's a grainy picture from the yearbook, but you can barely make out either of them. Mr. Kenley has glasses and is bald. Brock might be blond? In this photo, he's wearing a white basketball jersey."*

I take one final step back from the forest and swallow down the rising fear. The white figure makes sense now; it's Brock in his white basketball uniform. The glassy stare from within the forest could definitely be Kenley, though I can't be sure.

Looking back to where I left Aunt Josephine's car, and then to the shadowed curve of the road, I wonder just how far I can run before either try to grab me. Can I make it to the gas station hidden beyond the bend before they make me—or the car—disappear?

Spirits with enough dark energy can do a lot of damage, and if Brock and Kenley were bad alive...then dead they are much, much worse.

"You still there?" Aunt J asks, her voice buzzing in my ear. The Bluetooth earpiece whines, and I press down on one of the buttons.

"Yeah. I'm still here." But the whining continues until it's screeching in my ear. I pull the piece out and look down at it in my hand. Faintly, I hear Aunt Josephine warning me, but I already know they're here.

I can't bring myself to turn around as a hand caresses my back, while someone else's fingers run through my hair. Closing my eyes, I calm my breathing, even though my chest hurts with every icy breath and thump of my heart.

I've done this a thousand times, I repeat, over and over again, until the words are nothing more than a hum inside my head.

"Aren't you pretty," a voice whispers. I feel their energy, shapeless and dark, full of rage and...something else. I swallow. *"So, so, pretty."* The hand in my hair tightens until they're tugging it.

Quickly, I try pulling away, but the hands keep me in place.

"*Scared?*" the spirit asks. Their face comes into focus in front of me. Bald and glasses. Unassuming. Kenley.

The other says, "*We won't hurt you...much.*" I know this one is Brock—the way he touches me reminds me of the slimy boys from my last school. His voice is higher, too, like he didn't finish puberty before committing murder.

The air around us chills significantly; my breath almost freezes in front of me as goose-bumps line my arms. I shiver, but it's not from the cold.

One of my hands is still in my pocket, and I quickly shove the Bluetooth into the other. My left hand grips at a spirit bag tightly, and under my breath, I chant:

'Hear me spirits as I speak,

Be trapped in fire,

Within the veil,

And hold until you are no more.'

Neither Kenley nor Brock understand what I'm doing; they never do, and they don't care. I'm merely another body to add to their mass grave.

That's their fault, though.

I drop the spirit bag from my pocket and watch it fall to the asphalt. Flames erupt from the maroon velvet, reaching the two spirits beside me.

The flames circle them and form a barrier they can't cross. The fire is seen only by me, a kind of magic in a way. Developed by psychics back when spirits roamed more freely, Hunters like myself and Aunt J have been using the technique ever since. It's a much easier method to trap a spirit until you can burn their vessel—body, a token, a lock of hair—but it isn't always this easy, and I'm not always so lucky.

With a shaky hand, I reach for the Bluetooth and hook it back into my ear.

"You still there, Aunt Josephine?" I ask, voice barely a

whisper.

I hear a sigh of relief from her end. "*Yes. I am. Did you do it?*"

Looking back down to the spirit bag, I smile at the unburnt surface. For now, it's working and will keep my new friends locked in place. But if it burns, they're free...and I die. Horribly. "It's done."

On the other end, Aunt J grunts. "*Give me a minute and I'll find the bodies. Get ready.*"

The other end goes dead silent, and I back away from the two spirits planning my death, leaving the spirit bag on the road with them. That should keep them trapped long enough for me to burn whatever is left of them and make sure they never come back.

Aunt J is still quiet, even as I bounce impatiently, the pack on my back growing heavier and heavier. I play with the torch and swing it around the forest like I'll see their skeletons just hanging out inside one of the bushes.

I shudder. Around me, I feel *them*.

Dozens of spirits, trapped between the world of the living and the Afterlife. They aren't violent, not like Kenley and Brock. These were normal people, people who just happened to be caught in the maniacal cycle that belonged to a couple of serial killers.

"*Got it. Same MO as the other town. Cabin in the woods. Head straight into the forest, and you'll find an overgrown path. That'll lead you straight to the cabin. It's small, but you'll find a trap door that'll lead you into a cellar. Boom. Bodies everywhere.*"

I grimace as I settle the pack more comfortably on my back. "Can I torch the whole cellar?"

Aunt Josephine snorts. "*You can try.*"

The whole place will *stink*. How have the authorities not found it? I voice my question, though I don't expect an answer.

"*It could be a lot of dark, spiritual activity,*" Aunt J responds, startling me. "*Enough of it can keep anyone away. Police likely didn't know where to look and probably knew they shouldn't go near the cabin. Human instinct."*

"Too bad that's not something either of us listen to," I mutter, entering the trees. Like Aunt Josephine said, there's a decrepit trail that leads straight to a small, moss-and-ivy covered Hunter's cabin maybe fifteen minutes from the road. The door has pretty much been forced into place with a large bolt, but the hinges are rusted so bad that one level kick to the frame sends it tumbling.

I take in the space: an old refrigerator with a broken door hangs open to my right, the contents spilling out with a nasty smell. My nose crinkles, but it isn't the worst thing I've had to deal with. The countertops are covered in a thick film, and something dark and sticky lines the sink. I step further into the cabin and the door slams behind me.

"Great," I mutter. Not much time now before my two murderous friends break free then.

There are no other doors in the cabin, though from the outside it didn't look very big, so I start searching for a cellar door.

I push at a rotting couch and trip over the corner of something heavy. Taking a step back, I survey what has to be the makeshift living room.

An old rug, left askew covers the floor in front of an old fireplace. A table has been pushed aside, and the only other thing covering it had been the couch. I hadn't noticed it at first because the colour has been washed out so much it blends into the dark ground.

Bingo.

I kick it aside and locate the door that leads into the cellar. Before opening it, I make sure to wrap my scarf around my face several times. My eyes are watering before I even open the trap door.

Bodies are piled within, some huddled together, others splayed on the floor. Men, women, and children. Trapped below.

And in the centre, leaning against one another, is Kenley with his wide glasses and Brock in his white jersey.

Rocking back, I pull the pack from my back and open it. I unscrew the lid of the salt and throw it into the cellar, squinting to make sure I hit all of the bodies. Because of the purity of salt, it aids in helping the spirit cross over and leave this world—or so Aunt J says. Mix it with holy water and a little bit of lavender to dispel the negative energy, then burn, you remove any unwanted spirits.

The space is small, but there are so many corpses in there; over the course of at least twenty years, there should be well over thirty bodies based on the reports, maybe more from what I can see. Some are piled on top of others, and I'm sure if I go inside, I'll find more.

Swallowing thickly, I pour the gasoline over as much as I can. I just have to hope the two in the middle burn quickly. Once they're released, the others are free.

I take pleasure in lighting the match and dropping it onto Kenley's smug face. The fire catches him, this time real, and as it spreads onto Brock and his white jersey, I can't help but smile.

I close the hatch to the cellar as the bodies burn, the sound of cracking bones carrying on the chilling breeze. Eventually the night warms with the fire as it carries the stench of burning flesh. I make sure to wipe away any trace that I was here.

On the way back to the car, I make an anonymous call into the local fire department, alerting them to the fire in the national forest, and that they should hurry.

"*Is it all done?*" Aunt Josephine asks as I set the Bluetooth piece back into my ear. She knows it's done; she probably watched me do it in a vision.

But I reply either way. "Yeah, they're gone."

"*The other bodies were in there?*"

I sigh. Slowly, the feeling of spirits seem to disappear into the next world; the afterlife, netherworld, whatever it's called. As I start the car and it churns to life, I hear the sound of sirens in the distance. In the rear-view mirror, smoke crests the tree line and looms over the forest, the soft glow of fire illuminating the sky.

"Yeah, they were in there."

"Good, now, come home. I don't need you getting into trouble. Again."

I laugh and pull away from the curb.

But my stomach churns, and the smile on my face drops. Lining either side of the road, spirits watch. Their energy is something else, something I don't understand. They disappear, one after another.

It feels like a warning, one I shouldn't ignore.

2

VISIONS OF FORT CALDWELL

AUNT JOSEPHINE LOVES TO COOK, especially when she's stressed or after a particularly bad hunt.

I, on the other hand, think last night went *splendidly*.

She disagrees, but at least the town can rest easy.

As Aunt J pours over the stove, I swing my legs back and forth. Sitting on the island in our small, temporary kitchen is probably her least favourite habit of mine, but it's a hard one to kick. When I was younger, Mom and Dad would sit me on any uncluttered counter so I could listen to what happened on their hunts, or learn about their dull day jobs.

I close my eyes and breathe in. Whatever Aunt J is making, it smells *amazing*. There are hints of cinnamon, nutmeg, and apple. Though that might be her newest shampoo.

Whenever Aunt J leaves to scope out a new town, I always

have a stocked fridge and freezer of her food, from soups to pastas, and anything else she conjures up. If she wasn't a psychic, she could have been a chef.

"Are you excited for school to start?" she asks, not looking up from her pot. "Only a couple of weeks now!"

I roll my eyes. "Not at all."

This forces Aunt J to look up and frown. Or well, pout. She isn't old by any means; she's actually four years younger than my mom, and when I'd been born, Aunt Josephine had only just left high school. If anyone were to guess, they'd assume Aunt J is in her twenties, and I would think so too; she keeps herself looking proper, no matter what type of day she's having. Sometimes, I wish I looked more like her and Mom; they both had the same wild red hair and milky skin, whereas Dad had dark hair and eyes, like me. In another life, they would have been model's, Dad would joke.

I shrug and pick at the rips in my jeans. "I just don't see the point..." I trail off and shake my head.

Aunt J sighs. A common argument in our household. But there's something off in the way she looks at me. Her eyes narrow and she reaches up to touch my temple. A jolt shudders through my body, rushing down my spine. My eyes close involuntarily as a vision pounds in my head.

A house, four storeys high. An iron fence blocks us off. Ivy and vines crawl along the stone exterior. A plaque by the door.

And a man. His clothing is old, fashion from over two-hundred years ago. He tips his hat at me, while the other reaches into the pocket of his vest and pulls out a watch...

I pull away and suck in a breath as Aunt Josephine takes a step back. Her eyes are still closed, pain contorting her face.

"What the hell was that?" I breathe, voice shaking. My fingers are cold as I shove them between my thighs, trying to stop them from shaking.

Aunt J releases a breath. "That's not good."

My brows furrow as I watch her. I remain on the counter as she goes about finishing dinner—like it never happened.

I shake my head, a frustrated sigh leaving my lips. "What's not good?"

"That."

I sigh loudly in irritation as she opens drawers and pulls out forks and serving spoons. Totally normal, like I didn't just have a vision against my will.

"I'm going away for a couple of days to check that out." She doesn't look up at me as she starts serving the food. "I'll send for you if I need to."

Shaking my head, I jump from the counter. "What do you mean? What was *that*?" My stomach turns over again as her eyes meet mine.

"Morcant. That was Josiah Morcant."

My breath is knocked from my lungs. I stumble back, bile rising in my throat. *Josiah Morcant.* He was an evil son of a bitch. So bad, he manages to kill anyone and everyone who gets trapped inside his monstrous house. He's been on my hit list for four years.

"The vision was a warning. Yesterday I had one too." I look up and meet her stare as she leans against the bench. She purses her lips, and the colour drains from her face. I've never seen her so rattled.

I run my hands through my hair, pulling at the tangles. I can feel Aunt Josephine's eyes on me as I do, but there's no comfort in that. My breath hitches in my throat, and my heartbeat escalates. "What does it mean?"

She sighs. I don't hear her move, but she's suddenly in front of me, her face close to mine. "Breathe, Huntliegh. Breathe."

But I can't. My chest is so *tight*. My lungs are being crushed. Every breath screams.

"Breathe." *I can't.*

My mind flashes to a fight in our old house, a phone call and all our clocks stopping. Police officers and search parties.

Aunt J wraps an arm around my shoulders and leads me towards the couch where she sits me down. She kneels in front of me.

"Head between your knees," she says softly. I do as I'm told, my hands still in my hair. I tug at the roots anxiously.

Josiah Morcant. His name rings through my head. I've done a lot to keep him out, and yet he walks back in and *ruins* me. How can I face him if I can't deal with a stupid vision? If I can't even hear his name without freaking out? I took down two serial killer spirits last night and survived.

As my airways clear, my breathing returns to normal. Aunt J has her hands on my back, rubbing soothing circles and patterns up and down my spine. "The vision could mean nothing," she murmurs, voice soft and steady.

I snort and try to sit up. "When has it ever meant 'nothing'?"

Lips still pursed, she looks away. "I know... Let me look into it first, okay?"

"Do you think it's that dangerous?" Aunt Josephine usually leaves me behind to scope out possible threats, though she's never gone for more than a couple of days. The Morcant case is a state over, a couple of hours away.

She offers me a smile. "Of course I do. He is a very powerful creature."

I frown but don't argue, because she's right. He's probably *the* most dangerous spirit in all of Northern America. "When will you leave?"

"Soon. I know you're ready to get out of here."

The job is done. There's no reason to be sticking around; I have no friends besides the Hunters we infrequently encountered—which aren't many. Even though I'm enrolled in school here, I barely went, and the new school year is coming. It's time to move on.

The doorbell ringing pulls us out of our thoughts, and Aunt J and I exchange looks. "Expecting anyone?" I ask, looking back towards the old timber door.

Her eyes widen. "Shoot!" Standing, Aunt J rushes around the living room, throwing old magazines into a still unpacked, yet open, box behind the couch. "Darren and Tate. I knew they were going to be passing through town!"

I smile broadly and stand from the couch, heading towards the door. Darren and Tate Clifton are two other Hunters, like Aunt J and me, though they mainly stick to Canada while we traipse around America—probably because Aunt J hates paperwork and doesn't want to get a passport. Occasionally, though, they pass through the states and drop in whenever they get the chance. They were friends of my parents, and from a young age, I've considered them family.

"Hey, kiddo!" Darren says, large arms reaching out for a hug. I can't help giddiness that rushes through me at the sight of them. He encloses me in a tight bear hug and pats me on the back. His husband, Tate, hugs me too, but he's a little softer.

"How have you been?" I ask, leading them into the living room. From the kitchen, Aunt Josephine shouts 'hello'. Within moments, our loungeroom looks cleaner; the boxes are somehow hidden, all the pillows fluffed, and there are glasses on the coffee table.

Tate shrugs, but Darren gives me a broad smile. "We just finished a job up north, and it just so happens to be our anniversary. Thought we might come visit."

"Good thing you did. I just finished the job here and Aunt J is going to check out another one."

Both men smile, but it doesn't reach their eyes. They have reservations about me going on this path, but...they understand, because they're doing the same thing for the same reasons.

Like most Hunters, *something* catapulted them into the life. For Darren and me, it was family; Mom and Dad were in the life, though how they'd gotten there has always been a secret they promised to tell me when I was older—though, of course, that never happened. And Aunt J won't budge. Tate's story is a little more complicated, and one he doesn't share lightly.

Tate clears his throat and sits back, closing his eyes. "We're going to take a break for a couple of weeks, we think. Maybe go on that honeymoon we never did." He stretches his long legs out in front of him; as a child, I always thought of him as spider-like with his long dark limbs and thin fingers that were always quick to grab me when I passed, always finding that ticklish spot on my stomach.

Darren smiles sheepishly. He's laid back compared to Tate, and you can see it his face; he always has a smile on his lips, and his dark eyes always sparkle. He looks scarier, though, with a long black beard and a biker-bandana around his head—usually red, sometimes blue—and he's bulky, especially around the middle. He looks like he could kill you, but he's actually just a cinnamon roll.

Tate opens one dark eye to look at his husband. "That was my fault," Darren confesses. "There was a case, really bad. I took off to try and stop the Big Bad and ended up needing this lovely fellow to come save my stupid ass."

I laugh with him as Aunt Josephine carries a tray of stew and sweet tea into the living room, offering bowls to the guys before handing one to me.

The four of us sit in silence for a couple of moments, each entangled in our own thoughts. Mine stray to the vision, to Morcant and what it all means. For years, I've been training, taking on the lesser spirits so that I can eventually face him. Taking down Brock and Kenley in this town was only a small step towards taking down my own Big Bad—the nightmare that got me into hunting in the first place. We all have one, a Big Bad that got us into the life. I was always going to follow my parents, but Morcant and what he did...that had given me a new perspective. Now, I fight to take him down, no matter what. Is the vision telling me I'm ready? Or is it a warning?

"We have...news," Tate says, eyes passing over me. "About Morcant."

My back stiffens, and beside me, Aunt J sits back. "I'm going there," she says.

"It's looking bad, Jo," Tate replies, pursing his lips. "Do you remember Carol and Skye?"

Aunt J nods, but I have no idea who they're referring to. "They went in, didn't they?" she asks. "They were taken?"

This time, Darren nods. "Before them, it was Roderick Pine."

I know that name; he had been at our house once, back in Salem. When Mom and Dad were still here. I remember his voice, so loud and angry. I'd spent the entire encounter with Aunt J in her bedroom as she'd combed my hair in an attempt to distract me from the story of death he'd been telling my parents.

I look to Aunt J as she nods and breathes a sigh. "He's gone too, I take it."

"Three in the last year." Darren and Tate share a look. "Not to mention the two regular folk," Darren adds.

Regular folk usually refers to anyone who doesn't know about our world. Morcant has two hundred year's worth of spirits in his grasp—there's no telling what he'll do with them all.

"Hunt?" I blink and meet Aunt J's worried stare. "Can you start cleaning up? So I can talk to the guys?"

That's code for: we're about to talk about Hunter things that you're too young to know about, so eavesdrop from the kitchen. Maybe she'll tell me later, but there's a look in her eyes that tells me otherwise.

There's no use in arguing—because the last time I did that, I ended up exiled to my room like a child.

Sighing, I take the bowls into the kitchen. They wait until they hear the water of the kitchen tap turn on before continuing their little discussion in hushed tones.

"You shouldn't go there," Tate murmurs.

Aunt J sighs. "You know what she's like. If I don't go there first, she'll just go herself. And *will* get herself killed."

"Then take her far away, at least for a little while." Darren's voice gets lower so I can't hear anything.

I spend the rest of the conversation in the kitchen, waiting for something to happen, but they stay quiet for the remainder of their time here.

Tate and Darren leave at nine, heading out to their black truck with waves and full bellies. Even as they climb into their cars, I see the worry marring their faces. The smile even vanishes from Darren's lips.

I swallow thickly and close the door, leaning back against the cool timber.

"You okay, hon?" Aunt J asks. She crosses her arms and leans against the door beside me.

Sighing, I shake my head. "I just…" I don't know what to say. "I need to go to bed. Last night just wore me out." *Not to mention the fact that Morcant is now sending me visions, and there are three Hunters now missing—likely taken by that demonic son of a bitch.*

She nods in understanding, but there's worry in her eyes as she watches me go up the stairs of our old townhouse. There's always worry in her eyes these days.

The old brass doorknob is cold as I turn it, the door whining on old hinges. Darkness consumes the room, but I push through it straight to the bed.

Kicking off my boots, I pull the duvet over me, not bothering to change out of my clothes. I can't stop my thoughts from dissecting everything that happened tonight; Morcant's vision, the arrival of Tate and Darren, the revelation of the three missing Hunters along with two more likely dead *regular folk.*

How much longer is Morcant going to be allowed to reign? How many more deaths?

How is he going to be stopped?

~ ~ ~

Packing my room only takes a couple of hours; and helping Aunt J with the rest of the house takes a couple of days, even though she disappears for half of it to check out the small town of Fort Caldwell.

There is a simplistic easiness to throwing cutlery and kitchenware into a box while listening to a true crime podcast. It's monotonous, and simple, a routine I know all too well.

The podcast stops abruptly as my phone rings. I look down and see a picture of Aunt J flooding the screen. "Hey, what's up?"

"Hey, hon, I'm in Fort Caldwell. Passed Morcant's house on the way here and let me tell you, that place gives me the chills."

"Everything gives you the chills," I reply, shoving a pan into a box.

Fort Caldwell, home to the scariest mo-fo I've ever heard of.

She sighs from the other end. *"I don't like the feel of this town. I had two visions when I entered the town! Two! I'm lucky if I even have two a week!"*

Frowning, I stop and perch on the edge of the bench. "Were they about him?"

I'm not sure if it's fear or something else that makes me ask. Over the last four years, I've been training, hunting, and fighting my way through some pretty bad spirits. Kenley and Brock aren't even the worst of the batch. I've been locked in abandoned hospitals with crazy doctors, houses with old ladies who didn't like being disturbed, caught in forests with enough bad energy to take out an entire block of New York, but I've done the job.

Morcant shouldn't be any different.

He is though. The thought comes bitterly, leaving a sour taste in my mouth as my thoughts go back to what Darren and Tate said about the three missing Hunters.

What can an almost-eighteen-year-old do that a couple of seasoned Hunters can't?

"*No,*" she replies, the sound jarring. "*The visions had nothing to do with him. There's a woman in white trapped out on a back road near the lake, and a ghoul terrorising an old house that's been foreclosed.*"

"Wait. That's just in town?"

Aunt J is silent for several moments, though I can hear the bustling of people on the other end. Her voice is quiet when she replies, "*Yes! And then I watched them both just disappear. Not in the way of moving on, but like they were sucked away. There's something dark in this town. I'm trying to figure out what it is. I called Tate and Darren and asked if they'd help you move the stuff here. I found a place, but...*"

"But what?" She's quiet for a couple more moments, and I realise she isn't even listening to me anymore; on the other end, I hear the voice of an older woman talking to Aunt J, welcoming her to the town. Despite the definite dark energy surrounding that Ford Caldwell, she sounds...normal.

"*I'm going to stay here and get a start on figuring out what this town is hiding. Like I said, Tate and Darren are going to help us move. Not like they're happy about it but, oh well. I have to go, hon. Going to organise the house and such. I've already called about our move and I'm enrolling you in the local high school. It seems nice.*"

I groan. "We'll only be there for a couple of months at the most. Is it really worth going through all the trouble of enrolment?"

Aunt J tsks and hangs up without a reply, leaving me in silence while the podcast starts up again.

School. The bane of my existence. Should have been Morcant, but I hate the process of high school even more. The only reason I go is because my parents wanted it—and my grandfather, an imposing man who never seems to be happy and always has something to complain about, makes sure Aunt J knows that as soon as I slip, he's swooping in to take me away. *To a better life*, he says.

I shake my head. Harrison Parrish has no problem taking me all the way back to Australia with him, if it means taking me away from Aunt J and spirits. So, I go to keep him quiet and happy. It relieves some of Aunt J's stress. But it's all around just boring.

My thoughts snag on Aunt J's visions. *A woman in white and a ghoul.* In the same town?

I go back to packing, mechanically wrapping breakables and playing Tetris to make sure they all fit. The podcast drones on, but I'm not longer listening; at some point it went from serial killers in the US to what kind of wine should you drink while watching True Crime documentaries on *Netflix*.

I think of that stupid town. From what I know, Fort Caldwell is small and unassuming, despite the high number of missing persons. That has everything to do Morcant, but having more than one angered spirit in the same town causing trouble? You only hear about that in cities, where the dead are feeding off the energy of the living. I've been to Fort Caldwell once, when my parents went missing. From the outside, it looks completely ordinary.

For a spirit to come back and cause these kinds of hauntings...they were completely messed up in life, or their death was violent enough for them to stick around. Kenley and Brock were examples of both; in life they were killers, and they probably died slowly, which contributed to their after-death activities. It was enough to trap them in this state of half-death, and it allowed them to grow strong enough to continue what they'd started.

A woman in white is usually a product of both; a violent occurrence causes her to do something drastic—like kill her spouse, children, or parents—and then commit suicide. She'll haunt wherever she killed herself and recreate what happened to her before the time of her death.

A ghoul, though...they're parasites, creatures born from sorrow and destruction. Usually children, but sometimes—rarely—they're old people, forgotten by those around them, lost. Ghouls usually just torment the living into leaving their home, and sometimes kill if they grow annoyed.

I took one out when I was fourteen; an old man surprisingly, who killed a woman and her husband because they wanted to knock down a wall.

Is Morcant responsible for the creation of these dark spirits? And for them just...disappearing, as Aunt J said?

Sighing, I become more vigorous in throwing kitchenware into boxes.

I shake my head. Finished with the kitchen, I walk into the living room and stop.

Aunt Josephine and I hadn't given much thought into decorating; we hung a couple of photos on the wall, and there was a tapestry full of protective symbols behind a bookshelf. Nothing too special, though, because we could never stay in just one place. I'd joked about getting a caravan once, selling all our furniture and living on the road.

But everything we own...it used to belong to my parents. So, we lug it around.

I turn in a slow circle, lips pursed, as I take in all the photos; they're relatively normal looking, except for the ones with me in them. They've been flipped upside down, and my eyes are scratched out. A bad omen, Aunt J would say, but I know it's a warning.

A warning against me going to Fort Caldwell.

I pull the photos from the walls and the shelves and stack them into boxes. I take a moment before releasing a heavy breath. "I'll find you, Morcant," I whisper. "I'll find you, and I *will* free my parents. I promise."

3

LIFE AFTER DEATH

DARREN AND TATE HELP ME pack the rest of our belongings into the back of a U-haul. Their incessant muttering and little jabs about going to Fort Caldwell give me the impression that they aren't happy about our next move.

Part of me doesn't blame them. Fort Caldwell is *bad*. My parents died there, claimed by Morcant. And there were probably dozens of Hunters like us who were taken by the devil himself.

"Are you sure you're ready for this?" Tate asks quietly as we carry boxes out to the truck.

I shrug. "Are any of us ever ready?"

Tate shakes his head and turns to me. "Cut the crap, Hunt. This is your revenge. You've been working your way up to this for years, but are you really sure you're ready to take him on?"

Biting my lip, I look away. His stare burns as it rests on me. "I don't know. Honestly, I think I have to be."

"Why's that?"

Finally, I meet his gaze. Inside, Darren calls out for help, but we don't move. "That town has high spirit activity; Aunt Josephine says it's off the charts. Women in white, ghouls... Something is going on, and Morcant is at the centre of it all. If I can take him out, it all stops."

Tate's lips form a straight, thin line, and his eyes darken. "I know of five different Hunters who have gone in and never gone out; two were your parents, Hunt." I flinch, and his eyes soften. "Please, don't add yourself to the list. Because I'm afraid Darren and Josephine will jump straight on it and get themselves killed too. Play this game carefully. Morcant has had hundreds of years of experience, and you're seventeen years old with a whole future ahead of you. Don't blow it."

I bite down on my lip as tears burn my eyes. He sounds too much like Harrison, telling me I shouldn't waste my life fighting ghosts.

"Fine," I mutter, but my heart isn't in it. My stomach churns as he watches me for a moment, and I remember that he didn't come into this life the same way. It's something he doesn't talk about often, because I know it hurts. But he loves Darren more than anything, and he...he's stuck, like the rest of us.

How am I supposed to turn my back on this world?

Tate looks as if he isn't sure if he believes me, but he sighs and goes back inside to help Darren, who shouts again for help.

The sun beats down on us, warm and peaceful, but a chill dances through the air. Summer is coming to an end, allowing autumn to burrow in and take hold. Leaves have already started to change, red and orange, a spectacular array of colour that clashes with the bright hues of greens and blues that make summer almost bearable.

Taking in a shuddering breath, I cross my arms and let the sun warm my face. Our street is quiet, almost like it's caught in time. Most are probably out drinking in the final days of summer break before school goes back.

It takes Tate, Darren, and I a day to completely pack the U-Haul and their truck. Aunt Josephine has thankfully taken her car with her, which means I'm free to drive myself to Fort Caldwell.

Mom's old Honda NT650 bike.

It's a 1988 model and the first thing I ever learnt how to ride. Mom used to take me out with her on it; I would clutch onto her for dear life while she'd laugh and take me on little adventures. Dad used to call it a death trap—he'd always been the brain of their little operation, finding the jobs and researching, like Aunt J does for me. Mom was the brute force that finished the job.

When they were taken by Morcant, Aunt J didn't have the heart to sell the bike, despite Darren and Tate constantly telling her to. So, when I'd gotten my motorcycle license, I'd made the obvious choice to ride the bike instead of getting a car, so that it wouldn't be collecting dust—because it's what Mom would have wanted.

I make my way to the garage, where it sits with a dark grey leather cover protecting it. It's all sleek silver and black, with new tires and lights. It needs a long ride; since the last move, it's been cooped up in the garage save for a couple of *special* rides, though they haven't been spectacular.

It deserves some love.

"You sure you want to ride that all the way to Montana?" Tate ask, dark brows raised as he enters the garage through the kitchen door.

I nod excitedly. "I barely got to ride it while we were here, and I'd rather be riding this than be stuck in the car. Anyways, Seattle isn't *that* far from Fort Caldwell."

Throwing a leg over, I strap the helmet over my head. My heart thumps wildly in my chest, a rush of eagerness washing over me.

"Okay, we'll lead the way kiddo," Darren calls, jumping into the U-Haul truck. He revs the engine, and the truck bursts to life.

Tate is a little warier as he gets into their black truck. "If anything happens, we can make room and put the bike in the truck, alright?"

I give him a thumbs up as I start the engine. I listen to it purr, feel it jolt beneath me as the smell of gas fills the garage.

I don't give Morcant or this town a second thought as I peel out of the driveway and onto the street. I bask in the freedom, and the thrill of open road. The guys are behind me, and yet I feel absolutely alone out here.

Twelve hours and seven hundred and thirty-five miles of road between me and my revenge.

~ ~ ~

Forest surrounds the entire town, though I'm not surprised. Fort Caldwell backs up onto a large lake that looks like a looming death threat. Around the lake are several large houses and cabins, and small boats are out on the water, probably enjoying the final days of summer before autumn—which I can already feel—finally sets in. People jump off a dock and swim despite the chilly air and dark sky.

I shudder and turn towards the town. We drive down the main road slowly. After about six hours, I'd thrown the bike into the back of the U-Haul and settled into the cab seat with headphones.

It gives me a chance to take in the long stretch of storefronts; there are at least three cafés, two bakeries, a bank and post office side by side, more restaurants spread down the road and other little storefronts that look like boutiques and other novelty shops. Wedged between a real estate agency and a news company looks like a store dedicated to the Morcant Estate. It's weird, but anyone interested in the supernatural or seasonal tourists would eat it up.

It makes my spine tingle and stomach flip, so I force myself to look away.

It's Friday, so there are plenty of people wandering the streets; there's a lot of teenagers making up the populace in the cafes, sitting around laptops or talking over coffee. The further we go, the more I realise just how little I'll fit in here.

We pass the local sheriff station, and my heart plummets into my stomach. I can almost see myself sitting out on the front bench as Aunt J and my grandfather go inside to talk to the officers about my parents' disappearance. I didn't cry at all that day; I'd wanted to be brave.

A police officer—a kind, older woman with dark skin and pretty eyes—had tried to comfort me.

I tear my eyes away from it as we turn down a residential road.

Aunt J waits outside of what would be our temporary home. The cookie-cutter townhouse is at the beginning of a line of them—around six in total, all with their own porches and garages. The exterior has three windows I can see and no front yard. They're wedged between basic suburban homes.

Darren parks the U-Haul out front with an elated grin as Aunt J waits for us. When he jumps out, she envelopes him in a tight hug before rushing to where I sit.

"Oh, I missed you!" she says, crushing me to her body.

I laugh, the exhaustion and churning in my stomach disappearing as her arms tighten around me. "Missed you too, Aunt J."

Tate clears his throat as he steps out of the black truck, which he parks behind us. "Do I get a hug?" he asks, grinning wide despite his own fatigue.

Aunt Josephine makes a show of rolling her eyes, but she goes over and hugs him just as tightly. "Thank you for helping and bringing her here," she says.

Tate replies too quietly for me to catch what he says.

A cold wind picks up and brushes over me. Above us, the sky looks just about ready to break and dampen all our good moods. I look away and take in the neighbourhood. Darren had refused to take us past the Morcant House, though I have a feeling I know where it is. His property would be surrounded by the old town, further in the forest. It's blocked off and abandoned, apparently watched by security twenty-four-seven. When we'd entered into town, I'd noticed a security car pass us.

"Do you like the house?" Aunt J asks, pulling me out of my thoughts. She wraps her arm around my shoulder again. I smile and look up at the building.

I shrug. "It's nice, I guess."

Her smile falters, but she tightens her grip on me. "We're going to be here for a while, Huntliegh. You might as well get used to it."

I sigh. "Yeah, I know, but—"

"No 'buts'," she interjects, grinning. "Anyway, we happen to be living right next door to a lovely young man who has already offered to help you on your first day of school."

My eyes widen, and I turn to her. "You're joking, right?"

"Nope!" She just grins, like what she did was totally okay.

"You can't just make friends for me!"

Darren snorts, and Tate laughs more than I think I've ever heard before. "Sure she can, kiddo," Darren teases, ruffling my hair. I swat his hand away.

"No," I say, emphasising the word as I step away from her. "She can't."

Aunt J grins wider before changing the subject entirely. "Why don't we start getting the furniture inside? Before it starts raining? Hunt, there's a space in the garage for the bike. Just push it up in front of the car."

Rolling my eyes, I help Darren open the back of the U-Haul. Together, we get the bike out, and I push it to the back of the garage. I throw the cover over it with a heavy sigh.

'Til next time, I think, frowning. I didn't think I'd hate this town any more than I already do. Autumn and winter are going to *suck* if it's always crappy weather.

Tate and Darren start with the furniture while Aunt J lugs boxes into the house. I pull my Hunter-pack over my shoulder, then my duffel. My school bag is wedged between Tate's bag and Darren's pack—full of brand-new books.

"Need a hand?"

I jump, dropping my duffle.

The guy behind me watches as I pick it up; dark, tousled hair falls over his forehead, and his hazel eyes shine as they meet mine. He's at least a head taller than me, with broad shoulders and a sweater that looks *a little* too tight around his arms.

"Hey, I'm Weston." He holds out a hand for me to shake. It takes me a moment to register, but I shake it, blinking in confusion. "I live next door. You must be Huntliegh?"

I nod, dumbfounded. "Yeah, I, uh, I am."

He grins, and his face lights up. I hate to admit it, but he's cute. In a *small-town boy* kind of way. In a *I'm not going to be here long enough so I shouldn't care* kind of way.

"Ah, Weston!" Aunt J calls as she rushes over. Her red hair bounces as she does. "I'm glad you could finally meet my niece."

His grin shifts as he greets Aunt J, who is quick to introduce him to Tate and Darren.

Behind Weston's back, Darren gives me a thumbs up and I scowl. Weston might be cute, but there is no way I'm buying into whatever Aunt J is selling. I don't even *know* what she's planning, and I'm too afraid to ask.

The last time she'd had a *bright idea*—like coming up with a foolproof plan to keep us in one town for longer than a couple of months—we'd accidentally burned down a house. One that *hadn't been haunted*. A regular folks home!

And I thought we decided we weren't *going to try that again!*

"So," Weston starts, turning back to me. Aunt J grins broadly—oh-so-proud of herself. "Are you excited to start school?"

I bite my lip. "Not exactly," I say. "Being the new kid sucks." That's only half the truth. How can I explain that I won't be here long enough to really care?

"It won't be too bad," he says, giving me a half smile. "Everyone knows everyone here. You'll fit right in."

I look between him and Aunt J, who quickly goes back to unloading the truck. *Tricky woman.* I hope she knows I won't let this go.

Sighing, I smile awkwardly up at him. "Yeah, I guess. Still, new town, new people, new school. Gets a little...overwhelming sometimes."

"I'll be there," he replies. "If you ever need anything, you can always ask. I mean, we live right next door to each other." That insufferable grin of his only grows. Is he this nice to everyone who moves in next door?

Or is this his ploy to embarrass the new girl before she even steps foot in school? It doesn't escape my notice how *charming* and polite he is. High school boys can be terrible, especially the pretty ones. They're egos are usually inflated like a weather balloon—and their skulls are twice as thick as a regular one. I've broken my fair share of noses because of guys like *Weston*.

"Thanks," is all I can manage. I forcefully clear my throat. "I should get back to helping unpack, but again, thank you for your offer."

Weston nods happily. Is there even a mean bone in his body? That grin of his reminds me of a puppy dog. Is everyone in this town like this? Or is it just him?

Or am I reading into it?

It's all a ruse, Hunt. Don't fall for that—again.

"Alright, well, I'll see you later, or tomorrow maybe. Definitely Monday. Do you want a ride to school?"

Aunt J speaks before I can, and says, "We would definitely appreciate that, Weston. Thank you so much for offering. I'm afraid if I let her take my car she'll get lost."

"I doubt it, Aunt J," I reply through gritted teeth, but I don't rebuff the offer. For whatever reason, I want to know more about *why* Weston is so nice. What's behind that grey pullover of his? The nice boy he lets everyone see, or is there more? A decent heart or a heart of ice?

He is suddenly very interesting, and I hate myself for thinking so.

Weston waves awkwardly as he walks back towards his house; a two-storey blue suburban home, with black shingles and white details. Behind the front door, a dog barks excitedly.

Guys who have dogs are usually nice, right?

Turning back to Aunt J, I shake my head. "I can't believe you."

Her grin widens, and she picks at her white sweater. "But isn't he lovely? Did you get a reading of him?"

No, I hadn't, though now I wish I'd tried. Spirits are easy, but it's possible for me to do the same to the living. I'm so attuned with Aunt J that I know she's proud of herself without even having to open myself up to her.

"What do you get out of this?" I ask, narrowing my eyes. I shoulder my duffle, school bag, and pack and head inside while she follows. Darren and Tate are carrying my mattress up the stairs when I enter, muttering to themselves about the stairs.

Aunt J leads me upstairs as she speaks. "Well, you didn't really have any friends in that last town." We stop at the top of the stairs, and Aunt Josephine points to a door so Darren and Tate can drop the mattress inside. "Morcant will take time to defeat.

Your parents mistakenly thought it would only be a couple of weeks. Now we know it'll take much, much longer. I don't want you to rush into it. So, while we're here, you should get to know the people more."

"But they'll just become distractions," I say frowning. "If I befriend anyone here, I'll just end up leaving in a year anyways."

"In a year, I'd hope you'd be going to college."

I purse my lips. Darren and Tate stop behind Aunt J and cross their arms. I reach out to them, and feel their agreeance with Aunt J.

Out of the two of them, Tate is the only one with a college education. Occult studies, like my dad. From what I know, it ended up with Tate being disowned for not going into medicine or law like his parents wanted. He was the first man in his family to afford getting into college.

Darren, on the other hand, was already hunting. That's how they met—how they met my parents and Aunt J.

"What?" I ask, folding my arms over my chest. They share a look. "What?"

"Have you even thought about what you want to do after you get your revenge?" Tate asks.

In all honesty, I haven't—I never allow myself to. My focus is on removing Morcant from the face of this earth, once and for all. After that...then I'll see. I have to *survive* first, so making plans for a life I might never have seems useless. My parents made plans, and then they died.

Darren sighs and closes his eyes, rubbing them tiredly.

"Why can't I continue hunting?" I ask honestly. I can't imagine myself *not* travelling and helping spirits or defeating them. That's what I'm good at.

"You should do more with your life," Aunt J says. "Continuing down this path can lead to an early grave."

I shrug. "Then I'll go down doing what I love, doing what I'm good at. I'll be helping people doing this. Anyway," I continue, "what else would I do?"

Aunt J shrugs dramatically. "Oh, I don't know. Maybe you'd have a life? Have friends? Maybe get married and settle down? You could become a detective or something! I don't know!"

"I have friends," I snap, pointing to Darren and Tate. "They're my friends, my family. So are you. Do I really need more than that?"

She sighs in exasperation and throws her hands up. "I'm hoping that, maybe, we can stay in this town, and you can go to the local college. Maybe, just maybe, you could do your own thing and let all of this crap go. After you do what you need to do."

I shake my head. "I can't, Aunt Josephine, you know I can't. *This* is my life."

Her face darkens, and she pushes past me. Both Darren and Tate remain silent as they go back down to the truck to finish unpacking.

~ ~ ~

Eyeing the boxes in the corner of my room, I give them the finger as I flick through one of my new textbooks—courtesy of Aunt J. I found them sitting in the closet when I went to unpack my duffel. History, English, Calculus, PE, and Chemistry. So normal that it hurts. Boring, because I could be doing something better.

Is Aunt J feeling pressured by Morcant? Or maybe Grandpa? He left when I was thirteen, walking away from this life because of what it did to Mom and Dad. He wanted me to go with him, but I'd chosen Aunt J and the life of hunting.

Is he back, making it hard for Aunt J? I know over the years he's called and made threats about taking me away. Maybe he's doing the same now.

Midnight clicks over on my phone. Aunt J is already sound

asleep in her room, while Tate and Darren have set up the sofa bed in the living room. At dinner, they decided that they would stay for a couple of nights until we're settled and until we have a plan of action.

A chill shudders down my spine, and my breath fogs in front of me. Chest tightening, pressure builds on my ribs.

I fall from the bed and hit the ground, my phone dropping before sliding out of reach. I grasp at my chest, trying to get the phantom pressure to release, but it doesn't. I don't have a protection bag on me—they're in the closet in my pack, but I can't even crawl over to it.

The door to my room slams open and Aunt J rushes in, protection bag in hand. She shoves it into the pocket of my pyjamas and the pressure lifts.

I suck in a shuddering breath, coughing as I do. I can't hear her over the ringing in my ears, but her mouth is moving, asking me questions. I can't answer though.

Stars dance in front of my eyes before everything goes black.

4

WATCH THE DEAD

THE VISION CUTS THROUGH ME LIKE A knife, slamming into me before I can even take a breath.

I peel my eyes open and find the world around me hazy, blurry, and yellowed like an old photograph. People surround me, children primarily, running around a group of adults who don't seem to care. Most of the children are little boys who wear grey uniforms and have their hair slicked back. The adults wear a mixture of different clothing, and one woman passes wearing a ruffled baby-blue dress straight out of a Victorian period drama.

I blink and try to move. Every muscle hurts, but I manage to sit up. Ghosts mingle with the living, wearing nightgowns with capped sleeves; I see sores scattered on their arms from infections., and bruises different shades of purple blotching their skin.

There are ghostly children, too, but they only watch while the others play. Their attention is on a large woman who floats between the living adults.

What is going on?

Pain pulses in my temple, but I ignore it, instead focusing on the brightest spirit. She wears the clothing of a nun, her habit askew, but she isn't old, maybe my age. Around her neck hangs a crucifix, vines crawling all over Jesus's body and around the cross he's nailed to. The only reason it catches my eye is because it's hanging upside down.

Either it's some kind of joke, or there's something else going on. She watches the larger woman as she makes her rounds about the room; the larger woman ignores the children, but when the nun acknowledges them, she sneers like they're beneath her, and they sneer back.

Either they're running a school or an orphanage, but I know where I am.

The Morcant Estate.

The realization shudders through me and sends the skin of my arms puckering. Back in the forties or fifties, the house had been renovated to suit an asylum, but everything in this room looks original.

How the hell are there spirits of patients mingling with people from the late eighteen hundreds?

What kind of vision is this?

As if I ask the question aloud, all eyes fall on me—or at least, the eyes of the spirits. Five little ghost boys surround me, then the patients. Behind them are even more. Anyone who is supposed to be alive disappears, leaving me with the dead.

The crowd parts to reveal him.

Morcant, dressed all in black, holds the arm of the nun I'd seen before. No, not nun. She's his daughter. I vaguely remember her from an old painting my parents found. There was a rumour he'd murdered her, but seeing it for myself...

She looks almost afraid, standing with him.

'You haven't much time,' *she whispers, voice eerily close to* my ear. 'It's all coming to an end. Soon.'

"Soon?" I ask. "What's coming to an end?"

Delilah Morcant appears in front of me, fear alighting in her dark eyes. "Times up."

The vision blurs and falls away.

5

DEATH AND UNREST

I REMEMBER THE VISION IN excruciating detail. It feels more like a dream, rather than something that happened in the past. As an Empath, I usually get a taste of the spirit through emotion and memory—the emotion usually tying in with whatever they show me *through* a memory.

But this time... It was different. Maybe because Morcant is different.

And what the hell did it mean?

"Are you sure you're okay?" Aunt J asks. I jump in my seat and turn to her, startled; since last night, she hasn't slept—and to be fair, neither have I. But out of stress and worry, Aunt J cooks; there's a month's worth of soup already in the freezer, and she has some kind of casserole in the oven and pasta sauce simmering in a pot.

I shake my head. "I'm fine. We don't even know if it was a

vision or just a bad dream." I don't say anything about the weirdness of it, how oddly out of place I'd felt, or how I think it's some kind of warning, maybe from Delilah Morcant about her father. Her appearance just doesn't make sense.

Aunt J purses her lips before returning to whatever concoction she's working on. "It was a vision, alright," she mutters, probably more to herself than to me.

"I don't think so," I reply, slouching in my seat. My response earns me a quick, over-the-shoulder glare. "I don't know how to interpret it. Right now, I'm going to focus on all the facts. And that's Morcant."

Aunt J visibly flinches, taking a step back from the stove. "I don't think this is a good idea, Huntliegh. I really, really don't." She picks at a hanging string on her sweater, her hands trembling. "You're being targeted. Not just by him, but by other *things* in this town..."

I swallow and look away. I've tried to never to give in to fear—something that would undoubtedly get me killed if I don't control it. "I know, but...if I'm not the one to stop him, then who is?"

She sighs and heads into the adjoining dining room. I follow behind slowly, my throat burning as I sit. Reaching out, Aunt J takes my hand. Her soft fingers wrap around mine and squeeze gently. "There will be other Hunters."

"And there will be more deaths!" I reply, pulling away. I run my hands through my hair, chest tightening. "There are more dead Hunters, Aunt J. Who knows how many more civilians lost inside the estate? Morcant needs to be *stopped*."

"Why does it have to be you, Huntliegh? Why should you be responsible for all this?" Anger fills her voice, an emotion she doesn't usually reveal.

I swallow and avert my eyes; I pick at my fingernails and the chipped black paint I'd coated them in only a week ago. "No other Hunter will go *near* this place, Aunt J. You heard Tate and

Darren; only fools go into Morcant's house."

Aunt J heaves a heavy breath and shakes her head, red curls bouncing. "So, what, you're a fool now?"

"Might as well be," I mutter. I meet her stare, then quickly look away as fear flashes within them. "Someone has to do it. Who better than me?"

"It should never have to be you, Hunt. I should have listened to your grandfather."

I stand silently, shaking my head. My heart skips a beat at the mention of my grandfather, who I know hates this world, hates how my parents were taken. "Well, it is," I reply, ignoring the jab.

Standing, I stalk out of the dining room and grab my jacket before leaving the house. Something hits the ground; I look down and see a protection bag.

I don't realise I'm having another vision until it's too late. I only get a word, scribbled in blood on a wall caked in old wallpaper that peels to reveal layers of paint and grime beneath.

West.

It comes and goes in a single moment, but it's enough to have me hesitating on the front porch.

West. I have to make sure to see what's west of the property when I track down a map of the Morcant estate. Is it a clue or a dead end? The location of the bodies maybe? Or my parents?

I swallow bile that rises in my throat.

"You good, kiddo?" Darren asks from the driver's side of the truck. Tate stops at the hood, the sleeves of his beige sweater rolled up to reveal the dark skin of his forearms. Both men emit worry so strong I close myself off to it.

"Yeah," I reply, "I'm fine."

Tate looks between me and the house before releasing a breath. "We're going sightseeing. Come on."

Anything to get out of the house, I think. Even though it's a lie; they've been out all day. Tate's only offering because he thinks it'll help, and it will.

Shoving my hands into the pockets of my leather jacket, I make my way to the truck and climb into the back seat. I take the middle seat and buckle in. Leaning forward, I poke my head in between Tate and Darren, who say nothing as we pull away from the curb.

For a Saturday, Fort Caldwell isn't nearly as busy as I expected. The sun casts a pleasant warmth down on the town, so I expect the lake to be a hot spot, but when we pass down the main street and I catch a glimpse of the dark blue waters, I don't see many on the shore or out in the lake.

"So," Darren starts, one hand on the wheel while the other rests on the window. "You and your Aunt had a fight."

"How'd you know?" I ask.

He shrugs. "You had that look about you."

I don't question that any further and instead sit back. Aunt J and I don't fight, at least not often, and I wouldn't call our argument that.

The town around us shifts from buildings to trees. Thick forest surrounds the road as it circles around the lake. It isn't the same stretch we drove down yesterday, so I'm not sure where we're going now.

A strange tingling sensation cascades over my skin, like the misty rain that seems to always be at the edges of Fort Caldwell. Every muscle in my body tenses, a range of unrecognisable emotions ploughing into me, so sudden I almost forget to breathe.

I lean forward and stare out the windshield, waiting, but I'm not sure for what. A sign, a spirit...

Through the trees, I spot a flash of light, something hidden in the shadows.

"Pull over up here," I say, and point to an old motel sign ahead. Darren and Tate share a look but don't say anything as they pull into the all-but-abandoned parking lot. There's one other vehicle parked in front of an office, but otherwise, we're alone.

I climb out of the truck and look up at the motel; shaped like an L, the building has two levels, and looks like every other basic back road American motel. With a half-illuminated sign on the side of the road reading 'motel' and 'vacancy', I almost get horror movie vibes from the place. It doesn't help that all around us is forest. According to a big sign across the road, a couple of miles up is a gas station and diner.

A shiver races down my spine, and my stomach drops. I swallow back a bout of panic that hits me faster than a bullet-train. "Something doesn't seem right about this place."

Darren turns to me with furrowed brows. "You getting a ghosty feeling about the place?"

I can only nod, mouth dry.

Tate and Darren share a look. "If anything jumps out at us, then we'll do what we always do. You got your pack?" I nod, and hurry to the back of their black truck. A go pack sits on the back seat. The heavy bag offers me a sense of security, but it does nothing to stop the chills that run down my back and arms.

"Alright. We stick together. Anything jumps out at us, we shoot first, ask questions later." Tate and Darren nod to one another, and I try to wipe the look of panic from my face.

Whatever's here is letting me know about it.

Although this place looks like the setting of a horror movie, I'm not overly afraid of it. I can handle myself quite well in these situations. But the spirit—or spirits, should there be more attached to the location—all seem to be in a state of panic and fear.

"Act natural," Tate murmurs. "We'll stay the night. Shouldn't be a problem."

Unless Aunt J finds out. Although, she might already know.

Quietly, I follow the men to the receptionist; a woman with grey hair and black eyes. She smiles at Tate and Darren warily, and narrows her eyes at me.

"How many rooms would you like?" she asks, her tone sharp.

I notice Darren and Tate share a look. While they speak with the old woman, I look around the small office. Divide and conquer.

The receptionist sits behind a desk covered in papers, but there are no pictures that I can see—of herself or the building, like most motels have. Behind her, wallpaper peels at the corners, and water stains the ceiling. A fake plant sits by the door, and beside that is a battered, old chair. To my right, a door that reads 'private' and to the left, just a blank wall.

"Thank you," Darren says with a large smile. Tate merely nods. I look back to them, only to see a key in Darren's hand.

I walk outside first and embrace the cool air. "She wasn't very nice," Tate says, crossing his arms over his chest. "Didn't like the look of you, Hunt."

I roll my eyes. "No one likes the look of me. Apparently, the leather is just a calling card for trouble."

Darren snorts loudly and heads in the direction of a staircase, leading the way up. He stops at room twenty-one and unlocks the door. "We'll hang around here for a bit. Should start getting dark soon enough. Hopefully we can get an idea of what's haunting the joint, or maybe it's another one of Morcant's tricks." Darren steps into the room before passing the key to me.

I take it and hesitate. It feels like ice in my hand. Another wave of panic washes over me, and I double over, coughing. I can't get enough air in my lungs, and every breath I take burns like ice down my throat.

'Help me,' a voice whispers, crackling like a bad phone line. The pressure on my lungs becomes stronger. 'Help me.'

The panic intensifies. Suddenly, I'm not at the motel anymore. I'm sitting outside of a cops station while Aunt J and my grandfather talk to the police about my parents' case. I know they're dead, I can feel it deep in my bones, but the cops are certain they'll find them, and I hate that they don't know the truth.

I hate that they were ripped away from me.

Tate grabs the key from my hand and drags me into the room. Darren pulls a protection bag from the pack and shoves it into the pocket of my jacket. The release is almost immediately; the panic dissipates, fear dissolves, and I can *breathe* again.

"The hell was that?" Tate asks, arms wrapped around me still. Against his chest, I shudder.

I clear my throat and pull away, swallowing. "I don't know. But they want our help."

"How can you be sure, kiddo?" Darren asks.

I look up at the ceiling and close my eyes. "Because they asked for it. And I want to help them. I *need* to."

Tate casts Darren a quick, wary look, and asks, "Why's that?"

"Because I need to defeat Morcant." His name tastes bitter in my mouth, but I say it over and over in my head, because I need to feel a sense of resolution. "And every spirit I help or destroy will help me. Especially here, in this town."

Opening my eyes, I look back to Darren, because I know he'll understand. "Please."

He runs a hand over his beard and sighs. "Fine. Let's figure out where the little ghosty is and cross it over."

6

THE CASE OF AMBER MARSTON

WHILE WE WAIT FOR NIGHT, WE RESEARCH.

The old receptionist frowns as Darren and I wander back into the office, looking every bit suspicious with our too polite smiles. I shove my hands into the pockets of my leather jacket, clutching the protection bag that keeps me safe from the spirit's emotions.

"I'm sorry to ask," Darren starts, a winning smile spreading across his round face, "but you wouldn't happen to have any old newspapers lying around, would you?"

Her eyes crinkle, and I smile broadly at her. "I forgot to grab some on my way in, and I have an art project I'm working on." The lie rolls off my tongue easily, and I smile a little wider at her, pleadingly.

The old woman's frown only deepens, but she shrugs nonetheless. "I might have some in the back. Just give me a moment." She hobbles around the desk and reaches for a set of keys from the pocket of her pink cardigan. On the ring is probably a master key to every room, though an old iron one jingles oddly amongst the bunch.

There's a whisper that follows the movement, one that curdles in my stomach.

She shuffles into a small, dark room, and closes the door behind her.

I turn to Darren with a frown. "Weird. That iron key looks suspicious." I don't mention the odd feeling, not yet anyway.

He rolls his eyes but doesn't argue. "We'll have a little look around later, okay?"

I nod. After a few moments she returns, her arms full of newspaper. Some are water-stained, while others look, for the most part, untouched. At least it's a start.

Giving her a winning smile, I take the papers from her arms. The stack is massive and heavy, which almost causes me to drop them. "I hope there's enough there for you, dear," she says, voice low and unimpressed. She gives me a bored look before hobbling back to her seat behind the counter.

I notice the charm bracelet on her wrist then; compared to the rest of her ensemble, it looks too *new*. Too shiny. The Eiffel Tower, the London Bridge, and several other charms dangle from the bracelet.

"I love the charms," I say, nodding to the item.

The old woman is quick to cover it with the sleeve of her cardigan, and she glowers at me. "Anything else you two need?"

Darren and I share a quick glance and shake our heads. She sighs and looks down at her paperwork, dismissing us.

Rain starts falling from the heavy clouds as we make our way back to the room. Any remnants of summer have disappeared in the short time since we stumbled across this place.

Darren, thankfully, takes half of the newspapers before we

climb the stairs. The mist that now curls over the bitumen gives me a shiver.

"We'll look for any missing persons," I say as soon as the door is closed and locked. "See if any might connect with this place."

"Alright." He drops his half of the stack onto the rickety old table in the corner of the room. Outside, the rain steadily grows louder, angrier.

The first three papers I look through have nothing interesting; a litter of kittens for sale, a missing car, and three job ads. The local politician is threatening to demolish some community centre, which includes an old skate ramp and park. These three are dated over the last year, which probably means either the spirit is older, or no one has noticed they've gone missing.

The fourth one, though... I swallow thickly as I gaze down at the photo of a young woman, the words 'MISSING' printed across the front page. Oddly enough, her eyes have been drawn over with marker.

"I've got one," I say quietly as Darren drops his newspaper to scoot closer. "Amber Marston. Went missing fourteen months ago. Twenty-one, road tripping alone, originally from England. She was supposed to meet up with friends when she stopped at the gas station up the road and was never seen again."

Below her photo are several surveillance images from the gas station; she's filling up her car in the first photo, then walking out of the station in the second.

"Could be a Morcant one," he says. I release a breath. He's right. She could have made a wrong turn and gone to the estate. Made the mistake of going inside. Never to be seen again.

Darren and I share a look as the door opens. Tate swears loudly, his dark hair dripping. His pack drips water on the already stained floor.

"Bit wet out there?" Darren asks, laughing as Tate grimaces

and drops the bag onto the table.

"Did either of you find anything?" he asks, dropping into a chair. He stretches his long legs out in front of him. "Because I noticed a missing persons photo in the window of the diner. But then again, Fort Caldwell has a lot of missing persons."

I wonder if this place even classifies as Fort Caldwell. We're far enough away from the main town that this could be a whole other world.

Instead of voicing those thoughts, I hold up the paper to show him. "This one?" I ask, and he nods, frowning. "I have a feeling something happened here, in this motel. I think she's haunting the place."

"Are you sure?" Tate asks. "There could be others. The old lady could have had a husband who died here, or a child or family member. They might not even realise they're trapped here and could be completely harmless. We don't know the reach of Morcant's influence yet, if he has any influence on the spirits here."

I shake my head as a feeling of...*relief* shudders through me. I continue reading. "He does," I reply, though I'm not sure if I believe it myself. "Says here that amongst her personal effects should be a charm bracelet. Her friends said she was collecting charms based on countries she visited. France. England. The states. The old woman was wearing the exact same one." I meet Tate's eye, then Darren's. Both are quiet as I let the words settle. Somehow, the receptionist is involved, and somehow she's gotten away with wearing the evidence on her wrist.

Talk about being caught red-handed.

"Maybe she found the bracelet and never realised it belonged to the girl?" Tate tries reasoning. "Maybe it's just a coincidence?"

"When is it ever *just a coincidence*?" I ask, standing. "That woman knows something. I bet Amber's body is here on the property somewhere, and I'm going to find her."

I pull the protection bag from my pocket and drop it on the bed. Darren watches with pursed lips as I rifle through my pack, checking the rest of my tools; flashlight, salt and lavender, a small bottle of gasoline, a box of matches. Three different spirit bags are ready to be used, and a tin box has the necessities I need to make them on the go. I pull a small box from one of the inner pockets and slip it into my jacket.

Quickly, I tear the photo of Amber from the newspaper and shove it into my bag.

Panic rushes through me, though it isn't as bad as before. Thankfully, I can still breathe.

"Keep an eye out for the old lady." I shove my Bluetooth earpiece into my ear. I'll use the panic to guide me. "Call me if she comes looking."

With a sigh, Darren nods. Tate looks between us and stands. "I'll keep watch. Darren, you should go out and make this hunt end quickly so we can go home."

I look over to my bearded friend who grins, like he was waiting for his husband to give him the okay. Darren quickly shoves a pack over his back and takes out a flashlight.

Tate opens the curtains of the room; he takes a seat where he can see the inside of the office and the silver-haired crone who sits at the desk.

"I'll call you both in an hour," Tate mutters. He kicks his feet up onto the second chair.

That's good enough for me. I open the door to the room and hurry to a different set of stairs, the ones furthest away from the office, hopefully out of sight. Darren follows, and we both carefully descend as rain continues to pour heavily from above.

Together, we creep around the side of the motel. There's nothing but forest back here, though I can make out an old, dried up pool and a storage shed. From what I make out through the haze of rain, there's no security cameras overlooking the back of the building, though I hadn't seen any sign of computers in the office anyway. Everything is done by hand in there, it seems.

"I'll check the shed and pool area," I say over the rain. Darren nods, keeping close to me. "You should check and see if there are any other buildings."

"Alright. You got your phone on and that Bluetooth thing working?" I nod and press at my ear. The piece beeps, connecting with my phone in my pocket. "I'm going to call you now, so we're connected, okay? I don't want to lose you, kiddo."

I offer him a tight-lipped smile as he struggles to get his phone to connect to his own Bluetooth earpiece. It takes several moments, but soon enough, we're connected.

Nodding to one another, we both set off; I head straight towards the pool, keeping my eyes peeled for anything out of the ordinary. I keep my senses open, too, giving Amber the chance to reach out if she needs to. But the panic has settled into the back of my mind—I know it's there, aware that it's now a part of me until I help her, but it doesn't overcome me.

Darren walks close to the motels wall, heading towards the back and into the forest. I watch him vanish, then wait for his flashlight to switch on. When I can see his light, I continue on.

The pool area is fenced off, though the gate swings open easily when I unclip the latch. The old thing makes no sound, though I rush to stop it before it can smash into the fence that surrounds the pool. When I do, I breathe a sigh of relief. For some reason I fear making any sound, aware that one wrong move could scare Amber away. It's the last thing I need—we don't have much time before Aunt J catches onto us.

Water coats the uneven paving of the pool, turning the stone slick. I stick to the fence, constantly checking to see if anyone is watching—maybe hoping to find Amber hovering nearby.

The hairs on my arms stand on end, and I wait for something to come over me; a feeling, a vision, *something* that connects

Amber with this pool.

I suck in a hesitant breath but nothing comes.

As the sky continues to grow darker, I'm forced to rely on my flashlight. The wide beam of light coats the pool yellow, revealing muddy stains at the bottom and on the sides.

Muddy stains? Or blood?

I shudder as a cold wind sweeps through the trees. It has to be mud, grime, something. Amber went missing fourteen months ago. Any likelihood of finding harrowing evidence like *that* would have washed away with the first storm that visited this town.

"*Find anything?*" Darren asks, his voice crackling over the earpiece.

I shake my head, despite him not being able to see me. "Maybe. Maybe not. Brown stains at the bottom of the pool."

"*Could be blood. You feel anything?*"

The panic still resides in the back of my mind, but nothing new comes to me. "No. Nothing. Have you found anything?"

"*No other buildings out here. I can see you from out here though. There's something strange about these trees.*"

"What do you mean?" I ask. I walk over to the pool shed, careful of the wet stone, and try the door. Locked. Last Christmas, Darren bought me a lock picking set. I pull it from my pocket and set my flashlight between my legs as I focus on the lock. I align the pin inside the tumbler and feel around for the springs.

"*I think there used to be something out here,*" Darren continues, his voice comforting in my ears. "*Little clearing here has foundations.*"

I look over to him and spot the flashlight as it glances over the forest floor. "Any hidden doors?" I ask.

"*Nope. Nothing. What about you?*"

I jiggle the pick, feeling the lock give way beneath my hands. "Checking now."

We both remain silent. I hold my breath as I enter the shed, letting the beam of my flashlight skim over the interior. The metal walls are cleared out and leaning against one side are a couple of cleaning implements. The ground itself is concrete.

I release a heavy breath. "Nothing."

I feel it then, fingers of ice running down my spine. I shudder, the sensation of panic washes over me again, this time in tenfold.

'*Help me,*' a voice whispers. British accent, young, feminine. Amber. It sounds exactly like the voice I'd heard earlier.

Other than the panic and fear, there is no anger in her energy. Not like Brock and Kenley. They died and came back the same—terrible monsters who took lives—but Amber is one of the few who seek justice and peace. It's why she asks for help. She could have easily absorbed the bad energy of the old lady, but revenge isn't something she wants.

I turn slowly, backing into the shed. She stands behind me, her neck bent at an odd angle. Her eyes aren't on me, but rather on the pool, and the smudges at the bottom.

'*Help me,*' she whispers again, and vanishes.

Breathing heavily, I leave the pool and head towards Darren, whose back is to me. "She was here, definitely. I think she broke her neck falling into the pool."

Darren turns to me with raised brows, his eyes going to the pool. "Poor girl."

I nod. We stand together, eyeing the pool. Her early grave. I shudder again.

From the corner of my eye, it looks like a hand, barely distinguishable, reaching from behind me to point into the forest. It trembles, then disappears. I follow it and run my light over the area.

There, in the distance, is a tree. It looks newer than the ones here in the forest, maybe only a year old. A sapling, with a thin trunk and branches.

I swallow thickly. "That tree there. That's where she was

buried."

My stomach turns as Darren turns his flashlight onto the tree, grimacing. "Stupid woman, putting that there." I see her again, Amber, without the bend from her broken neck, wearing a turtleneck and jeans, smiling in relief. Slowly, I lift my hand and wave. She does the same.

Darren lowers the flashlight and motions for me to follow as Amber fazes out of sight, the panic and fear finally washing away with her. "Come on," he says, touching my arm lightly, "we better call the police."

7

REMNANTS OF DREAMS

UNLIKE YESTERDAY, TODAY IS uneventful. We didn't stick around to talk to the cops, only leaving an anonymous tip after digging up most of Ambers grave.

There she was, wrapped in the pool tarp.

I leave the dining room and take the stairs two at a time, heading up to the spare room. Aunt J claimed it as an office, and during her time here, she's begun piecing together the story of Morcant; spread across the white walls are photographs and sketches, newspaper clippings and post-it notes, all pointing towards the Morcant estate. Even a map of the town has been pinned up with his house circled in red.

Fitting my earbuds into my ears, I choose a podcast on hauntings, specifically about the Morcant house.

"Morcant House was first built in 1849, in the establishing town of Fort Caldwell," the presenter, Alby, starts, his voice deep

and soothing. *"Josiah Morcant could only be described as a cruel son of a bitch. Know why, Jen?"*

"No, Alby, I don't," his wife replies sarcastically.

I do; Josiah Morcant dabbled in Satanic worship while living in England and brought his beliefs with him to the Americas. While Fort Caldwell's old sector was being built, he started a church under the guise of preaching 'God's' word. Instead, he practiced human sacrifice in an underground cellar.

To this day, no one can find it, despite it being so well known. Over the past one-hundred and sixty-nine years, well over a hundred people have disappeared by entering that house—though the final number is still unknown.

"Josiah had no heirs, except for his daughter. Who, apparently, was sacrificed alongside other young men and woman her age," Alby continues in my ear.

"That's just disgusting, and horrible. Who does that to their own child?"

Psychopaths? Serial killers? There are a few options, there, Jenny.

Rolling my eyes, I pick up a card that Aunt J wrote:

Morcant Estate belongs to local council and is a heritage site. Was once almost burned, but the flames mysteriously disappeared. Morcant's doing, probably.

Well, fire doesn't seem to be a good option if he's powerful enough to extinguish the flames. So, there goes that option. Also known as the easiest way to get rid of pesky spirits.

I sigh loudly and eye a stack of missing persons reports, frowning. The file is much thinner than I would have guessed. When I pick it up, a sticky-note drops to the floor.

Definitely not Morcant House.

I bite my lip as I flip through the pages, noticing more notes written on the pages: possible woman in white, ghoul, ghost hitchhiker, and so on. Relatively easy spirits to get rid of, like

Amber.

"Those are cases that I found." I jump, dropping the file, and turn to where Aunt J stands in the doorway. "Not directly related to the Morcant House, but I believe Morcant is somehow *amplifying* spirit activity in the town. Like the spirit you decided to take on without me..."

I ignore the comment, but it makes sense. "Do you think that has anything to do with what happened with my vision?" I ask, pausing the podcast as I do, cutting off Jenny before she can say something totally scripted about how evil Morcant is.

"Of course I do." Aunt J steps into the room and walks towards the wall, pointing to the map that she has pinned to the wall. "I decided to pinpoint areas in town that may or may not have spirit activity. The road to the Morcant House is very...odd."

"How so?"

She purses her lips, shaking her head. "Over the last couple of years, locals have sworn they've seen...*people*, dressed in all types of period clothing heading towards the house."

"That is odd..." I look back down at the file, noticing that it dates back at least a hundred years. "Did anyone get close to see the spirits? Was it just an apparition?"

Because if regular folk are actually *seeing* the dead...that's a problem.

Aunt J shrugs. "I know *someone* in town saw it and tried getting closer. Only, when they rounded a bend, the people were gone."

A shiver courses down my spine. I step away from the board. Not out of fear, but intrigue; spirits normally aren't visible to regular folk, so either the one who saw it is a sensitive with a willpower about questioning the unbelievable, or Morcant is making other spirits strong enough to be visible.

"I don't get it. I don't get any of it," I say quietly.

"Don't stress over what you don't understand," Aunt J

murmurs. "I'm here to help, and Darren and Tate will always be a phone call away should anything happen, or if we need backup."

I nod, but it still eats at me. What does all this *mean?* Morcant is undeniably powerful, and that power seems to be *spreading* through town. But is that even possible? I don't remember anyone ever talking about it, but there is still a lot we don't know about the world of spirits.

Fort Caldwell has a lot more going on than just whatever is happening in that godforsaken house, apparently.

"How are we supposed to stop all of this, Aunt Josephine?"

The façade of strength she worked onto her face falls. She sighs, pulling out the desk chair, every movement sluggish. Falling into it, Aunt J eyes me warily. "I..." Her face goes blank, and the colour drains from her cheeks.

"Aunt Josephine?" I ask tentatively. She doesn't respond.

Clenching my jaw, I wait; when she has a vision, it usually means she'll be out of it for a while, sometimes maybe an hour, depending on the severity of the scene she witnesses or the power of the spirit that gives it to her. If it's the first, then it'll take her a couple of minutes to recompose herself, but if it's the latter—if it has anything to do with a spirit—then I can only wait, though after last night, worry eats at me.

After a moment, Aunt J blinks; once, twice, three times, before the colour comes back to her face. She clears her throat loudly and shakes her head.

"I hate when that happens," she mutters, rubbing her forehead. "It never gets any better." A chill courses through the room, almost like someone decided to blast the air conditioner. Goosebumps rise along my arms.

"What happened?" I ask, rubbing my arms.

Aunt J looks up at me warily before looking away. "A death, down by the elementary school."

I swallow thickly and look down at our file. Oh, how it will grow now that Morcant is getting even more powerful. I release a heavy breath and set the papers down. "Do you know what happened?"

Aunt J stands and runs her hands down her pants. They tremble, the effects of the vision still clinging to her. "Yes, and the police won't find the body unless we go down there."

"We?" I have no problem with skeletons and spirits, but a 'just dead' body... I shudder. But it gives me the chance I need to get out of the house again, to really see what else is going on out there.

My aunt nods sadly before heading to the door of the office. I follow her out, but she hesitates by the front door. "If it becomes too dangerous," she starts, "then I want you to get out, okay? Whatever is in that house...it doesn't want to be disturbed."

I nod. My pack sits beside the front door, partially open to reveal the contents. Pulling two protection bags out, I hand one to Aunt J before pocketing the second, and zip it shut.

"If it turns out to be too dangerous in general, then we both need to get out of there, okay?" I say, shouldering the pack.

Aunt J offers me a tight-lipped smile and tucks her protection bag into an inner pocket of her jacket. "Of course, Hunt."

Her words don't sit right with me, but I don't voice my concern. She steps outside into a misty rain, red curls becoming instantly damp. I can't help but stop and watch as she climbs into the driver's side of the car, buckling herself in. My feet won't move though, and I'm locked in place.

A wave of panic shudders through me for a split second before disappearing, and I take an unintentional step back.

What the hell... Aunt J honks the car, breaking me out of my thoughts, out of the panic. Sucking in a breath, I brave the weather and run to the car.

Time to take down a spirit.

8

THE UNDEAD

MY MIND WHIRLS WITH THOUGHTS I can't dwell on, that disappear before I can latch onto and ponder them further; about Morcant and Amber and how the spirits of Fort Caldwell haven't already left this cursed place.

Beside me, Aunt J hums along to a song in her head as she drives us down a back road, past the elementary school, and towards a house that doesn't quite fit into the look of Fort Caldwell. Nestled between ancient oaks and pines, the small house looks to be just as old as the town around it; dark brick exterior meets old iron fencing that signifies the property line; the windows are darkened with age, some of them blown out. Wood covers the broken ones, and in some areas, I see old newspaper covering the glass.

"Someone is freshly dead...in here?" I ask, squinting through the rain. I can't make out any lights, nor can I feel anything remotely paranormal coming from the building. Though based on how old it looks, I'm not surprised it's haunted.

My aunt nods sadly and turns the car off. Resting her hands in her lap, she her fidgets with the rings on her fingers, the tension so thick I can cut it with a knife. "Not a nice death, either," she says quietly.

Swallowing the lump in my throat, I double check my pack, pulling out two medical face masks. Handing her one, I say, "Better to be safe than sorry." My nose crinkles at the thought of walking in on the body, and the *smell*...

She looks down at it before taking it from me, strapping it over her mouth and nose. I do the same, and together we get out of the car.

Overgrown with weeds and thorny brambles, the yard looks like it hasn't seen care in twenty years. Behind the fence, I make out an old swing set that sends a shiver down my spine. An old building sits in the back of the yard—an outhouse, maybe, or some kind of shed. Vines grow over the exterior, making it hard to tell.

"Why don't we just call the police?" I ask as we step hazardously over broken bottles and old, decayed toys. Something squeaks beneath my boot, and I jump back. A dog's chew toy. I shudder again and step over it.

Aunt J shakes her head, pulling her hair back with a rainbow scrunchy. "The spirit in there is angry, malevolent. If any normal person went in there, I'm afraid they'd end up like poor old Mr. Heckney." She sighs sadly when we make it to the porch.

Mr. Heckney? The dead person, I'm guessing. I step cautiously, fully aware that half the wood is rotted and ready to break.

Good thing I'm up to date with my tetanus shots, I think, grimacing.

The wood creaks beneath me, and I stop. "Are you sure anyone even lives here?"

My aunt spares me a look before walking to the door in two, long strides and tries the handle. Locked. Aunt J rams her shoulder into the decaying wood with no luck and frowns.

"Let's try around back," she suggests, already leading the way back down the stairs and through the knee-high grass. She walks around a large stone, and I stop to look at it.

The epigraph reads: '*My beautiful daughter. Though you may not be here, you are at least with the angels.*' A headstone, sitting in the front yard. Something doesn't feel right about it.

"Aunt J," I call, beckoning her over. I kneel down in the grass and rub at the stone, hoping for more information, for the girl's name or what happened. At the bottom, though, are a set of initials: *J.M.*

Aunt J halts, kneeling beside me, eyes narrowing. "The spirit must be his daughter," she murmurs, so quiet I almost don't hear her.

I run a hand through my hair and back away, feeling that same terror slice through me. It isn't as strong as before, though, probably being filtered out by the protection bag in my pocket. But I still feel it, burrowing down into me.

Something is seriously wrong.

"I don't think that's what happened here, Aunt J," I say, rubbing my hands together. A chilling wind picks up, lifting my hair off my face. Aunt J turns to me with darkened eyes. I swallow thickly before saying, "The initials at the bottom of the headstone say *J.M.* I don't think that's a coincidence."

Somewhere in the house, glass smashes. I jump back in surprise, while Aunt J rises in one single motion and dashes to the gated fence, swinging the rotted iron thing open.

She's off, heading into the back yard before I can even blink. Something else smashes in the house, and over the rain I think I hear someone speak. They scream a name, one I can't quite make out, but it sounds human.

"Aunt Josephine!" I shout, swearing as she waves me off from somewhere in the long grass. I take off into a sprint behind her, wincing as my foot catches the side of something large—a washing machine, I think. The whole back yard is as bad as the front; broken furniture and appliances litter the overgrown yard, making it extremely hard to manoeuvre. There are at least two broken cars—or at least, the shells of them—taking up residence amongst the grass.

Aunt J is already climbing the back stairs, jiggling the door when I finally catch sight of her. "Hey!" I say, trying to get her attention. "What the hell?"

She doesn't even look at me as she pushes the door open, almost falling into the house as she does.

Mr. Heckney's home, oddly enough, looks *nothing* like his yard; clean white walls dusted with photographs and framed news clippings, recently cleaned wooden floors, and the kitchen—or what I can make of it from where we stand—looks brand new, like he installed all the new countertops and oven recently, and threw the old crap straight into the yard.

"There is something seriously wrong with this picture," I hiss, pulling at Aunt J's arm. Finally, as if hearing me for the first time, she takes a step out of the house.

The door slams in her face, and we both jump.

Something else smashes. Somewhere within the house, someone howls, swearing colourfully as they do.

We share a look; something is *definitely* wrong.

Aunt J and I ram our shoulders into the door as another shout sounds from somewhere inside of the house. There's a gargle, but... I'm not sure. The feeling I'm getting from whoever is inside doesn't make any sense.

"Not that one!" an old man shouts as something else crashes. I flinch, slamming back into the door. It doesn't budge.

Stepping away, I scan the porch; two windows look out over

the yard, both of them boarded up. I try both, using all my strength to kick at the planks of wood, but it's no use. They've been nailed in place, by either Mr. Heckney or the spirit.

Running from the back porch, I head around the side of the house and climb atop the old stove. It creaks beneath me but doesn't give way as I slam my fist into the unbroken window above. The glass rattles, meaning I can break through it with enough force.

A smile splits my face. *Victory will be mine,* I think. Jumping from the stove, I search the yard for something hard and heavy; an old microwave oven scattered in pieces at my feet is no help, and neither is the doll head lying beside it. I carefully dig through the grass and find a heavy rock.

"Good enough," I mutter. Standing just below the window, I aim the rock at the glass, and throw it.

The sound echoes in my ears, rattling me to the bone. But it does the job; glass falls in, creating a clear entrance for me to climb though. Climbing the stove once again, I take my scarf off and wrap it around my hand, using it to break the rest of the glass. From here, I can hear the man's voice clearly.

"No!" he shouts as something else breaks.

I glance over to the porch, where Aunt J is looking over the railing. "Come on!" I say.

I climb through the window with Aunt J hot on my trail, careful not to fall into the pile of glass I created on the floor. I kick the rock out of the way and pause. Much like the back entrance, this area is just as neat; a clean dining room, fit to seat a family of eight, with a glass cabinet full of expensive looking dinnerware and glass. Several of the display plates are missing; their fragments are on the other side of the room, smashed pieces of porcelain imbedded in the wall.

Dropping my pack to the ground, I pull out a couple of spirit bags and whisper their enchantments. This whole situation sends a shiver down my spine, almost like a warning.

A warning for us to leave and never return.

We creep into the hallway, tiptoeing up the stairs where most of the shouting and shattering is coming from. Glass covers the wooden stairs, and there are two broken picture frames at the top.

I stop and look down at the smiling faces; one is of a little girl, with red pigtails and a bright smile. A man has his arms around her; he is clearly her father, with the same red hair and smile.

Looking over to Aunt J, I point to the picture. She sighs sadly and shakes her head.

I turn into the hall, where the little girl appears. Blood runs from her eyes as she fazes in and out of focus. Much like Amber, she points in the direction of a door, mouthing, *'go'* before disappearing once again.

Tightening my grip on the spirit bag, I shoulder my way into the room, throwing the bag at the first otherworldly creature I see.

The thing stops mid step; the dark body of the man grows clearer, and it swivels to where I stand. I only get a brief look at him before he goes up in flames, trapped.

Aunt J throws the next bag, and it hits an older man straight in the stomach. He looks down at the bag, shock highlighting his aged features, before looking between us. When I glance at Aunt J, her eyes are wide and mouth agape.

"Who are you?" I ask, turning back to the man.

He looks back down at the bag. "My name," he wheezes, clearing his throat, "is Albert Heckney. And I can assure you ladies, I am *not* dead."

9

MR HECKNEY'S GHOSTS

I TAKE A CAREFUL STEP BACK AND BUMB into Aunt J, who looks as shocked and uncertain as I feel. Her hand wraps around mine, almost as if she's ready to run and take me with her. I almost don't mind if she *does* take off with me in tow.

I'm still not even entirely sure what's happening here.

Mr Heckney stands before us with his arms crossed over his chest, lips pulled in an unsatisfied smile. He holds the spirit bag in his hand, and I have the feeling he won't be giving it back. Every once in a while, he glances over to the one trapping the spirit.

He looks nothing like the photographs; age has clearly taken over the man. His hair grows in thin silver wisps, and his once angular face now droops, kind of reminding me of the old man from *Up*. He's dressed in grey slacks and a beige sweater vest, and basically looks like a traditional grandfather—though, ironically, nothing like my own.

We stand in silence for another moment, the air thick with tension.

"Ghost Hunters, I presume," he starts, "You might as well give me your names." Mr Heckney drops the bag and rifles through his pockets before pulling out a cigarette and putting in his mouth. His hands shake as he flicks a lighter and lights it.

Behind me, Aunt J takes a step forward. "My name is Josephine Rhodes, and this is my niece, Huntliegh Parrish. We thought...*I* thought you were dead, Mr Heckney."

The old man coughs and laughs, the cigarette almost falling from his lips. "And what gave you that idea?" he asks, eyes crinkling.

"I...had a vision," Aunt J explains. "I saw you die by that spirit's hand. You were supposed to be dead for days."

His face drops as he glances between the two of us. I continue, "When we got here, we heard you shouting. That thing was a ghoul, wasn't it?"

Mr Heckney shrugs. "You tell me, little girl."

"And your daughter?" I ask, watching as his eyes widen. "What about her?"

The old man's face drops, the cigarette hanging from his cracked lips at an odd angle. He stares at me in a way that almost has me fidgeting. "Excuse me?"

"A little girl pointed to *this* door. Same little girl from the photos. You're obviously aware of the ghoul, and you obviously know what we do, so you must be aware of her protecting you. You're a sensitive." I turn to Aunt J. "Is there a chance she *sent* you that vision as a warning?"

Aunt J looks from Mr Heckney, to me, then out into the hall where we saw his daughter. She was no longer there, but that doesn't surprise me. Something about her doesn't sit right with me either; nothing about this house or situation or *anything* about this town does. I don't even know where to start with figuring it out, but I'm sure it all leads back to Morcant. Does this?

Mr Heckney starts shaking his head, pulling the cigarette from his mouth. "I don't believe it." He looks down at his hands and drops the cigarette to the floor, stamping it out. I flinch. When he looks back up at me, his eyes are full of hope. "So, you've seen her? My little Bonnie?"

I nod hesitantly and stamp down on the residue emotions emitting from the old man. "What happened to her, Mr. Heckney?"

The old man sighs and turns away from us, lowering himself onto the bed; the room, like the rest of the inside of the house, looks pristine, save for the broken glass scattered across the floor and the stamped-out cigarette. "My daughter went into that house."

A shiver courses through me. *That house.* He means the Morcant house.

He looks up, though he isn't staring at us. His gaze drifts behind us, lost in a memory. "My beautiful little Bonnie. She was seven when she went in there."

"I don't understand... How is she *here* then?" I ask, directing my question to Aunt J, who shakes her head, just as confused as I am—I feel it as she opens her emotions up to me, though only partially.

Mr Heckney continues, "My property backs onto the Morcant estate, is almost part of it. I've seen many spirits wander through the forest, lost and trapped. My daughter is amongst them."

"Is there a chance that you've seen my parents?" I ask. Aunt J tugs on my hand sharply.

He meets my stare sadly. "If they were like you, then they're trapped only in the house. The ones Morcant finds useful stay there. His estate is large, and I've spent most of my life documenting it."

I narrow my eyes. "You're going to try and find the bodies,

aren't you? You're looking for your daughter."

Mr. Heckney nods sadly and points to the door behind us. "My daughters room. Sometimes...sometimes I can hear her playing in there. I want to put her to rest. Like you clearly want to do with your parents."

Mouth dry, I can only nod.

"Sometimes, Bonnie brings a friend with her to play. I see them in the yard, and they run around with each other, like normal children. A little boy, not much older than her. The poor child; his parents don't know what happened to him. I remember when he went missing."

I cast Aunt J a quick glance; tears shine in her eyes, and she remains uncharacteristically quiet, like she isn't sure what to say. I squeeze her hand, and she blinks furiously.

With a groan, Mr. Heckney stands and gestures to the hall. I pull Aunt J with me as we step out. The old man strides past us, and we follow him down the stairs and to a basement door. Using a key that he has tied around his neck, he unlocks the door and lets it swing open. Lights immediately come on, casting a yellow glow over the cement stairs.

"Down the rabbit hole we go," I mutter, grimacing as Mr Heckney makes his way down the stairs. I glance back at Aunt J, who shrugs. Isn't this the part where we go running from the house? For all we know, he's a serial killer on Morcant's side.

As if reading my thoughts, Aunt J narrows her eyes and points down the stairs.

I sigh and follow the old man down, my hand still clutched in Aunt Josephine's. We descend into the darkness together. From here, I can't make out much other than shadows. Despite the strangeness of the situation—and how *dangerous* it is—I don't feel fear. The logical side of me berates the curious side.

At the foot of the stairs, Mr Heckney stops and flicks a switch, illuminating the rest of the basement. As light floods the secluded space, my mouth drops open, surprise coursing through me.

Covering the walls are hundreds of newspaper clippings and police reports, with a detailed diagram of the Morcant estate directly in the centre of the room. There are a couple of large computer screens mounted on the walls, all attached to a single desktop computer at the far end of the basement. Built into the wall beside me are bookshelves filled with hundreds of books, all about spirits, the dead, and Morcant.

I release a breath and study the room, striding to the closest wall. Above the papers and photographs, in bright red letters, reads **'THE BEGINNING'**; directly below that is the only known photograph of Morcant.

He looks exactly like he did in my vision. The same dark hair and manic look in his dark eyes, the same pale skin and sunken face. In this picture, though, he wears a tailored suit, standing on the steps of the massive house after it was finished. Morcant himself wouldn't have arrived in America yet, having sent an architect ahead of him to build his new home.

It had taken almost five years to complete, and the house itself had claimed the lives of many workers and even the architect himself, who was arranged to marry Morcant's only daughter, Delilah. The arrangement had then, of course, ended, and Delilah was to be given to another man to marry shortly after they arrived in Fort Caldwell.

She never even made it to her wedding day; at the age of seventeen, Delilah Morcant had been sacrificed alongside five other girls in Morcant's demonic church.

I shudder, looking over the same information I have drilled in my head. I've been compiling everything since my parents were taken.

"I have spent *years* gathering this information, so that someone like you could carry out the task of destroying the demon himself," Mr Heckney says, walking over to the diagram. I follow—at a safe distance—and look to where he points from the other side of the table. Aunt J clings to my side like a child I can't shake, but I don't mind. I take comfort in her presence.

"Here," he continues, gesturing to a destroyed building off in the wooded area of the estate, "was the church, where he apparently claimed the lives of sixty-six women, and sixty-six men. No one can say they ever saw him do it, but you know...when one-hundred and thirty-two people go missing in town under 'strange circumstances', fingers tend to be pointed. Every one of his victims went to this church, too, and their names were written in his book."

I glance over the diagram; the house itself stands four storeys high, with an attic and multiple cellars down below. Rumour has it, there are even tunnels that spread across the property, so that if anything were to happen, Morcant could easily escape.

Instead, though, he vanished within the house and ordered his staff to close the doors forever.

Ten years after his disappearance, the house was remodelled—though only slightly—to accommodate a new use; an orphanage, run by Matron Ellis. After six months of running the house, she went missing, along with five children. Officials at the time claimed a copy-cat killer was running around town, so they closed the house to be safe.

Locals, though, claimed the spirit of Morcant still ran the house, and killed to satisfy his god, Satan.

Another shudder crawls over my skin as images from my vision flash across my eyes; the Matron talking to families, the children who watched with dead eyes, Morcant and Delilah standing amongst the spirits, preparing to take more.

"Are there any other buildings out there?" I ask, pointing to the woods. I shove the vision from my mind and focus on the diagram.

Mr Heckney shakes his head. "I've walked these woods for

years, and I have only ever found the remains of the church. No trap doors, either. No hidden passages under there."

I purse my lips. "What about sewer entrances?"

"Why?" he asks sceptically, raising a silver brow.

I lean into the diagram, looking for any ways into the underground, where he might stow the bodies. But if Mr Heckney ever found any, he never bothered to note them in his extremely detailed diagram.

"The only way into the house is through the front door, isn't it?" Aunt J asks, voice nearly a whisper. I squeeze her hand, and she squeezes back.

Mr Heckney nods. "As far as I know, any who enter the house and stay once midnight strikes rarely ever return."

I look down, feeling my throat close. In my chest, my heart thunders against my ribcage so hard I'm surprised it doesn't fracture. After the house had been emptied of its orphans, it remained empty for sixty years. The town turned it into an asylum for the criminally insane, and after sixteen disappearances, they transferred all patients to another location. It happened again when they turned the house into an all boys boarding school. Too many disappeared, and the house closed entirely.

Morcant had been taking large numbers at a time while the house was full, but when it shut down entirely, he began taking anyone who was stupid enough to go in.

Like Mr Heckney's daughter, like my parents.

I shudder violently and take a step back from the diagram and away from the elderly man. "So, you've never gone into the house?"

"No." He laughs darkly. "I was never stupid enough to. I took my time with the rest of the forest, decided he wouldn't bother trying to take me in broad daylight. Something about the sun really pisses him off, I think. After I got started with my research, I became too old to go in there and risk it. Lots of people have come by looking for information, but they never returned."

My stomach drops as I glance at another side of the wall, where a bold header reads **'*HUNTERS*'**. Below it are pictures and news clippings. My parents are amongst them. "You saw them?" I ask, walking to the wall in three long strides. I pull the paper from the wall; I have the same one, tucked away in my bag. It keeps me going, helps me keep fighting. I gave an identical one to my grandfather the day he said good-riddance to Aunt J and I. "They were here?"

Mr Heckney scrunches his brows, his eyes widening as the realisation hits him. "They were your parents?" he asks, taking the clipping from me. I nod, hands trembling. "Good people, they were. I thought they might be different." He shrugs and pins the clipping back up on the wall.

I watch as he does, lights flaring behind my eyes. My parents had *been* here, in this very room, doing exactly what *I* am doing...and they still died.

We're missing *something*, something crucial, but what? What could be so important that got my parents killed? They were far more skilled and knowledgeable than I am, than Aunt J. What had *they* missed?

"Hunt? You okay?" Aunt J asks, pulling me from my thoughts.

I shake my head and run my hands through my hair, trying my hardest to keep my breathing even, to keep my heart rate steady. But I can't do it.

"I need some air," I whisper, running for the stairs. I don't bother listening as she yells for me, don't even flinch when Bonnie appears in front of me. I just need to get out.

~ ~ ~

I suck in a chilling breath, relishing in the cool air that washes over me. I soak in the soft caress of rain as it washes away the trapped feeling and smile as thunder cracks overhead, the end-of-summer storm finally reaching our little pocket of the world. Out here, despite the landscape, a calmness washes over me.

Though, I'm not sure if it's me, or the spirit that stands beside me.

The little boy has to be no more than twelve, with dishevelled black hair and dark eyes that probably once sparkled. His photo had been pinned to Mr Heckney's wall, so he could be Bonnie's little friend.

He looks up at me, blood smeared across his youthful face, streaming from his eyes in a similar manner to Bonnie's. Much like her, there is something...*different* about the way he conducts himself, almost like he knows he's dead and doesn't mind it one bit.

The little boy never speaks, though, and I don't want him to.

"You alright, girl?" Mr Heckney asks, waddling over to where I stand beside one of the car shells.

I shrug, looking out into the forest. Night slowly descends upon us, turning the woods into a giant shadow that only seems to grow, inching closer and closer. Amongst the trees are spirits, wandering aimlessly between brambles and branches. All I feel from them is confusion.

"What's west of the estate?" I ask, cocking my head. If I try hard enough, I think I might be able to see it from here.

Mr Heckney coughs loudly, chest rattling loud enough for me to here. "The church. Why?"

"A vision," I say, shrugging again. "Someone wrote the word '*west*' on a wall with blood."

The old man stares at me before turning to the wood and squinting. "Strange."

Strange, indeed.

"Huntliegh!" Aunt J shouts. I turn and watch as she comes

around the side of the house, sighing as she spots Mr Heckney and I standing in the back. "Oh thank God, I thought you took the car for a moment there, or that you ran straight into that forest." She visibly shudders, and I don't blame her.

I also don't admit I'm too afraid to step foot in there after dark.

"Come on. We should go home," she says.

Turning back to Mr. Heckney, I watch as he pulls the spirit bag from his pocket and holds it in front of him. "Do you know what do with that ghoul up there?" I ask.

He sighs loudly. "It's my brother, the son of a bitch. Been dead twenty years, wish he'd stay that way. I'll handle him."

I can't help but smile at him. "Alright." Reaching over, I close his fingers around the bag.

I step away, dropping my hand from his. Before I can fully turn, he says, "Make sure you come back some time, alright? I want to help you, little girl."

This time, I grin as widely as I can. "Okay, old man. I'll be back."

Mr Heckney nods and waves as I take Aunt Josephine's hand once again. As we make our way back to the car, I look back to the house and wave to little Bonnie and her friend.

10

THE DEAD DON'T TALK

I MAKE ABSOLUTELY NO SOUND AS I roll the bike out of the garage. Despite the floodlights lining the street, an impenetrable darkness smothers the town, almost like the night knows this is Morcant's dominion.

Rain continues to fall in a steady rhythm, splattering against the seat of the bike and my helmet, which is locked tightly on my head. I can already imagine what Aunt J is going to say if she finds me out of bed, breaking curfew, with the bike.

I take the bike two houses up before I sit and start the engine. A crack of thunder masks the sound, and I sigh in relief as it purrs to life, surprised that neither Tate nor Darren thought to empty the tank.

They will now, though. Note to self, don't mention it.

I kick off. Midnight in Fort Caldwell means everyone is in bed—though I'm not surprised, since it's Sunday—or technically

Monday?—and the responsible adults have to work. Part of me wonders if the kids my age are having one last party before school goes back. Down by the lake, I imagine, where they can swim and build a fire and be away from everything.

Part of me doesn't care, as long as they aren't at Morcant's estate.

I carefully pick up speed and drift through the sleepy town. My body knows where to go, even if my mind doesn't. I pass Heckney's house and slow. Everything is dark, the yard even more terrifying at night. The forest beyond looks like a dark wall that seems impossible to cross.

I take a right and pull out onto the service road that leads to the estate. On either side of me is darkness, the single light on the front of the bike doing little to illuminate the shadows. I drive for maybe ten minutes before I see the fence that blocks the road and stops people from crossing the estate line. No security team there, but I'm sure they aren't far away.

Cruising to a stop, I kick out the stand and pull my helmet off. The bike still rumbles beneath me, just in case.

The thick forest stops the harshness of the rain from hitting the road, which is somewhat of a relief. My insides are like sludge as I search the trees. Hope sparks within me, like maybe, if I'm lucky, I'll see my parents.

Bile rises in my throat, and the hope quickly disappears. The last thing I need to see is the ghosts of my parents, who probably won't recognize me, who are trapped in the house until Morcant is finally defeated.

I shudder. The darkness around me thickens until it's almost impossible to see through, despite the headlight still glaring into the night. I release a breath and prepare to put my helmet back on.

Until *something* comes over me.

I still, fingers tightening around the helmet. From the corner of my eye, I spy a grey figure standing just off the side of the road. The only clear details I can make out is a cane and a top hat.

Morcant.

I'm not sure why I think that, but it feels like a correct assumption.

Behind him, I see *them.*

Spirits.

But they aren't *coming* from the estate. I look behind me, around me. I see at least a dozen from varying periods of time, floating in the direction of the house. Their gazes see right through me, and when I reach out to feel for their emotions, I sense nothing.

Slowly, I swing my leg over the bike and approach the last spirit. He's a young man, no older than twenty-five, with a moustache and glasses and the beginnings of a beard. His clothes are splattered with blood, half his body mangled. A car accident, maybe. He could have been a teacher; his eyes are a kind shade of brown, and he has that *good-with-children* vibe about him.

I wave my hand in front of his face as I walk backwards. But he doesn't stop. "Hello?" I reach out again for him, hoping that maybe I'll get a vision or something to understand what the hell is going on.

But it's like he's a blank slate, a shadow of his former self. I step aside and watch as he disappears beyond the property line.

Slowly, I turn to face Morcant, but he's already gone.

~ ~ ~

The door to the garage clicks shut softly, hidden by the pounding rain. I slide the helmet off and shake out my hair, the ends wet from where it had stuck out from beneath the helmet.

As I enter the kitchen, a light flickers on, and I squint from the sudden brightness.

Crap.

I look up expecting Aunt J but instead find Darren's burly figure. When I'd left, he'd been asleep on the pull-out couch with Tate, both snoring enough to match the crescendo of the thunder. But now he sits in front of me at the island with bleary eyes and a frown that means trouble.

"Sit," he commands, and I do so without arguing. It's hard to get him angry but even harder to disappoint him, and I think I managed to accomplish both in one night.

Fan-freaking-tastic.

"Were you at that house?" he asks, jumping straight to the point.

I sigh. There's no use in lying—sensing lies is one of his talents, or so he claims—so I nod. "Yeah, I went out there to get a look."

Darren rubs his eyes tiredly. "Why?"

I shrug. "I just wanted to see it. At night, when the spirits are more active. It was...strange." I shake my head, thoughts going back to what I saw. "There were spirits that weren't trapped there entering the grounds, like they were being pulled there somehow. They didn't even notice me."

I wait for Darren to snap or get angry, but he watches me with the same confusion I felt early. "What did you feel from them?" he asks, surprising me.

I suck in a breath and dredge up the memory; Morcant watching me from the side of the road, the dozen or so spirits walking through the trees and across the border between the estate and the rest of the town. When I'd felt nothing from the approaching spirits.

"Nothing," I say quietly. It's been a while since I've felt absolutely nothing from a spirit. "I felt nothing from them. I tried, I actually sought one out. But whatever they were doing, it wasn't...right."

Darren nods and looks away. "Jo said you saw your parents on that wall, in the old man's house. Is that why you went tonight?"

I swallow bile that rises in my throat, and slowly nod. "Yeah."

He remains quiet for a moment before sighing. "Go to bed, Hunt. You have school in the morning." He rises and looks back at me. "And don't think about sneaking out again."

I watch him return to the living room, listen as the sofa bed creaks as he climbs in. They've stayed longer than they wanted, but I know it's just to make sure we're alright. I release a heavy breath and make my way through the house. With every step, the house creaks, as if letting me know it'll snitch the next time I try anything.

As I close my bedroom door behind me, I shut my eyes and lean back against it, and know full well I won't be sleeping tonight—or any night until Morcant is gone.

11

IS THIS HELL?

***I LOOK LIKE AN IDIOT*, I THINK AS** I cock my head, looking over my second-choice outfit. The frayed skinny jeans look strange on me for some reason, and the sweater I'd stolen from Aunt J looks too...*new*, like I'm trying too hard to fit in.

The alternative is a pair of shorts and a plain t-shirt, but that seems *too* casual to wear on the first day. I find comfort in the stolen sweater; after the weekend I've had, the idea of school feels wrong and foreign.

I give myself a tight-lipped smile in the mirror and sigh, throwing my dark brown hair up into a bun. It's good enough.

My mind strays to Mr Heckney and last night's little adventure. What else does the old man know? What can he tell me? I itch to go back there, to even walk through the forest myself—in daylight, of course. But the thought sends my brain into overload.

"You look nice. Any reason in particular?" Aunt J asks from the doorway, still cosy in her pyjamas. She winks. "Are you excited for your trip to school?"

I narrow my eyes and huff, tucking my shirt into my jeans. "No. I just hate having nothing decent to wear in this town. And I'm tired as hell."

Aunt J makes a sound in the back of her throat. This morning I've had two coffees, so I'm running on a caffeine high and anxiety over this whole ordeal. The distraction of *clothes* is welcome.

"How so?" she asks, head cocked. Her smile is all-knowing, and I glower at what's behind it.

"Every town is different, especially when it comes to style," I say, throwing my books into my bag. "Last school I went to, wearing anything 'hipster' was fine. Here, it could be entirely different. Flannel might be in, and if I show up in something that screams 'outsider' then I'll have to live in this stupid town with 'kick-me' stamped across my back."

Aunt J rolls her eyes dramatically and falls onto my bed with a sigh. "Well, I think you look nice. Even if that's my sweater."

"Nice won't cut it, Aunt J."

"Since when did you care?" she asks. I remain quiet for a moment, staring down at my socks, then over at my boots. I still can't shake that old man and his daughter from my head or the strange spirits from last night. "Hunt?"

"I just..." I trail off and frown. "I thought about what you and Darren and Tate were talking about. And after going over that information, I...I realised just how *hard* this is going to be. And I know now that this is going to take some time to do." I also need more of a reason to stay, for Mr Heckney and my parents. I need to stay as long as possible to get the job done. There's too much riding on this—on me.

Aunt J raises a brow, sitting up. "Are you...are you telling me you're prepared to stay? In this town? And make friends?"

I purse my lips and nod, the lie a bitter sensation that crushes my heart. There's no way I'll also admit to staying up all night locating any and all possible spirit attacks from the last three months, while also pouring over a map of the Morcant estate—which is massive, by the way—trying to figure out what the hell is going on with the ghostly population of this town. I keep trying to recall the detailed diagram Mr Heckney had created; I wish I'd taken a photo of it. If I can get myself used to the place, then maybe I'll have more of a chance in going up against Morcant.

Based on the information we have about Morcant, there has to be a cellar where he's stored all his victims once he's sacrificed them. And I'll bet that's where my mom and dad are.

The thought sends chills down my spine.

"You alright, Hunt?" Aunt J asks, breaking through my thoughts.

I force a smile. "Yeah, fine."

Downstairs, the doorbell rings, echoing through the townhouse.

"Oh, that'll be Weston!" Aunt J says, a wide smile spreading across her face.

I grimace and look back over my outfit before grabbing the cardigan and my bag. I shove the protection bag into one of the inner pockets, careful to close it before turning to my door. Down below, I hear someone—Darren or Tate, whoever is up this early—greet Weston.

"Wish me luck," I mutter.

Aunt J laughs loudly. "Good luck, honey!"

~ ~ ~

Heart racing, I smile up at Weston as we walk towards his silver truck. From the moment I saw him, standing at the door with Darren, I couldn't quite...*speak*; whether it was because of pure exhaustion, or because of something else, but every moment spent with him gives me pause.

I'm not here to meet boys. I am here to defeat Morcant.

I'm not here to meet boys. I am here to defeat Morcant.

I repeat the mantra three more times in my head before climbing into the truck. I drop my bag to the floor of the cab and sit back, pulling the seat belt over my body and clicking it into place. The movements feel robotic, unnatural. But it means I don't have to look at him or smile as pleasantly as he does. It means not getting distracted, so that I can really analyse what happened last night.

And yet, I can't help but look over to him; the look of pure concentration on his face as he turns the car on and the way he tilts his head, his hair falling into his face.

Weston glances over and smiles again. I quickly look away, and curse myself; caught looking? Really? I'm almost tempted to slap myself.

I'm not here to meet boys or make lasting connections. I'm here to defeat Morcant. And when that's done...

I look back over; my cheeks heat up.

"Are you excited? Nervous?" Weston asks, pulling out of his driveway.

Shrugging, I avert my eyes and concentrate on the street. We head down the main road, passing the little coffee shops I noticed when we rolled into town. "Aunt J works in different towns quite a lot," I explain. "I'm used to being the new kid."

"That kind of sucks," he replies. A police car cut us off. Weston slams the breaks, swearing. An ambulance follows just as quickly. I think back to Amber, to the arrival of police. They must have been relieved to have a win.

They head around a bend, towards the lake. I turn to Weston. "Does this happen often?"

Lips thin, he checks me over. "Not really, but..."

But something's off in this town. He doesn't have to finish the sentence or thought; whatever power Morcant has, it's influencing any and all spirit activity in Fort Caldwell. Spirits who haven't even had the time to cross over are somehow being trapped here, forced to relive their deaths. Or somehow, they're drawn to the house.

Maybe it's an epicentre of sorts? Sensitives like Hunters are usually drawn to areas with greater spiritual activity. Could spirits sense that too and be drawn towards that? But what about Amber?

Weston and I remain quiet for the remainder of the ten-minute drive to school; the campus is located on the other side of town, situated in a neighbourhood full of new, shiny houses—completely different to the neighbourhood we live in.

Fort Caldwell has one high school, a middle school next door, and an elementary school two blocks from our house. There's a college campus about an hour away, in the next town over, Aunt J explained when we first arrived.

But Fort Caldwell High is nothing spectacular; a multi-storey complex made of strangely placed square buildings, it looks ugly compared to the houses that surround it. Of course, the sporting field looks new. Across the front of the building, someone is hanging a banner that reads: '*Go Demons!*'

I shudder. Funny how they chose *demons* as their mascot when their own town has a resident demon living in the forest.

"I'll show you to the admin building, okay?" Weston says, dragging me from my thoughts. His smile is wide once more but not as beaming as it was before.

Giving him a tight-lipped smile, I step out of the truck, releasing a heavy breath. Time to be the new kid once again.

A feeling of terror washes over me then, suffocating me. It spreads deep in my mind, branching off until it's all I feel. There is no wind, and yet a chill seeps through my sweater, leeching into my bones.

I shudder and step back.

"Hey, are you okay?" Weston asks, coming around the side of the truck. He has my bag in his hand. Did I drop it?

People watch us; a guy in a letterman's jacket stops, probably to talk to Weston. The guy has his arm wrapped around a pretty Latina girl, who stares with piercing hazel eyes; overall totally gorgeous in a *I can and will step on you* kind of way.

I push the terror aside; whatever spirit sent me *that* is powerful, though I doubt Morcant is responsible for it. That emotion was pure and raw; it can't be transferred unless the spirit itself felt it.

Shaking my head, I try to smile. "Yeah, fine, I think I just got up too quickly."

"Did you eat this morning?" he asks, my bag still in his hand. I reach for it, and he gives it up. I don't reply straight away; I hadn't, despite Tate giving me the side eye when I looked at his scrambled eggs.

Instead, you downed two cups of coffee.

I shrug. "I didn't…"

My next-door neighbour shakes his head in disappointment. "It's the most important meal of the day."

"Okay, Mom, I'll remember tomorrow," I reply. I stop myself from laughing.

I'm not here to meet boys. I am here to defeat Morcant.

The bright smile that had been on his face earlier returns, and it sends a strange flutter down my stomach and washes away the rest of the panic.

The letterman-jacket guy clears his throat, finally approaching. "Hey, man," he starts, looking between Weston and me. "This the new girl?"

I offer the guy a smile, if only to be nice. "I'm Huntliegh."

"Connor," he replies. "This is my girlfriend, Blaire."

The girl—Blaire—steps away from him and smiles widely. "Blaire Contreras. It's really nice to meet you," she says. Overhead, a bell rings, and she sighs. "I have homeroom. Do you have your schedule yet, Huntliegh?" I nod.

Connor gestures for us to follow, leading us towards the front of the school.

I turn to Weston, who dons his own letterman jacket. "You're a jock?" I ask. Am I really surprised? Weston is *definitely* the type of guy to join football. Hell, he probably has a cheerleader girlfriend.

Weston laughs, opening the door for me. "Football jock," he says.

I thank him and we push our way into the busy hall. He takes my arm and leads me towards an office—Admin, obviously— where I'll most likely get a rundown of all the school rules, appropriate dress code, and other things I already have drilled into my head.

The office is quiet compared to the shrill hum of the hallway. An older man sits behind the desk, black rimmed glasses sitting on the tip of his nose. He doesn't bother looking up as we approach. "Weston Mackenzie, please go to class."

Behind me, Weston sighs. "Yeah, I'm going. Thought I'd show the newbie here, though."

The man—Mr Contreras, his nametag reads—frowns and looks between us. He has the same hazel eyes as Blaire, and I realise this must be her father. Where her eyes are critical, his are kind, full of amusement.

"Well, well, well," he murmurs. He offers me a wide smile, reaching for what has to be a school-approved 'newbie' package. I take it robotically. It'll just go in recycling when I get home. "You must be Huntliegh. I had a *lovely* chat with your aunt when she came in to enrol you. Lovely woman."

I smile and look down; school map, handbook, a newsletter. I already have the rest.

Another bell rings, and Mr Contreras gives Weston an impatient look. "I think I can handle Miss Parrish's induction, Mr Mackenzie. Please, go to class."

I feel Weston's hand—warm and steady—rest on my elbow. "I'll give you a lift home, 'kay? And if you want, you can sit with me at lunch."

Despite myself, I nod; I already plan on sitting in the library to pour over as many newspaper clippings and police reports I can concerning Morcant. Sitting with Weston would be nice, but I don't fit in with his crowd; I'm not popularity material, or a cheerleader, or a sport star. I coast in the middle of school, keeping decent grades so teachers won't point fingers and my grandfather doesn't say anything.

Clenching my teeth, I watch as he leaves the office, abandoning me with Mr Contreras. "He's a nice boy, doesn't know when to stop."

I look back to him. I haven't even spoken once. "Thank you, uh, for this," I say, waving the pile around.

Mr Contreras rolls his eyes. "Doubt you need it. You look like you know what you're doing, no offense."

I shrug. "You're right."

Eyes narrowed, he watches me for several moments; I've fought serial killers, women in white, serial abusers, and *more*, but for whatever reason, this man's gaze makes me squirm, like he somehow knows everything I've ever done in my life. Like he knows why I'm really here in Fort Caldwell.

"Well, how about I show you to homeroom? Doubt you need any induction. You've heard it all before. Don't wear revealing clothes. Be at school on time, otherwise the doors will be locked. Your schedule is in that little bundle. Oh, and school spirit!" He pumps his fist into the air with a sarcastic smile.

Mr Contreras walks around the desk; he isn't overly tall,

probably only an inch taller than I am, but he manages to fill the space with a kind air that should make all new kids comfortable.

"Now," he starts as we enter the now quiet hall. "Unfortunately for you, you have homeroom and calculus with my horrible daughter, Blaire. On the bright side, you have PE with my *other* horrible daughter, Riley. Don't let them confuse you, though; they are twins, but one rebelled and has pink hair, so you should be *fine*."

I let a smile form on my lips; maybe Fort Caldwell High won't be as bad as I first thought.

~ ~ ~

Not only do I have PE with Mr Contreras's daughter, Riley, but I also have it with Weston and Connor, and it's right before lunch, which means sneaking away to the library will be much harder than I thought it would be.

Naturally, as per school sexism, girls and boys split up; boys are out running track in a misty, summer rain, while the girls are in the recently refurbished gymnasium playing basketball.

We're automatically put into teams, and I've been placed with Riley. She sidles up to me, pink hair pulled up into a long ponytail. "I'm Riley, Blaire's less talented twin, who you met this morning standing beside the Ken doll."

I snort. Connor does, in fact, look like a glorified Ken doll now that I think about it. I shake my head. "Thank you for putting that mental image in my head. Now, all I'll see when I'm forced to converse with him is Ken and Barbie."

Riley smiles. "You got a name, newbie?"

"I'm Huntliegh," I reply, grimacing.

She shrugs, turning to the coach. "Interesting name, Huntliegh. Any particular reason your parents chose *that*?"

"They liked the sound of it," I say, though the mention of

them sends a pang into my heart. I clear my throat. "My aunt chose it, though. Said it meant 'protector' or something. I don't know, she's into all that kind of stuff."

Riley doesn't reply, and instead motions for me to follow her to the other side of the court. The athletic girls take control quickly, and we're left in the back, forgotten by both our peers and the coach, who keeps her eyes on the 'worthwhile' students.

"You like it here?" Riley asks, arms crossed over her chest.

"I guess? Small towns all look the same after a while."

She looks over to me. "Move around a lot?"

I nod. "Yeah. My aunt packs us up whenever her job moves her," I lie. The words slide from my mouth easily—too easily. I know I have to, but something in my gut churns with every lie I'm forced to tell. But it's better than the truth.

"What about your parents?" she asks, narrowing her eyes at me.

"They died a couple of years ago," I say. At least I don't have to lie about this.

Riley looks away, arms dropping to her side. The ball bounces towards us, and I grab it before it can go out of bounds—and before the P.E teacher gets pissed. Dribbling, I pass it to a girl I recognise from my team.

"My mom died from cancer a year ago," Riley says as the group rushes to the other end of the court. "I know what it's like; that's why I have pink hair. They might be dead, but they never really go, do they?" She touches the ends of her hair, frowning.

I nod silently, any response dying on my lips.

The rest of PE drags; Riley and I talk the rest of class about the woes of small-town mentality and only join in when the ball comes remotely close to where we stand. About ten minutes before the bell, the boys come running in, shoulders wet with rain and drenched in sweat.

Weston and Connor jog towards Riley and I, grinning.

"Enjoying yourselves?"

I shrug, but Riley says, "We *were* before you stinking morons decided to come over here."

"We're sorry we interrupted," Weston laughs wholeheartedly, unshaken.

"Enjoy the weather out there?" I ask, giving him a half smile.

The doors to the gym open, revealing the dark sky and mist; several more boys rush in—the slower of the lot, clearly—followed by the other coach.

Connor shrugs. "It wasn't too bad out there. I mean, it would have been nicer in *here* where it's *warm*."

"Yeah, I can't feel my toes," Weston says, grinning.

Our coach blows the whistle and shouts for everyone to clean up before the bell goes; I face Riley, who sighs and takes her sash off, pulling me along with her.

"Hey!" Weston calls. "Will I see you at lunch?"

Connor doesn't look all that stoked at the idea, and Riley turns around with a sour look on her face.

Facing Weston, I shrug helplessly; a part of me feels disappointed at the idea of not sitting with him, but another—larger—part sighs in relief. I shout back, "We'll see!"

When I turn around, I can't seem to get Weston's smile out of my head. I know I can't—no matter what Aunt J or Tate or Darren says. This town... I'm not here to stay. I'm here to defeat Morcant.

12

THE LIFE OF A HUNTER

"WAIT. WHAT DO YOU MEAN?" I ASK, propping the phone between my ear and shoulder. I cast a quick glance around me to make sure no teachers are around.

Aunt J sighs on the other end as I pull local history books from the shelf. There are quite a few about the Morcant property and what happened to it a hundred years ago. But I doubt any of them talk about the underground church and sacrificial chamber and where it would have been located.

They aren't nearly as detailed as Mr Heckney's works, which I no doubt need to read.

Aunt J makes a sound in the back of her throat. *"The vision was extremely clear, Hunt. This town is a hot spot because of the doorway."*

"How?" I ask. Someone at the desks shushes me, and I sneer. Quieting my voice, I say, "I don't understand. What kind of doorway?" I can't help but think of my earlier guess: that the town—and the house—are some kind of epicentre drawing in spirits.

She sighs again and somewhere in the distance, a car honks. *"In some areas around the globe, there are...breaches in the fabric of our universe that give spirits easy access to the living. When you're on a job, you burn the bones of the spirit you're hunting, right? Well, they have to go somewhere. That could be heaven or hell or whatever you want to believe. Now, the spirits that are trapped here, where are they? We don't normally see or hear from them, and if they are restless enough to cause harm like Morcant does, then where are they during that time?"* Aunt J pauses, whether it's for dramatic effect or to get an answer out of me, I'm not sure. But I don't have an answer.

I wonder if Mr Heckney does but shake my head.

"I don't know!" I say finally, breaking the silence. I drop my stack of books onto a desk and flinch when other students shush me again.

"They're behind a...curtain, of sorts. A veil. When they're here long enough, or become restless and dangerous, then they can break through and become corporeal. When they do, they can attack, kill, do all kinds of things to the living. In some places, that veil—or curtain—is thin, or broken enough for spirits to easily slip through and take a more physical form."

"Is that what's happening here?" I whisper, taking a seat. I flip through the pages of the first book, eyeing the ancient photographs and the massive walls of text. Before being abandoned, the Morcant house had been many things: an asylum, an orphanage, and a boy's school.

But strange occurrences continued to close down the many different operations. Which meant Morcant probably has *hundreds* of spirits trapped in there with him. And they're not all dead because of him...

If I consult Mr Heckney's walls, then I can probably count all the victims that fell prey to Morcant. Though, I doubt I'll have the time to. It won't even count the spirits he collects from outside the estate.

I shudder. "Aunt Josephine?"

"*Hmm? Oh, yes. I believe, with the growing strength of Morcant, that the veil is growing weaker. Any spirits trapped on this plane will be able to come and go as they please, I'm afraid.*"

"Meaning Morcant won't be trapped in his home anymore?"

"*No,*" she says quietly. "*I don't think he will. If my vision is correct...*"

Silence falls on the other end, and I hear nothing. Looking down at my textbooks, I realise my hand is shaking.

"*I think we have until Halloween to keep him locked in his house, Hunt.*"

My breath leaves me at once, and I slump in my seat. "That's less than two months away, Aunt Josephine."

"*This... It's more serious than I ever would have imagined. I am so sorry.*"

I run my fingers through my hair and continue to stare down at the book in front of me. Two months, if she's right. Two months to keep him trapped in that house. If I can keep him there, keep him *locked away*, then it could give me more time to find a way to kill him. But if he gets out, if he manages to enter the world of the living for a *second* time, then what is going to stop him from killing everyone in this town?

Releasing a shuddering breath, I close the textbook and sit back. "Is there any way we can stop it? Stop him?"

"*I'm working on that,*" she says proudly. "*Tate and Darren are going to stay until we sort out this mess, okay?*"

"Yeah, okay," I murmur, shaking my head, "sounds good. We're going to need all the help we can get."

She says something else, but I don't quite catch it. The doors to the library open, and I look up just as Weston enters with Connor in tow. They both have amused grins on their faces and duffels tucked under their arms.

I forgot about our shared study period.

I look back down quickly. "I have to go, Aunt J. Text me when you find anything else out, okay? I'll talk to you when you get home. Bye." I hang up before she can get a word in, and I place my binder over the history books as Weston makes his way to me.

Swallowing, I force myself to smile up at him. "I didn't think jocks like you would be caught dead in the library."

"I say death to that stereotype. I happen to be very studious," he replies, smirking.

I shake my head and point to Connor. "What about him?"

Weston subtly turns around to catch a glance of his friend before turning back to me. He shrugs helplessly. "Okay, *he* falls into the stereotype, but I'm trying to get him to change his ways."

Once again, I can't help but think there's something different about him.

"Are you still good to come home with me?" he asks.

"Huh? Oh, yeah, definitely, thank you." I smile as he perches on the desk in front of me, dropping his duffel to the ground.

He narrows his eyes at the stack of books. "What are you reading?"

I look down at the history books, eyes widening. I don't have time to stop him from moving my binder out of the way so he can read the title.

"*A History of the Unusual; The Life and Story of Josiah Morcant.* You're a local history buff?" Weston's brows shoot up, and I cover my eyes in embarrassment.

"Maybe?" He laughs, the sound filling the library. "Shut up, there's nothing wrong with looking into the town you live in. Anyway, the story of Morcant seriously freaks me out," I reply. Half lie. Morcant does freak me out.

His laughter dies down, and he leans forward, oddly close for this to be friendly, but he still has that smile on his face. "He's just a ghost story."

I shrug. Unfortunately, he's way more than just a *'ghost story'*. He's painfully real and painfully ready to take over this town if he gets the chance. "Yeah, well, it's also interesting how no one picked up on his wrong doings until *after* he killed fifty people and sacrificed his daughter to Satan."

Weston sighs. "He killed one hundred and thirty-two before taking his daughter," he corrects, eyes glimmering. I raise a brow. "What? You're the only one allowed to be weirdly fascinated with this town?"

"You were *literally* just laughing at me about it," I point out. I don't mention how his daughter had been specifically sacrificed with five other girls her age, and that the general 'one hundred and thirty-two' is only a cover up, and that it also didn't include the many who died while building his home.

No one really knows how many he killed before Delilah.

"Yeah, well," he says, shrugging, "let's just say that dude was seriously sick in the head."

Yeah, you have no idea. He's still sacrificing people beyond the grave—my parents joined that list.

We remain quiet for several moments, each lost in our own thoughts. With him here, sitting in front of me...my mind doesn't immediately jump back to the case or to Morcant and the difficult task of trapping him back in his house on Halloween. It's peaceful, despite the very real threat of Morcant.

Overhead, the bell rings, calling for last period. Weston clears his throat and stands, snatching his bag from the floor. "I'll see you at the car, okay?"

I don't get the chance to reply as he rushes off, grabbing Connor by the back of the neck. Together, they enter the hallway and disappear amongst the rush of other students.

Sighing, I gather my binder and bag. I look back down at the textbooks and those fears and worries come rushing back. What if I can't stop Morcant before Halloween? What happens then?

~ ~ ~

The car ride home is oddly quiet, save for the radio playing and Weston humming along as he drives. When I met him at the truck, he opened the door for me, asked me what I thought about school, and then shut up after that.

I look down at my phone as we pull up to his driveway; no new messages from Aunt J about her miraculous plan, but I do have four texts from Riley about some party this weekend.

"Are you going to Simone Barlow's party?" I ask, breaking the silence. I look over to him, and he pauses, pouting slightly.

He scratches the back of his neck. Weston's fingers tangle into the dark curls of his hair as he says, "Maybe? I mean, it depends on the weather, and whether or not I'll have something to wear. Oh, and not to mention whether a certain new girl will be going..." He turns to me with a hopeful smile.

Shaking my head, I sit back, rolling my eyes. "Why would you want to go with me, Weston? Not to sound cliché or anything, but...you don't even know me. Well, not enough to warrant anything."

He shrugs as he turns the truck off, leaving us to sit in silence. "Isn't that the point of hanging out? Getting to know one another?"

"I suppose," I reply, glancing down at my phone. Another message comes through from Riley, who continues to impatiently ask if I'll be going on Saturday and if she needs to pick me up. She lives on the other side of town, closer to where the party is. It'd be a real pain if she has to drive here, get me, then go back. But...if Weston goes too...

"Like I said, Hunt. I'll go if you do. I'm not much of a party person. You know, weather, clothing choices..." I meet his stare, see that friendly, charming smile, and match it.

Finally, I concede, nodding. "I'll go if you take me. I doubt I'll be allowed to borrow the car and my aunt would probably drain the tank of my bike if I even asked. If I mention you taking me, I'll have a better chance at escaping."

Weston's brows shoot up, and he looks between me and the townhouse. "You have a motorcycle?"

Grinning, I nod. "What? Don't I look like I biker chick?" I gestured to my sweater and skinny jeans. I look like the complete opposite, honestly.

"No, I never would have thought," he replies, running his hand through his hair. "Mind taking me for a ride sometime?"

My heartbeat accelerates, hammering in my chest. I'm not sure why it even *matters* this much, or even why my palms are sweaty now just *thinking* about riding with him behind me... My God, I'm turning into a ninny—like in a stupid rom-com.

Clearing my throat, I smile. "Sure. Maybe when the weather clears up a bit. Again, Aunt J will drain the tank if it looks too dangerous outside."

Weston's eyes crinkle at the corners as he smiles. "Great. I'd love that. Uh, text me if you do end up deciding on going to the party. I'll definitely take you."

Biting down on my lip, I contemplate saying anything else, but before I can, Aunt J pulls up in front of the house, her old car roaring to a stop. She jumps out, wearing some horrid mustard-coloured sweater and blue jeans, matched with converses and a beanie.

"Huntliegh!" she calls, waving me over.

Sighing, I give Weston a smile. "Thank you, again, for the rides. Once we're settled, I'll be able to drive myself..."

"Anytime, Hunt."

Stepping out of the truck, I wave as I cross the grass between our two houses. Behind me, Weston says something to Aunt J, but I ignore it and head straight for her.

The worry and fear seeps back into my bones, growing stronger the closer I get. "Anything?"

She purses her lips, waves to Weston, and wraps an arm around my shoulders. "Let's talk about this inside. We have a lot of work to do."

The house is quiet when we step across the threshold; in the living room, Darren and Tate are reading over whatever information they've managed to get today. Steaming cups of cocoa sit on the table, practically forgotten.

"Anything, Jo?" Darren asks, finally looking up. He pulls his reading glasses off his face. "How was school, Hunt?"

I shrug. "Fine. School's just...school. Where are we at with our new deadline?"

Tate glances at his husband with a look of disdain, shaking his head.

Meeting Tate's stare, Darren continues, "We've been looking into whatever we can find, kiddo. Only problem is..."

"What?" I ask. I drop my bag beside the couch and fall to the floor, crossing my legs beneath me. Suddenly, I feel like a child again, sitting at their feet.

They share another look. "There isn't much documentation about these kinds of...*occurrences*," Tate says, visibly uncomfortable. He runs a dark-brown hand over his shaved head. "There are so many contradictions in the lore...at this rate, we're going to have to try everything."

Furrowing my brows, I bring my knees to my chest. This has to be rare, no doubt, but I never expected it to be *this* hard. And contradictory? I rub my eyes. How can it be contradictory? Math is contradictory, English and History are contradictory. But lore? Fighting the bad spirits? That should be simple.

"How many different things do we need to try?" I ask, looking at the table. "At this rate, two months are going to go quickly, so I don't think we have much of a choice. We don't have time to try everything."

Tate shuffles his papers while Darren says, "There is still a *lot* we have to look through, kiddo. We aren't sure yet."

I heave a breath and run a hand through my tousled hair. "What about you, Aunt J? What did you find?"

"Another psychic who confirmed what I saw," she murmurs. "Said she got a call from a friend of hers. The same vision. They know something's going to happen, but they don't know how to stop it."

I close my eyes. *We're screwed.*

13

THE DEADLINE

THE RIDE TO MR HECKNEY'S HOUSE takes longer than usual, though for the most part it has nothing to do with sightseeing or being lost in my own thoughts.

It has everything to do with Morcant and the games he's playing.

Thoughts of our new deadline strike against old and new fears that I would much rather keep buried, but at this rate they're all going to come flying from the woodworks. So, if they're going to hit me, better now than later.

Better now than when I'm facing down the devil himself.

Pushing my bike behind the house, I cover it with brambles and grass, attempting to keep it out of sight of any who might poke around. Mr Heckney has promised to keep the back door unlocked, but when I try it, it won't give.

"Bonnie!" I call quietly, hoping she's listening. "Can you

unlock the door?"

On cue, the little girl appears at my side, head cocked to the side. A moment later, the door swings open on silent hinges.

"Thank you." The little girl smiles and disappears.

I don't dwell on the strangeness, not when I'm here for something else.

I hear Mr Heckney before I see him; in the kitchen it sounds like he's trying to cook something, though from the smell... I grimace as I step inside.

Swearing, Mr Heckney drops a pan of burnt food into the sink, throwing his oven mitts in with it. With a shake of his head, he rests his hands on his hips in defeat.

"What did the mitts ever do to you?" I ask, leaning against the doorframe.

The old man jumps, swearing profusely again. "Ah, you again," he mutters, motioning for me to get closer. "I have no new developments for you, little girl."

I roll my eyes. "We have something for you, though. And, I brought food. Beef stew, if you want it."

Mr Heckney eyes me suspiciously before nodding, and I pull the still warm cannister out of my side-satchel. Grabbing a bowl from the cabinet, I pour the stew straight in, rifle for a spoon, and set it on the breakfast table.

"Thank you," he mutters, taking a seat. I sit across from him and watch for a moment. Mr Heckney, unlike my own grandfather, looks like the type of man who would spoil any child who came remotely close to him. He has that warm and inviting sense to him that makes it easy to like him, whereas my own grandfather is as cold as ice, and won't let that front go—not even for his own granddaughter, who he walked away from four years ago.

"Mr Heckney, what do you know about doorways to the spirit world?" I ask, leaning back.

The old man sips his stew and doesn't answer for a long moment. "Whatever do you mean?"

"Have you ever heard about spirits being able to...*cross* into this world by other means?"

Albert Heckney props his spoon in his bowl and clasps his hands in front of him. "Are you asking if I think this town is subject to more spiritual activity than others?" I nod. "Then yes, of course I do. I blame Morcant for that, though." He goes back to eating his stew, like he has promptly forgotten about the conversation at hand—or the conversations we still need to have.

Over the course of the day, I spent every moment I could contemplating what Aunt J told us yesterday. It's strange to think about, especially when I have Weston and Riley trying to be my friends, and I'm trying my hardest to—subtly—push them away. Though a big part of me knows I need to focus on Morcant and Halloween, a smaller part of me wants to see how these friendships play out.

I look away, tugging at the hem of my shirt. "I don't think this is Morcant's doing... I think this is what *drew* him here."

"Hmm?" Mr Heckney looks up, eyes narrowed. Stew drips from his mouth, and I point to it. He quickly wipes it away. "How do you mean?"

"I mean...it couldn't have been a coincidence that he chose Fort Caldwell, that he decided to build here. I just don't think *he* is responsible for the doorway. I think he sought it out and..."

"And what?" Mr Heckney asks, forgetting his stew.

I turn to the boarded window with a shake of my head. "I think he has something planned... I mean, I know he does. Mr Heckney, we don't have very long until Morcant strikes."

Fear replaces his questioning stare, and he almost jumps from his seat. "What do you mean?" The old man pushes the stew completely aside and stands carefully, hobbling towards the basement stairs.

I'm quick to follow. "Aunt J had another vision, and she went to see a psychic. I'm not sure of all the details, but the general gist is that the closer we get to Halloween, the stronger he's going to get."

"And then?" Mr Heckney pauses on the stairs.

A chill shudders down my spine. "And then, I'm not sure what. Maybe he leaves the house? Maybe he comes back? We don't know yet." Sadness washes through me as I watch Mr Heckney from the eyes of his daughter; she passes through me, sending me her memories, her emotions.

One particular image comes to the forefront of my mind, of a happy family, of a simple life where the grass is green and the house looks new, well-kept. I see a younger Mr Heckney with Bonnie's red hair, with another man at his side—his brother, the ghoul. Bonnie plays on the swing set that now decays in the yard.

In the background are spirits. Hundreds of them, trapped forever on the Morcant estate, unable to leave or cross over.

I shake my head, clearing the image from my mind. I look down to see Bonnie standing beside me, blood still dripping from her blue eyes. She watches her father sadly as he begins hobbling down the stairs once again.

"If Morcant can leave his house, then I am truly afraid of what that might eventually mean," the old man shouts from downstairs. I take the stairs two at a time to catch up. "Which means we need to start working quicker on locating his weakness."

"Does he even have one?" I ask, joining him at the bottom of the stairs.

Heckney gives me a pointed stare and then continues over to the diagram. He points to a shelf and says, "Get the book that says '*Crypts of the Damned*'."

Doing as told, I follow the line of books—of course, in alphabetical order—and pull it from the top shelf. Only a thin book, it fits neatly in my hands like a common paperback. The cover is of a cemetery, and the author's name is Eastern European, but I can't tell.

I hand it over to Mr Heckney. "How's that going to help?"

"Well," he starts, setting a pair of reading glass on the tip of his nose. "This book gives details about crypts in old estates, specifically royal families or in our case, the wealthy ones."

"So...?" I trail off, not catching on.

Mr Heckney sighs. "By using this, we can try and distinguish if Josiah Morcant had a family crypt, hidden beneath or within the house. I couldn't find one on the grounds, and every report I've read doesn't tell of any. But that doesn't mean it isn't possible." Looking down at the book in front of him, Mr Heckney begins flipping through the pages, scanning passages and headings that might be of use.

I release a breath and leave him to it. I wander over to a wall, pulling my phone from my bag, checking the time. Seven-fourteen. I purse my lips. I'd promised Weston I'd go to his place and study with him and a couple of others. My attempt at being normal to keep Aunt J happy, even if it means leaving Mr Heckney to go over the information.

I rub at my eyes; *this* is far more important than going to a study date, and I know I should text him and tell him I can't make it. But...I've barely spoken to him all day. My stomach churns at the thought of cancelling, too.

But I can't have it both ways.

Before I can text Weston, Mr Heckney says, "If you have somewhere better to be, girl, then go be there. This might take some time."

"No, I..." I shake my head. "I promised some people that I would study tonight."

Mr Heckney looks over to me. "So, why are you here?"

"Because this is more important," I reply automatically. "Because Morcant is a serious threat, and he needs to be stopped."

Heckney nods. "But what will you do once it is done? Once we have defeated the great evil, will you try and go back to the friends you pushed away?"

Although I want to see what happens here, maybe it'll be easier in the next town. Maybe I can start fresh *after* we handle Morcant and the doorway and everything else in between. But...is that what I really want?

Mr Heckney nods as if he understands the current war inside my head. "When I found out about my little Bonnie dying, I knew immediately that it was because of that house. I, too, was ready to die, ready to join her. But a young woman came into town and told me that I wouldn't be *able* to join her if she was trapped with Morcant.

"So, I learnt what was really out there, and I decided that it would be my job to do the hard work for her. So that she could go into that house and destroy Morcant and set my darling girl free."

"But that didn't happen," I say, furrowing my brows.

He shakes his head. "No. We thought we had cracked it, and she went in, and it started to *burn*, but the fire just...disappeared, like it never even happened."

My brows shoot up. "That was you?"

"Yes," he says, lips pursed. "That girl ended up dead, and I swore I would do what I could so that no one else had to die. I let go of any relationships I had, turned into the crazy old man down the road. Just so I could help any Hunter Bonnie brought me."

"Are you telling me I shouldn't end up like you?" I ask, crossing my arms.

Albert Heckney nods and waves his hand towards the stairwell. "Go on. Only one of us needs to be a hermit. You've given me something *new* to look up anyhow, and you are very distracting."

"How so, Mr Heckney?"

He looks me up and down with a critical eye before saying,

"You talk too much. Go."

I start for the stairs, where Bonnie watches me. I pause and look down into her sad, tired eyes, and realise I'm not just doing this for myself or the living—I'm doing all this for the dead, too, those who are trapped inside the house and can't move on. I think about Amber Marston and how all she wanted in death was peace and justice. That's all these spirits want, too.

Before I can move on, Mr Heckney clears his throat. "And be careful, will you? We can't go losing anyone else."

I nod but don't look back. A sick feeling enters my gut, and I'm not entirely sure why.

~ ~ ~

Rain hits Fort Caldwell as soon as I park my bike in the garage. The torrential downpour hits the ground and doesn't stop, picking up every so often to turn the street into a makeshift river.

"You're home early!" Tate shouts, entering the garage from the kitchen. He wraps his arms around himself, brows furrowed. "I thought you would still be with Mr Heckney." Since telling him and Darren about Mr Heckney, they've been more than...suspicious about the old man, even going to the extent of saying we shouldn't trust him.

But he knows more than *any* of us. So, who better than to get us in and out without dying?

Shrugging, I shoulder my bag. "I have a study session over at Weston's."

Tate's brow shoots up. "Is that so?"

I narrow my eyes and push past him into the house, heading straight into the kitchen. The old cabinets are all open, Aunt J still packing away pots and pans and plates that would normally be stowed straight back into their boxes in a couple of weeks— months at best.

Unfortunately, this kitchen is *much* smaller than what Aunt J is used to, and she keeps poking and hitting herself every time she turns, underestimating how much space she actually has. I watch her as she bumps her hip right into the corner of an open cabinet.

"Oh! You're home!" She shoves a pan into the bottom cupboard and smiles at me. "How is Mr Heckney?"

"Good. He's reading up on your vision as we speak."

She frowns. "Did you give him his stew?"

Nodding, I duck into the loungeroom. "He has it! I'm going over to Weston's!"

Saying the words creates a knot in my stomach as I dash up the stairs. Is it selfish of me to want to go over there? What would happen if something goes wrong? If maybe I don't succeed and Morcant makes me join my parents with him in that house?

Sighing, I open the door to my small room and duck inside, running a hand over my face. From my window, I can just see Weston's house, half-obscured by an old tree. Blue suburban and happy looking.

God, what would he think if he found out I hunted ghosts? Would he laugh and call me crazy? Or would he disappear from my life for good, like I'm planning to do to him in two months...

In my pocket, my phone buzzes. Weston's number pops up, and I swipe, looking down at the message:

Still on for tonight, right?

I smile down at my phone and type: *Yep! Be over once the rain calms down.* As I press 'send', the smile on my face falters, and drops completely from my face. Is it selfish of me to try this?

Maybe it is...but I grab my school bag and drop my satchel, kicking it under the bed. I check to make sure I have the right textbooks and my binder. My hand brushes over crumpled paper; the missing persons clipping of my parents. I swallow thickly and pull it out, sucking in a breath.

Meghan and Joshua Parrish, missing December 18th, 2012

Last seen in their hotel room; valuables still present in room. Believed to have 'run off', though family state they would never leave without their thirteen year-old daughter, who was not with them.

Their car was found off Morcant Road, cleaned out. Possible kidnapping. After searching the surrounding forest, officials were unable to find the pair, nor any of their belongings, save for a photograph (pictured above) by their vehicle.

Under their photos, I wrote 'open case' in red. They're still being searched for, like everyone else in this godforsaken town. Though, no one is ever found... I drop the paper onto my bed, closing my bag. The photo was our last family photo, taken by Aunt J in Washington. The police still have it, tucked away in evidence.

I'll find them, for the benefit of everyone in this town.

And I will *not* let Morcant get to me, or anyone, ever again.

That, I promise.

14

A PARTY TO DIE FOR

WESTON DOESN'T PICK ME UP UNTIL after eight, when the town is blanketed in darkness and the streets are starting to grow quieter. The early autumn rain that haunts the town keeps most people inside for the night, but not us, not as we drive towards the lake outside Fort Caldwell where Simone is hosting her usual back to school party.

Her parents, like half the town, own a cabin on the lake. Not one of the more extravagant ones, but it's far enough away from neighbours and prying eyes that she can get away with having dozens of kids from our year there without disturbing anyone. And in a small town like this one, not many care about what a bunch of high school kids are doing, so long as they don't drown in the lake or end up at the Morcant house, which is thankfully on the other side of town.

I clasp my hands in my lap as nerves eat at me. Despite the

many different schools, I've never been to a party. I've been invited—usually by nice popular girls hoping to get brownie points, sometimes by assholes who just want to embarrass the new girl—but I'd never gone.

Now, I can't help but wonder if I've made a mistake coming.

Weston pulls down one of the many dirt-packed roads that lead to the different cabins and lake houses. The tell-tale signs of a party glare at me; banners and streamers thrown across the bare limbs of trees, balloons drooping from branches and cars pulled over, engines quiet.

There are people—real people, and not spirits—walking through the woods, their voices loud, like they've already gotten into the beer.

My stomach churns, but I push it aside. I've fought serial killer spirits, ghouls with bad attitudes, and I've crossed over children who know nothing more than tragedy.

I can survive a high school party.

I hope.

The cabin comes into view; someone threw fairy lights through the trees here, illuminating the land, while a bonfire being fed by guys on the football team casts a great orange glow over everyone sitting around it. I can't see Riley or her familiar pink hair, but huddled beneath a blanket close to the fire is Connor and Blaire.

There are even girls in swimsuits, like they actually plan on braving the cool night to *swim* in the inky-black lake.

I see a splash in the water and realise they already *have*.

"Seriously?" I say aloud as Weston parks and kills the engine.

His hazel eyes dance from me to the water, then back, alight with amusement. "What? Forget your swimsuit?"

I grimace and shake my head. "They're going to catch their deaths out there! It's already cold enough." As soon as I say it, I regret it. "I sound so uncool right now, don't I?"

Weston laughs but doesn't reply. We climb out of his truck, chilly autumn air hitting me almost immediately. I wrap my arms around myself and suppress a shiver.

I spent the day with Tate and Heckney going over the Morcant estate lines, tracking the way it seems to grow with the lead up to Halloween. It's terrifying. I almost cancelled tonight because of it, because we don't understand what's going on. But Aunt J convinced me to come, to get out of the house and to not worry about all the things I currently can't control.

I wonder if this is something I can control, and if I even want to.

Weston brushes his hand against mine, which drags me away from thoughts of Morcant and Heckney and *things I currently can't control.*

"You okay?" he asks, guiding me through the small clump of trees and onto darkened sand. Someone erected a table and filled it with drinks, mostly cheap beer and some kind of fruity punch from the looks of it. There's a cooler with other drinks—hopefully something non-alcoholic—under the table.

I look up at Weston, into his kind eyes, and without meaning to, I reach out for his emotions to get a sense of what exactly I'm about to walk into. It's not something I normally do, especially since it's invasive and also draining when doing it on the living, but for him I do.

The first thing I feel from him is a nervousness that I wouldn't normally associate with him. He's always been so calm and collected, to the point where I think he's definitely aware that he's, well, *him*—popular football player with a genuine nice-guy demeanour who pretty much has everyone wanting to be his friend.

But he isn't sure of himself, at least not right now.

Finally, I give him a smile—soft, not one of the award winnings ones I'm so well known for. "Yeah, I'm fine."

"Are you sure?" he asks, a twinge of uncertainty entering his voice. "You've been pretty quiet since we left."

I sigh. I don't know how to answer him, not really, not without letting him know that there actually *is* something wrong. And the last thing I want is for him to worry.

So, I avoid the question and search the party for Riley's familiar face, and I'm surprised to find her sitting with her sister and Connor. As if sensing my stare, Riley looks up, her pink hair fluttering around her head, and waves.

I don't stop a smile from lifting my lips, though I can't help the small twinge of guilt that arises in my gut from not answering Weston's question.

Just one night, I think. *Just one night where I'm not a ghost Hunter, and I don't plan on leaving after the job is done. It's just one night of being normal.*

I can do that. I can be normal for a couple of hours. It's not like I have Morcant breathing down my neck or anything. Maybe even the fate of the entire town resting on my shoulders.

Totally. Normal.

The bonfire only seems to grow as more and more people arrive at the cabin. There's a peacefulness to it all, something I never would have expected from a town like this. Maybe it's because most people in Fort Caldwell are used to the strangeness and the unexplainable. Whatever it is, they don't dwell on it here. They thrive in each other's company, like yesterday never existed and tomorrow is just another day.

I take the chance to learn more about the people who have welcomed me into their little circle.

Riley and Blaire have lived their entire lives in Fort Caldwell and most of the people at the lake are people they've known their entire lives. They tell me in an offhanded way that for some reason, no one seems to want to leave despite the weirdness of the town.

I pocket that little titbit of information.

The twins are looking at going to college together—where, they don't know. Their dad just wants them to stay together, but neither are sure of what they plan on doing once we graduate. Blaire is thinking political science, which surprises me, but even Riley is considering the same thing.

I learn that Connor's parents own one of the restaurants in town, and that his older sisters are spread across the many high-end Universities in the country; Harvard and Yale, another goes to MIT and his eldest sister lives in England with her fiancé. He tells me that they're all destined to do great things, but he doubts he'll be able to live up to those expectations.

He's been drinking the entire time, though, lying across Blaire and me. She doesn't seem to mind, playing with his hair.

I've also learnt that he and Blaire have been together since middle-school. Power couple goals and all. Riley isn't much of a relationship person and prefers cats, which reminds me of Aunt J.

And Weston...he sits on the sand at my feet, his back against my shin as he drinks a Sprite, even though I've offered to drive us home if he wants. I don't drink, purely because if I do I leave myself open to attacks from spirits—not usually on purpose, but the last thing I need is to have a panic attack in front of half the school.

Beside me, Riley sighs and rests her head on my shoulder. "I promise these can be so much more fun," she whispers, voice sluggish, though not from drinking. She just sounds tired. "When Justin hosts—his parents are across the lake and have a huge cabin that fits all of us—we usually end up playing really dumb games like spin the bottle and seven minutes in heaven."

"Gross," I reply, smiling. "That's fun?"

She shrugs. "It is when it starts getting dramatic. I feed off that shit."

Shaking my head, I lift my drink to my lips. On my lap,

Connor shifts, spilling his beer on the sand. Weston laughs against my shin and Blaire, suddenly as tired as her twin, rests her head on my other shoulder.

From the ground, Weston twists and looks up to me. His features are highlighted by the fire, which splashes across his cheekbones and eyes. "Do you want to go for a walk?"

I nod, and with some help, manage to push Conner off enough for me to get out. And although both twins curse at me for leaving them, I can't help but laugh as they slur every word.

Weston and I walk in silence on the sand, following the lake's edge. There are fewer people along here, most keeping to the light of the bonfire so they don't get lost in the darkness that's blanketing our small town.

"You never answered my question," he says.

I watch him from the corner of my eye and swallow thickly. "I know."

He shoves his hands into his pockets and stops, twisting so his back is to the water and mine is to the trees. He's looking down at me like I'm some kind of puzzle, and it makes my stomach churn.

"You're a little bit weird, Huntliegh Parrish." He cocks his head as a soft smile graces his lips. "I just don't know if that's a good thing or not."

I blink and meet his stare. "Most will think it's a bad thing. You know, reputations and all that." For the second time tonight, I reach out to get a feel for his emotions, and find no malice or aggression within him. His intentions aren't rooted in anything bad, just curiosity. I pull away before I can feel anything else, heat burning my cheeks.

Weston chuckles and shakes his head. "I'm not worried about my reputation, most people here aren't." He pauses, heat entering his eyes as he looks me over once. "You're just something else."

"Now I think *I* should be the one wondering if that's bad or not," I reply, voice flat. But my heart betrays me by skipping a beat. "That doesn't sound much like a compliment."

"I'm sorry." He shakes his head again and rubs the back of his neck. "I'm glad you came."

I purse my lips and look back to the party. Deep down, I am too.

A cold, slithering feeling closes around my heart and throat. It feels like tentacles trapping me in place, made of ice and something else, something dark. My heart stops for a moment out of fear, and I can't move. I can't see anything beyond a blurring mass of darkness.

I can't breathe.

The protection bag in my pocket barely warms with the sudden attack.

A warm hand takes mine. The coldness recedes almost immediately, as if the physical contact scares it off. I suck in a sharp breath and blink until the world around me comes into focus.

"Huntliegh?"

I pull away and hug my hand to my chest. *What the hell was that?*

I clear my throat and force a smile onto my face. "Sorry, I'm fine. I zoned out a little." In my ears, my voice sounds weird, far off.

"Let me take you home."

I shake my head, but he's already guiding me back towards the party and his truck. We don't stop to say goodbye to anyone.

Sinking dread and guilt swim in my belly as Weston takes me home. And for the final time tonight, I reach out to him, and only feel concern—towards me.

~ ~ ~

The weeks pass slowly and with little incident; around every corner I expect to come face to face with a spirit or Morcant, but there is a strange...silence hanging around Fort Caldwell that chills me to the bone.

"What's up?" Weston asks, scooting his chair closer to mine. Dark hair falls over his brow, and he watches me with a critical eye.

"Huh?" I look up from my textbook. A smile spreads across his face. "Oh, uh..." I trail off, and he starts laughing.

Somewhere in the library, someone tells us to shut up. His laughter turns silent, though his body shudders as he giggles.

I roll my eyes and push the English book away from me, stretching. "I give up. This is even more boring than calc."

West snorts and pulls the book to him. Reading over the questions, he sighs. "This is pretty simple."

"Okay, Shakespeare, *you* do it for me." I cross my arms over my chest and watch him. Weston looks between me and the book, his eyes crinkled in amusement.

"Do my Chemistry, and it's a deal," he says with a grin. I roll my eyes again and jerk the book back to me, flipping it closed. I shove it back into my bag, feeling for my protection bag. I curl my fingers around it, then let go. His eyes dance with amusement, and the grin turns into a smirk. "Oh, come on, you're giving up?"

I shake my head and sit back, flinging my head over the back of the chair. "Yep. I quit."

"No, you don't." Before I can stop him, Weston is reaching over me for my bag, pressing his weight into my side. When I look up, his face is close, closer than it's ever been, lips only an inch away...

I swallow. I've spent the past couple of weeks *trying* to keep my distance from everyone, trying to focus on the job and Morcant. Every day after school, I go over to Mr Heckney's, whether with Aunt J, Darren, Tate, or on my own. And I spend what feels like hours pouring over books and files, trying to come up with some kind of game plan.

We know the spirits are trapped by the lines of Morcant's estate, and that come Halloween, those lines will forever be dropped, and our demonic friend will be free to do as he pleases. We know Mr Heckney's house is on the border of the Morcant estate, crossing into it, which explains why Bonnie and her friend can come and go as they please.

And we are certain Morcant himself is trapped in the house, unable to exit for whatever reason.

We just don't know how it works, or *why*.

I meet Weston's stare, swallowing thickly. He's still hovering over me, dark eyes on me. I've been staring at his lips...oh god.

Stupidly, I wonder if I should close the distance.

No, don't. No attachments, remember?

Clearing my throat, I shove at his chest, and he falls back into his chair easily, that laid-back smile on his face once again. His shoulders are tense though, and an awkward silence fills the space between us.

"I..." I don't know what to say; that I don't particularly mind if he had closed the distance? That, despite myself and the current circumstances, I *wanted* him to kiss me? More than once, the thought—the idea *and* the image—has crossed my mind. But I've shaken it off and tried to remember why I'm here in Fort Caldwell in the first place.

Morcant. Destroy him, destroy that house, set everyone free.

I am *not* here to meet boys or make connections.

At least, not *yet* anyway.

Other than spending time with Weston, I've spent time with Riley, and Blaire, and Connor, and over that time I've become better friends with them—something I wasn't really sure how to feel about. On one hand, it feels nice to have people outside of the life, who're innocent to the horrors that come with hunting.

They're regular folk, their only ties to the paranormal being that they live in Fort Caldwell.

But I also know how much of a risk they are. Getting close could lead to attachments, and if something happens on Halloween that traps me in the house? Will I become another nameless face on Mr Heckney's wall? Another person for the local PD to add to their endless list of missing persons? And if I succeed...I don't need to stay here. I can move on to the next town.

The day of Simone's party, I spent the morning in the pouring rain, walking around the entire Morcant estate, marking off where it starts and ends. I had Mr Heckney and Tate with me the entire time, the former ahead of us by several feet, keeping stride with little Bonnie who disappeared and reappeared in the forest.

Of course, after being soaked to the bone and going to a high school party almost straight after getting home meant I spent the entire day Sunday stuck in bed drinking soup and watching Netflix.

Weston and I drive to school together almost every day; sometimes in his truck, sometimes we're driven by Darren or Tate, and very rarely, I drive us on the bike. I know more about him than I ever thought I would, but at the same time, I know absolutely nothing about what's happening between us, and I can tell he's keeping something from me.

He's never explained why there's a small shrine in his kitchen, nor has he ever told me why his parents refuse to put up any of his childhood pictures. Though I've never asked, since he and his parents look like the most normal, happy family.

"Sorry," Weston says, pulling me from my thoughts. His voice is quiet, and he forces a laugh. Rubbing the back of his neck, he gives me a shy smile—one that makes my heart stutter.

I smile back, unable to remove my stare from his. There's a *very* large part of me that has enjoyed this time with him, especially when another part of me reminds me that it could very well be the last days of my life.

I try to push those thoughts away, but they always resurface.

"It-it's okay," I say, turning away. I heave a sigh and pick up my pen, but I don't make a move to write anything.

"Can I ask you something?" he says suddenly, dragging my attention back to him once again. I drop the pen, biting down on my lip. Waiting for him to continue, I nod, my heart accelerating.

Weston glances down at his hands, Adams-apple bobbing, and he swallows. "I, uh… Man, I don't know how to say this," he says, forcing a laugh. I keep my mouth shut, attempting to keep my face blank.

He continues, "Huntliegh, would you, uh…would you go on a date with me?"

My brows shoot up, and I sit back. *Not* what I was expecting, but at the same time…it is something I've *wanted*. My heart does a little flip in joy.

My mouth, though… "Why?"

I cringe internally. Another thing: I've never *actually*—properly—been asked out before. I'm never in one place long enough to warrant it.

And I'm a little surprised that he's asking, since I'm half-sure I weirded him out at Simone's party.

Weston's brows furrow together as he frowns. "Because I like you?"

Why couldn't I have just said yes! The awkwardness between us continues to thicken, and I'm at a loss for words.

"You know what? Forget I said anything." He turns away from me and runs a hand through his hair, shoulders tense.

"Wait, no." *God, Huntliegh, pull yourself together!* "Yes, I want to go on a date with you." His head shoots up, eyes wide as he smiles. "I just, I didn't know you liked me…like that?"

The small part of me that reminds me that I could die in the next month promptly reminds me that *this* is a bad idea and a serious waste of time. That if I *do* get myself caught up in a relationship with Weston, that we do end up staying together? There is still that chance that I can *die* and he'll never know what happened.

Can I do that? My brain—the ever-smart side of me screams '*NO*' while my heart... I want to take the chance, even with that looming threat hanging over my head.

Weston's eyes shine as he grins, taking one of my hands. "Why wouldn't I?"

I shrug. "Because we haven't known each other for that long? Because I'm the weird new girl, and I'm not just saying that to be cliché but seriously."

Weston rolls his eyes. "People on Tinder go out after a couple of messages. I've known you for a month, I see you every day. I think it's safe to assume a date wouldn't do much harm."

Except it will, if we let this unfold and I die *next month.* "You're right." But that nagging little part of me still says otherwise.

15

FACING DEATH

MR HECKNEY'S OLD IMPALA CREAKS as I climb over it so I can jump the back fence and enter the forest beyond. The emotions of spirits wash over me like cold water after a long day in the sun. Sadness and fear are most prominent, chilling me to the bone and sending shivers up and down my spine, but mixed in is anger so potent it turns bitter in my mouth.

I shake my hands out and look up to the sky; stars sprinkle the blue-black night, filling the space between darkness and clouds. They blink in and out of existence every so often, when the clouds blow over them. But they always reappear.

I shiver, tightening my hold on my scarf. Fall has definitely settled in after the summer storms; yellow and brown leaves scatter the forest floor, paired with pine needles and muddy puddles. I carefully step over one, feeling my shoes squelch underfoot—glad that I'm wearing boots instead of converses.

"Where are you going?" I turn to face Darren, who walks around the *side* of the house to meet me. He looks between me and the fence and shakes his head. "Always taking the hard way, I see."

I shrug. "I'm going to circle the perimeter again, see if I can spot anything different."

Darren sighs and shoves his hands into his pockets. "You know the rules. When it's dark..."

"Always be in pairs," I mutter in response. I pull my pack from my back, reaching in for my flashlight. I flick it on and wave it about the forest, double checking that it works. I hand Darren a plastic bag full of protection bags, ready to by tied to trees around the estate.

Extra protection, just in case.

As it grows closer to Halloween, we can *feel* the changes washing over Fort Caldwell; a month ago was timid compared to now. The past week, I've been out expelling ghouls and trapping spirits in town. Most haven't been vicious, but they are becoming a problem for the living.

I swing my light in an arc, finding the twine we'd hung around the property to show the boundary of the estate. It took two days to complete, since the estate seems to *grow* somehow; when I put the first line up, Bonnie watched me from the other side. The following day, she was beside me, on the same side, her friend in tow.

Whatever power is growing here, the Morcant estate is at the centre of it all.

Darren ties a protection bag on the branch of a bush, hiding it within the leaves. We can't risk some hiker finding and destroying the bags. We hope these help, even if it's only a little. Though they aren't as strong as anything Morcant is pulling together, the added protection might keep some spirits away. We're lucky most of the town is miles away from the estate line, but that doesn't seem to be stopping the rise in ghostly activity.

"You were quiet when you got home today." Darren meets my pace and stops to tie another bag into a bush.

We continue walking. I kick a pinecone into the darkness, shrugging. "I got asked out...on a date."

When I look over to Darren, his brows are so far up they reach his hairline. "By that Weston kid?"

I sigh and nod, pointing the light back up at the twine. "Yeah."

"Is that bad?" he asks, nudging me.

I stop. "I'm not sure," I reply, digging my boot into the soft earth. "I mean, I like him. But with all this happening, with Morcant and Halloween...I'm not sure if it's a good idea."

Darren drops the bags and cups my shoulders, giving me a light shake. "If this is because you're afraid, *don't be.* If this boy makes you happy, then you should fight for it. Don't just settle for this life, Huntliegh. Don't settle for death."

I swallow, biting down on the inside of my cheek. "I just...I don't know what to do. Is it selfish? Wanting to have something normal?"

He shakes his head, grip tightening. "No, not for you. You should have *everything*, Hunt. Be normal. Go to school. Date this boy and be happy. This job is not on you."

Pursing my lips, I nod. But his words don't eradicate the guilt swelling inside me for even *considering* anything other than this life.

Branches snap behind Darren, and we both spin towards it, guards up. Carefully, Darren bends down and picks up the protection bags. I remain still. We both have protection bags in our pockets, and traps ready.

As if in slow motion, something fazes into existence, bloody and white and *growling*. It almost looks like a zombie, with bared teeth and swollen, red eyes. The creature has no hair on its thin, creamy body, and when I meet its stare, I only feel rage.

"Run," I breathe, as the *thing* attacks.

I rip a trapping bag from my pocket and throw it, whispering the incantation as I do. Darren and I take off back towards Mr Heckney's house, back towards what we assume would be *safety*.

But that thing keeps running after us, crossing the boundary line as it does.

What the hell is this thing?

Darren is fast, despite his age, despite the injuries that would usually slow him down. I keep his pace, my breathing ragged.

I feel claws rip into my shoulder, and I scream, warmth seeping down the back of my jacket and shirt. Pain burns down my arm and through my entire body. Everything around me blurs.

Darren grabs my hand and propels me forward; the floodlights at Mr Heckney's house flash on, and in the doorway I see Bonnie coming closer, her father in tow.

Heckney cocks his shotgun as the creature digs its claws into Darren.

Shots ring out in the silence, and something falls to the pine needles behind me.

Real. It's real.

As the creature crashes into the forest floor, so does Darren. Blood oozes from claw marks down his back, half an inch deep and probably the same in width. My own wounds flare, the blood still trickling down my arm, but Darren...

He isn't moving.

I look up, but Mr Heckney is gone. In the distance, I hear sirens. At the front of the house, blue and red and white lights flash. Time is passing, but I can't move.

My chest tightens as I look back down at Darren; his face is white and smeared with blood, his hand reaching out to me. Is his chest moving? I can't tell. His eyes are shadowed in the dark; it's impossible to tell if life still flares within the brown of his iris.

I drop to my knees beside him; I can hear shouting coming from somewhere, but it isn't loud, and I can barely make out the words. Bonnie appears in front of me, but my vision blurs, and she fazes out of existence.

~ ~ ~

Flashes of white light and searing pain.

Someone screams beside me, hand clutching mine. Their grip tightens, then loosens, then disappears altogether.

"Huntliegh?" Someone flashes a light in my eyes, and I groan. "You need to remain calm, you're at the Fort Caldwell Hospital."

Memories of the white creature, of it attacking me, and *Darren*, his body limp beside me, blood pooling into the dirt below him. Is he dead? My chest tightens and my heart accelerates. I just want to scream.

Did Mr Heckney kill the thing? Or did it disappear?

I cry out, not in physical pain, but in terror. Despite everything, I only feel sorrow. My eyes sting, and I cry out again as waves of it slam into me. In here I'm not protected—I'm not protected anywhere anymore.

"Huntliegh, you need to calm down. Everything will be okay. We just need to stitch you up."

Doesn't he understand? There is so much pain, so much sorrow here, and it all floods into me. *Death* floods into me.

Peeling my eyes open, I meet the stare of a woman shaking her head.

Darkness hits me again, and I welcome it with open arms.

~ ~ ~

My eyes flutter open, and I'm met with blinding white light. I throw my hand up to shield my eyes, feeling a restraint around the other arm that keeps it close to my chest.

"Oh, honey, I'm sorry!" The lights flicker off a moment later, but I can still hear the buzz of electricity, and the piercing light leaves sun-dots dancing behind my eyelids.

Beside me, Aunt J sniffs, taking my free hand. I try to move the other arm, and groan as pain shudders through me. "Don't move, honey," she croaks, thumb stroking the top of my hand. "You'll pull your stitches."

Stitches? The night comes back to me; Mr Heckney's house, Darren and I talking in the forest and checking the perimeter, the *creature* jumping out at us and the attack.

I look down at my shoulder, which was *shredded* by the monster. White bandages cover most of my shoulder and upper arm, and I have a sling keeping my arm in place. I curl my fingers, breathing a sigh of relief when I feel the movement, feel the rough blanket beneath my fingertips.

Darren, the blood, his white face, pops back into my mind.

I suck in a breath as tears trickle down my cheeks. "What happened to Darren?" I ask, voice cracking.

Aunt Josephine's breath hitches. Her hands tighten around mine. "He's alive." I release a breath, but the tears keep falling. "Only barely, though, baby. He, uh...he sustained some serious injuries, and the doctors put him in a medically induced coma."

I shudder; this is my fault, *my* fault. "If I hadn't gone out..."

"Shh," she breathes. She reaches a hand up and strokes my face. "We didn't know anything like that was out there. The police just think it was a wolf that got you guys."

I sniff. "Mr Heckney, did he...?" I trail off. Did he kill the thing?

"He shot it, but when he went out after the ambulances picked you two up, there was no sign of it."

"He went out there alone?" I try to sit up but hiss as pain shoots through me again.

Aunt J forces me back down. "He had Bonnie watching over him, but he didn't even get close to the property line."

I shake my head. "That thing can get *past* the property line, Aunt J. That thing crossed it!" I meet her stare, watching her eyes widen. Her hand leaves my forehead, and she sits back.

"Are you sure?"

I nod. "It attacked us *off the property*. It was behind the line, then it wasn't."

A knock sounds at the door, and a doctor pops her head in.

Doctor Isabella Mackenzie, Weston's mom, gives me a soft smile as she looks over the charts. "How are you feeling, Huntliegh?"

I've met her on a couple of occasions, when I've been over at Weston's studying, but it's mostly been in passing. She works ridiculous hours, but she's always had a smile on her face whenever I've seen her.

She and Weston share the same unruly dark hair and wide, cheerful smile. Her eyes, though, are a scrutinizing blue.

I swallow. "Sore. When I move, my shoulder *really* hurts."

Doctor Mackenzie nods and steps further into the room, switching the lights back on. She lowers the intensity, though, and offers me another smile. "You are extremely lucky, Huntliegh. The damage to your nerves was minor, and you really only needed to be stitched back up. You'll have scars, though. They won't go away."

"I didn't think so," I reply quietly, averting my eyes. I bite down on my lip, tasting blood.

"You'll have to spend the day here tomorrow, miss school. I just want to keep an eye on you so I can be sure you won't get an infection. Even then, I can come check up on you when you get home."

Right. Neighbours. No escaping her. "Now," she continues, propping her clipboard beneath her arm. "I'm going to go tell

Weston and your friends that you're awake and fine, and that they need to go *home*. Do you want me to let them know they can come back tomorrow? Or do you want some peace?"

I look over to Aunt Josephine, who squeezes my hand. "I, uh...I think I'll wait to see them."

Doctor Mackenzie nods and slips back out the door.

I release a shuddering breath, removing my hand from Aunt J's, and I wipe my eyes. How can I even begin to explain this? Wolf attack my ass. It'd been hard before to lie about my life, but now this?

I have the blood and scars to prove just how dangerous this world really is.

"You should rest," Aunt J murmurs, patting my thigh. "It's *late*. Like, just after midnight. Try and get some sleep."

She stands, and I grab her hand. "How's Tate?"

"Holding on," she replies, bottom lip trembling. "But we'll get through this, we *all* will."

"Darren pushed me out of the way, Aunt Josephine. It should be *me*."

A tear slips down Aunt Josephine's face as she kneels down and kisses the top of my head.

It should have been me.

16

REAPERS DON'T WAIT

THE HOUSE FEELS EMPTY WHEN I WALK through the front door; Tate and Darren's truck is still at the hospital, no longer parked on the street, and their bags are no longer in the living room. The pull-out has been converted back into a couch and looks like it hasn't been touched in days.

When I was released, Aunt J and I stopped by Darren's hospital room before leaving. Tate didn't even look up at us, at Aunt J who left a cup of coffee on the nightstand beside the other ten empty cups. Hell, I doubt he even *wanted* to look up, to see me.

Darren was there because of me.

Swallowing thickly, I turn away from the living room and head up the stairs, ignoring Aunt Josephine as she calls out to me.

I can't fix what I've broken, and I hate feeling useless.

I drop my bag inside the door of my room and walk into the

adjacent bathroom, locking the door and falling to the floor.

Any food I'd managed to choke down in my hospital bed came right back up, filling the toilet bowl. Every heave burns my throat and mouth, the sour taste only forcing me to retch more. Sweat coats my brow, my face flushed. Tears sting my eyes, though I'm surprised I can cry anymore.

I cough and sit back, wincing as my shoulder jolts from the movement. But the pain is welcome.

All my fault. I went out to check the perimeter. *I* should have had his back.

Now, he's lying in a hospital bed, and I don't even know if he'll come out of it alive.

"Hunt?" Weston knocks on the door to the bathroom, voice soft. "You okay in there?"

Bile rises in the back of my throat, and I try to choke down a sob. I open my mouth to reply, but I vomit into the toilet again. The back of my throat burns and tears stream down my face. Embarrassment shudders through me as I vomit again, finally emptying my stomach into the porcelain bowl in front of me.

But I can't stop retching, and I can't stop the endless tears. Darren could have died, and that would have been on me. Darren could still die because I was stupid enough to think we were going to be safe.

And I was wrong. I was so, so wrong.

I can't let anyone else get hurt. "Just go away," I say, voice hitching. Hot tears enter my mouth, and I retch again.

"No. Just...tell me you're okay in there."

I flush the toilet and strain to stand. My shoulder throbs, the pain clamping my insides, but I have nothing else in my stomach to fill the toilet. "Fine. I'm fine," I reply, voice cracking.

He knocks quietly again. His concern is palpable.

What does he think happened out there? The same as everyone else? That a wolf came out and attacked Darren and me?

What would he think if I told him the truth? That some evil creature was what actually appeared, probably summoned by the evil spirit of Morcant. Would he run?

Swallowing, I turn the tap on and watch the water hit the basin and go down the drain, disappearing. If only I could do that; disappear. Maybe if I do, our problems will too.

"Hunt?" Aunt J, knocks once on the door and sighs. "He left. Said you locked yourself in here, that you were sick. You okay?"

Groaning, I cup my hand under the running water and watch my palm fill with cold water. I bring it to my lips and drink, swishing the water in my mouth before spitting it back out. I still taste the bile in my mouth when I finally unlock the door, coming face to face with Aunt J.

She crosses her arms over her chest. "You finished?"

I nod and push past her into my room, wincing as I remove the sling. I proceed to *try* and take my shirt off, but it gets caught on the bandages.

I feel Aunt Josephine's cool hands on my skin a moment later, helping me take the shirt off. Clammy sweat clings to my body, and I rifle through my cupboard for a clean shirt.

"Do you want to talk about it?" she asks, perching on my bed.

I shrug the shirt on, wincing as the sleeve brushes the bandages. "How long until I get this off?"

Aunt J purses her lips. "A couple of weeks. We have to take you back in two weeks to get the stitches out."

"We'll be cutting it close," I say, kicking my shoes off. "Halloween is coming up soon."

Her brows shoot up, and she eyes me sceptically from the bed, her hands white as she grips the sheets. "You cannot be serious," she snaps, getting up. "You could have died yesterday, Huntliegh. You will not be going back to that house!"

"Who else will?" I shout, throwing my hand up in frustration. "Whatever Morcant is doing...*that* is what will happen to the rest of the town!"

Aunt J growls and stalks to the door. "This is no longer your fight. We'll leave town as soon as your arm is better." She slams the door before I can reply.

I fall onto the bed, listening to the springs in the mattress whine. This is probably my only way to help Darren, and she's going to take that away from me? First Mom and Dad, then Darren...

Bile rises in my throat again, but I force it back down. That *thing*...that is because of Morcant, it has to be.

I wonder if she called grandpa and told him about all this. Would he care enough to call and check in? I almost laugh at myself. *That requires actually answering the phone.*

I rise and stride to my computer. Sitting down on the creaky desk chair, I open the search bar. I type in 'white-demons' and 'white-spirits', waiting as images and articles appear on the screen.

I click on the first one, and scroll through, searching for anything that remotely looks like the creature from the other night. Spirits that look like Bonnie pop up, along with silly ghosts that looked like it came out of a bad Halloween movie. Pictures of demons appear, though they have tails and pitchforks, rather than milky-white skin and red eyes.

My computer beeps, and I jump. An email from Mr Heckney.

Sighing, I rub my eyes and open it, mouth dropping open at the first picture I see. An illustration in a medieval text shows the same *thing* I saw last night; no hair, red eyes, long, lean body, and white skin. I swallow and scroll down to the body of the email, reading:

Said to patrol the afterlife, a Reaper is a protector of the dead, and a ward of the living. If you are touched by a Reaper, it is foretold that you will die within twenty-four hours.

The Reaper above, though, is said to have been summoned by a master of death and is controlled by its new master. This Reaper is not an omen, and if it attacks, it will kill you. The master can give it a name, and it will hunt its victim.

There are many theories...

My eyes water, and I cup my hand over my mouth. At the very bottom of the text, Mr Heckney typed out a warning: *it won't stop until it has you, Huntliegh Parrish.*

~ ~ ~

The vision surrounds me like ice water. Stale, damp air fills my lungs, tasting of mildew and decay. I recognize it almost immediately; an old building that hasn't been open to fresh air in over a decade. I've spent hours in places like this one.

When I open my eyes, I see a window with thick curtains, only a sliver of light penetrating the heavy fabric. Dust dances in that single glowing moat, and I follow its direction to a chest on the floor. An old, rusty lock keeps the lid closed. It sits at the foot of a four-poster bed.

Turning slowly, I take in the rest of the room: a tall set of drawers and matching wardrobe with peeling paint, a loveseat in the corner with a table covered with loose papers and open books. Finally, there's the vanity and mirror. Everything is coated in a thick layer of dust, though the mirror in front of me—sitting atop the finely made dresser—is clear, the glass in perfect shape.

I stare at myself and cock my head. The bed behind me has a body, but I can't see who it is. Standing beside it is Morcant, though, his dark eyes on it. He wears a top hat and a tailored suit, a cane in his hand. He leans heavily against it.

Almost directly behind me is Delilah Morcant. In another

life, she would have been pretty, excruciatingly so, with soft, mousy brown hair and bright blue eyes. She has soft features and a button nose, with pale skin. And when she smiles, she almost looks like she means it, but something about it doesn't quite meet her eyes.

Behind her, Morcant looks up from the body in the bed. His eyes meet mine briefly in the reflection before swivelling to his daughter. Anger radiates in his black eyes, directed at her. But...

No.

His eyes aren't on her, not really. I can barely turn my head, though when I do, I see something on the dresser. A book. It looks like a witch's grimoire, old and heavy, leather-bound with iron embellishments. There's writing I can't understand on the cover.

I look up again to catch Morcant's eye, then Delilah's.

Before I can think on it, the vision fades away, leaving me alone once more in my room. The cold doesn't disappear. Instead, it leaves me exhausted.

What the hell did he want? I wonder as I climb into bed. *And what the hell was that book?*

17

THE TOUCH OF A GHOST

"ARE YOU SURE ABOUT THIS?" AUNT J ASKS, slamming the page from his email down onto Mr Heckney's table. He blinks up at me, then directs his gaze to Aunt J, who looks just about ready to leap the back fence and hunt down that *Reaper* thing herself.

The old man shrugs helplessly. "What can I say?"

"Well, you can tell me that this isn't real!" she says. "That you misread the information!"

"I cannot do that, Josephine," he murmurs, resting his weathered hand on top of hers. She snatches it away and runs a hand through her unruly curls. "I will not lie, especially if it might put Huntliegh in more danger."

Aunt Josephine sniffs and falls into a chair, resting her head in her hands. Timidly, I touch her shoulder, and she releases a shuddering sigh. "What can we do?"

"We hope the protection bags you girls use is enough to keep it away. The only way it can be stopped, I believe, is by removing the 'master'."

I straighten, my lips pulling into grim line. "We need to get rid of Morcant."

Mr Heckney nods and begins pulling books towards him. "I've been reading over all the information we have, but because no one can really go in there without being trapped...I am merely reading the same material over and over again. I cannot find anything that will help, unfortunately."

I look down at the piles; I have the same ones, found the same articles online. Hell, I listen to any and every podcast that even *mentions* Morcant, and still, I've found nothing. No new information, no new interpretation of the same old legend.

When it comes to the legend of Morcant, the story is clean. Where most legends have different versions, like Bloody Mary or the Hook Man, Morcant seems to be nothing more than his actual story. His life, known by most who tell his tale, stays the same in every retelling, in every version. Sometimes when a different version is told, one can glean new information from it, because it isn't *changed* but rather told in a different way. Sometimes it includes details that would otherwise be forgotten about or glanced over.

Rubbing at my eyes, I sit down beside Aunt J and wince as my shoulder jolts. Pain lances down my arm and side. I swallow back a groan and suck in a breath, leaning forward. "What else can we do?"

Mr Heckney shakes his head. "I'm not sure."

"We have to go in there," Aunt J mutters, wiping her eyes. I blink, and her wet eyes meet mine. "*I* have to go in there. For you."

My throat closes up, and I fight back a slew of tears that'll do none of us any good. "No," I say, shaking my head. "You won't.

He'll take you, like Mom and Dad."

Aunt J gives me a tight-lipped smile, reaching over to cup my cheek. "I'll do anything to make sure you're safe. You know that, right?"

I nod and pull away, standing. The feeling of being useless closes in on me, so I walk over to the diagram and look down at the building. Two entries and exit points that we know of. Hundreds of windows lining the exterior, most of which are boarded up from the outside. On the first storey is the main kitchen and servant quarters, along with a formal dining room, a pavilion, a main sitting area, and a family room, and probably more rooms we don't know about. Upstairs are the bedrooms, with an attic above that. Beneath the main staircase is said to be a doorway to the cellar. Another staircase is rumoured to be located in the servants' quarters, though apparently when the orphanage opened, that was boarded up.

If I'm going to find my parents, they'll be under the house; Morcant probably has more stairwells that lead into the basement, but from the stories and books, we know of only two.

Swallowing, I kneel down at look at the front door, and an image of Morcant pops into my mind. My heart thunders as I watch him point his cane at me. The vision from last night stirs a new kind of fear inside of me. I haven't told Aunt J or Mr Heckney yet because I don't understand what Morcant is telling me.

Pulling back, I suck in a breath, closing my eyes. *He won't get me. He won't get me. I won't let him.* After Halloween, he won't be getting anyone, ever again.

"Huntliegh?" Aunt J calls. I look up and stand. She and Mr Heckney watch me with hooded eyes, the worry clear in their faces.

I offer them a smile, but I can't feel it, not over the thundering fear in my heart. "I'm fine. Tired."

Aunt J nods and stands from her chair, picking up her

handbag and pulling the printed page towards her. "We need to find a way to stop this, Albert," she said, "I can't lose her too."

The old man nods sadly. "We will figure this out. I'll read everything again, okay?"

She doesn't reply and instead beckons me towards the cement stairs. On her way, she drops a protection bag by the bookcase, and whispers the spell below her breath.

I swallow. Protection, because that *thing* can get in here too.

The walk to the car is quiet; I have no idea what Aunt Josephine is thinking about, but her brows are furrowed, and she has a spark of determination in her eyes. She climbs into the driver's seat and sits back, not moving to put the key in the ignition, even when I'm seated with my seatbelt crossed over my chest.

"What?" I ask.

She starts, blinking a couple of times before looking over at me. "Nothing. Just..." She shakes her head. "Nothing."

Narrowing my eyes, I don't press the issue and instead wait for the car to start. I sit back in the seat and close my eyes, seeing Morcant in front of the house again. There's blood now, and something in his eyes. They're sad, not blank or angry.

Just *sad*.

~ ~ ~

I throw my pillow to the ground and sit up, running a hand through my hair. Since hearing about my definite, upcoming peril, my stomach has been tied in a knot. Not because I'm going to die, but because I know I need to do *more* before that happens. Since my parents' death, since learning about their *profession*, I've been used to the idea of the afterlife, of death. It's never bothered me, and hell, it doesn't even really scare me like it should.

But I know I'm not supposed to die yet. I've settled for it, and now…

Sighing, I slump forward and reach for my phone. A couple of text messages from Riley, asking if I'm okay. One from Blaire, asking the same thing. Two from Connor, though his are about the homework I've missed and if I've done it yet.

I shake my head. None from Weston. I sigh and drop my phone onto the bed. Rubbing my eyes, I lay back down, hoping—*praying*, even—to sleep, to forget about everything, even for a couple of hours.

But the lack of messages or calls from Weston really hurts.

I sit back up and pick the phone up from the duvet and open messenger. I bite down on my lip as I stare at the keypad, unsure of what to type.

Are you awake?

Cheesy as hell, I drop the phone and groan. Really? 'Are you awake?' Is that the best I can come up with?

A moment later, my phone buzzes, and I look down at the screen.

Yeah. R u OK?

Closing my eyes, I clutch at my phone. What am I supposed to say now? 'Yeah'? And then what? Since the whole bathroom incident, he's been silent. Is he disgusted? Or does he realise that maybe I'm not worth it, wasn't worth the trouble?

He's probably been scared off, even though he tried so hard to be a good person.

The phone buzzes again, and I look down.

Do u want to talk?

I do, I really do. I send back a '*yes*' and climb out of bed. I throw on a t-shirt and a jacket, jeans, and my boots before pocketing my phone and a protection bag. My chest tightens as my heart races, and I suck in a breath.

"I can do this," I whisper, pulling my hair back into a ponytail. "I've got this."

The rest of the house is silent as I climb down the stairs; Tate is still at the hospital with Darren, and Aunt J's door is closed. The clock on the wall beside the stairs reads one AM.

Thanks to Darren, the front door doesn't squeak or slam, so sneaking out is easy. The floodlights out the front, though, flash on, and I wince.

Weston is already standing outside his house, arms crossed over his chest. His hair sticks up all over the place, and the sweater he wears is half tucked into his dark wash jeans. When he spots me, he offers me a tight-lipped smile, though his eyes drift down to my arm, which is tucked beneath my jacket.

Swallowing I race across the front yard towards him. "Hey," I say quietly, stopping in front of him.

His eyes skim over me, straight to my shoulder, before meeting my stare. "Hey."

A moment of silence passes between us as we look at one another warily.

"I'm sorry, about earlier," I say, shaking my head. "You were trying to help, and I pushed you away. I just..." I pause and swallow thickly, remembering the feeling of failure I felt when we got home.

Because I had put Darren in the hospital. Because it should have been me.

Weston places his hand on my neck, taking a step forward. "You have nothing to be sorry about," he says, shaking his head. "I shouldn't have tried to push you. I...I thought you might need me, but obviously you didn't."

I meet his stare. "Of course I need you, Weston. I just...it's all my fault. Darren's in the hospital because of me."

Before I can blink, Weston is pulling me into a hug, careful not to touch my shoulder. "None of it is your fault," he murmurs into my hair.

Pulling back, I shake my head and grimace. "It is, though. *I* went out, and he followed me. Darren pushed me out of the way and took most of the attack..." I rub my face and sigh. It would be so much easier if he knew the truth. "If I hadn't gone out there, he wouldn't be in there, is all I'm saying."

"Yeah, except you didn't know any of that was going to happen, Huntliegh. You aren't a psychic."

I'm related to one, though. Does that count?

I turn away and look over the desolate street.

"Don't punish yourself for this," he says quietly, so softly that it breaks me.

I'm surprised that the tears even fall. Haven't I cried enough over the last couple of days? Weston reaches for me, but I take a step back. I can't reply; my throat closes up with the truth on the tip of my tongue. How can I not punish myself for this? If he knew the truth, he'd probably blame me for everything too. Or, he'd run, and never talk to me again. And I can't lose him. I can't lose anyone else, not because of Morcant or because of this world I'm trapped in. I don't want to have to lose anyone else either.

Swallowing, I look back to him, meeting his stare. His wide, dark eyes meet mine without hesitation. "I really, *really* want to kiss you," he murmurs, eyes darting to my lips.

"We haven't even gone on that date yet," I point out, but my breath hitches in my throat. That normal part of me wants him too.

Weston shrugs. "I don't care."

"Then do it."

His lips meet mine carefully, softly, like he's afraid. My heart hammers in my chest as his lips move over mine. It isn't magical or like fireworks; it feels safe and like home. Like here, I don't have to face Morcant and death alone.

I lean in, deepening the kiss, loving how it feels to have his arm wrap around my torso while the other tangles in my hair.

In my pocket, my phone buzzes. Weston pulls away and looks

down at my pocket. I do the same, sighing, and pull it out.

Aunt Josephine. *I know you're outside. Please go to bed WITHOUT him.*

I bite down on my lip and turn back to the townhouse, unable to see her, but that doesn't mean she didn't *sense* it.

Swallowing, I turn back to Weston, who has a soft smile on his face. "Busted?"

I nod. "Busted."

"Totally worth it," he replies, leaning down and kissing me again quickly. "I'll talk to you later, okay?"

I want to say yes, but I can't. "Wait." My heart pounds for another reason now. *What the hell am I doing?*

When I speak, it's the truth, as bad as it is. "An animal didn't do this to us," I start.

His brows furrow. "What do you mean?"

"It wasn't something *alive* that did this." I motion to my shoulder as tears burn my eyes. "A Reaper did. A spirit."

Whether he means to or not, he takes a step back and shakes his head. I can already see the uncertainty in his eyes. Immediately, I regret everything, but I continue, because I can already feel my chest getting lighter. "My life *isn't* normal. You were right at Simone's party, that there's something weird about me. What I'm doing here isn't normal. And I'm afraid that if I tell you anything else, I might put you in danger. But I'm so, so sick of lying—especially to you."

"What exactly are you saying?"

I release a breath and shake my head. "I don't know. I just..." I purse my lips. "I don't want you to think I'm leaving here willingly."

I force myself to take a step back towards the house, where I know Aunt J is waiting.

"Wait, Hunt—"

I turn away and squeeze my eyes shut before making my way

to the door. I can just see him outlined in the streetlight. Weston doesn't move until I've made it to the front door, and from there I watch as he strides towards his own home.

The door opens underneath my hand, and I step back.

"Have fun?" Aunt J asks, arms crossed over her chest.

Sighing, I push past her. "Yeah, sort of." She remains quiet, and I take a step up the stairs. "I want to live through this, Aunt J. I really do. But I'm getting so tired of lying."

With that, I walk back up to my room.

18

GHOST GAMES

AFTER MY CONFESSION TO WESTON, I'm not entirely sure where we stand. It's been hard to find time to sit down and talk to him, explain to him what the hell is going on. I can't tell if he even wants to know. Part of me just hopes he thinks it was the pain meds talking, that I was just delusional after the events of the last couple of days.

He hasn't brought it up, and neither have I.

I spent a week at home, but that didn't mean I wasn't preparing for the upcoming battle with Morcant. Every spare minute has been about dissecting visions, learning about his estate, figuring out how Halloween ties into Morcant's plans.

Lore and mythology have always said Halloween is the day where the veil between the living and the dead is the thinnest. As Hunters, we've usually taken this particular lore as truth: sometimes some of the worst attacks on the living happens on this single day.

Aunt J drums her hands on the steering wheel as we drive back towards school. My stomach is in knots—not because of Halloween, but because today we're supposed to fit into normal society for a couple of hours. But it's hard to think about *normalcy* when the scars beneath my jacket burn as a reminder to what we have to lose.

"Are you sure you want to come?" I ask, pressing my hands into my lap.

I might be stressed, but she's taken it to a whole new level. Gone are the exciting clothes and cooking in bulk. Aunt J has turned into a recluse, surrounded by books instead of baked goods.

She's snappy, tired, and the visions are getting worse for her. Every couple of hours she complains of headaches and migraines. She downs coffee like it's going out of stock.

I've never been more worried for her than I am now.

Aunt J rolls her eyes. "I'm fine, Huntliegh. It'll be good for us to get out of the house." By *us*, she means her, because I've been back at school for three days despite our looming deadline.

I don't respond and instead settle back in my seat as we continue the drive to the school in silence. As we turn down the street, the traffic becomes heavy, filled with trucks waving flags for school teams, a mix of adults and students alike streaming onto the football field.

We pull into one of the few empty spaces. We're here to support Weston, but I'm also here because it's what Aunt J wants. She needs a break.

"Come on," I say finally, "we should go find Mr Contreras and Riley."

That brings a smile to my aunt's face, a soft one that shines a little bit of light in her tired eyes. "Of course. It's getting busy out there. Big turn out!"

I force a smile as we get out of the car. It's already getting dark with the sun setting over the lake. The stadium lights that surround the football field are beginning to turn on, illuminating the wet grass, guiding viewers to the main event.

We walk in silence towards the ticket area, where a booth has been set up to sell foam fingers and hats. Aunt J beelines there and gets herself a finger.

I spot Mr Contreras and Riley by the ticket booth. "Found them," I say, turning to Aunt J. For the first time in weeks, she smiles wide and brightly.

We meet them halfway; Mr Contreras also has one of the foam fingers tucked under his arm, face painted red, black, and grey for the school. He and Aunt J shake hands as we slowly file into the field.

"I still can't believe you actually showed up," I say, grinning over at Riley, who has a lollipop sticking out between red-painted lips.

Her smile turns to a grin as she meets my eye. "I can't believe I let you convince me."

"Neither can I." Mr Contreras glances between the two of us, the corners of his lips tipped upwards in a smile. His glasses slip down his nose as he bumps hips with Riley to get around her, a cup of popcorn in one hand and a soda in the other.

The smile doesn't disappear from Riley's face as she rolls her eyes. "Do you know how long my strike has been?"

"Since Blaire joined the cheerleading team?" I guess.

Riley nods sombrely. "I've done so well to avoid it. And now...now *you're* dating a *jock,* and suddenly I have to become *supportive.*"

I laugh. Butterflies erupt in the pit of my stomach as her words settle around me. *You're dating a jock.* It's strange *thinking* those words, let alone hearing them from *her* mouth.

I stop myself before I can say anything, but my cheeks warm, giving away my embarrassment. But Riley—ever the astute—catches it and gives my ribs a nudge.

"I hope you don't turn into a sap," Riley says, giving me a mocking once over. "Or a cheerleader. Please don't join my sister on the dark side."

Around us, the crowd thickens. We manage to stay together until we make it to the bleachers; the rows upon rows of people make my walls slam up to protect myself from wayward emotions. Too many might drive me nuts.

When we find an empty row of seats, we fall in with the rest of the crowd who begin to quiet down for the beginning of the game.

The teams fill the field; the Fort Caldwell Demons versus a school an hour away. I don't know the name, but their mascot is a wolf. There's a mix of fans for both teams, though I try to focus on finding Weston, who runs in with Connor at his side.

"What are their positions?" Aunt J asks.

I shrug. "I've never asked."

She gives me an unimpressed roll of the eyes. "Of course."

My cheeks heat with shame, but Riley sighs from beside me. "Don't worry. I don't know anything either. Dad pretends to but he's just here for brownie points and *school spirit.*"

I let a quiet laugh leave my lips as the game starts.

I watch with no idea what's going on. Football has never been a huge thing in our household, and until tonight, I've never been to a game.

So, I don't know what's going on.

After halftime, the inkling that something bad is going to happen hits me. At first it isn't noticeable, merely an ache in my temple. But it quickly turns into a sharp, throbbing pain.

The vision hits me faster than I can suck in a breath or reach for a protection bag:

Dark brown stains discolour the off-white panelled walls

circling the room. The window across from me has bars vertically welded into place, the gaps so thin it lets in little light, though the sky beyond is a similar dark steel-grey to the metal bars.

The light above me flickers and buzzes like a fly that somehow manages to avoid flying into your line of sight. The sound makes my ears ring, but something else brings a wave of panic that shudders over me.

I can't move my arms or legs.

I expect to feel pain in my shoulder from the Reaper attack, but there is nothing, the pain muted or gone—I can't tell. But something is wrapped around my wrists tightly, holding them in place on the bed, trapping me.

I wiggle and try to lift my head. A thin sheet covers my body, but beneath that, I'm in a night-gown, one that resembles a hospital gown from the 50s.

Somewhere behind me, a door creaks open. I try to look, but it's just hidden from sight.

Like a low hum, screams and cries for help reach my ears. I squeeze my eyes shut as the rush of emotions—terror, fury, anxiety—hit me. I'm not protected in this vision.

A nurse appears at my side. Her softly curled hair falls out of a white cap. Her cheeks are white, hands cold as they tighten the restraints around my wrists and ankles.

She wears an upside down cross around her neck. It's eerily familiar.

Delilah.

Footsteps, paired with a soft tapping, fill my ears when the door clicks shut, cutting off the screams of patients. It's not hard to tell where I am now, not when Morcant rounds the side of the bed. He stops beside his daughter and smiles down at me. He carries the same book from my last vision.

I glance between the two; there's something odd about the

way they're interacting, in the way they move.

Morcant flips open the book and starts reading over the pages while Delilah watches. Her gaze darkens with every moment he reads. They speak, but their words are inaudible.

The screams grow louder and start to penetrate the room. A wicked smile lights up both faces. I buck and pull at the restraints, but Delilah only laughs.

The vision clears, and I'm left gasping for breath. The world around me spins in and out of focus, blurring at the edges. I'm sure I'm going to pass out, throw up maybe, but I focus on the cold air of the football field.

And it doesn't work.

I stand with everyone else as cheers for our team replaces the screams of the asylum patients. Bile crawls into my throat. I push my way out of the bleachers and down onto the muddy ground between the stands.

Thankfully, there isn't a line outside the women's restrooms, and I sprint inside. The cheers become muffled as I collapse inside a stall and heave into the yellowed toilet bowl.

I can't escape the panic that filled the vision, nor the imprints of the restraints from my wrists. When I open my eyes and, with trembling hands, lift the sleeve off my left arm, dark blue and purple bruises glare back at me.

I throw up again.

Cool hands pull my hair back, but I can't hear the person over the ringing in my ears. Dampness hits the back of my neck, and I don't move, not with the screams still drumming in my ears, not when my own screams burn my throat.

The racing of my heart steadies as the urge to throw up finally recedes. I carefully touch my face and feel the hot flesh against my numb fingers. The air around me stinks, and yet I'm trapped back in that room, the stench of rubbing alcohol and sickly medicine clogging my senses.

The conversation between the doctor and nurse—*no*, between Morcant and *Delilah*, the daughter he'd murdered, had tortured.

I grip the edge of the bowl and push away from the toilet, my ears no longer ringing with the screams of patients and instead with the words of the spirits who haunted me. At my side, Riley says something. Shivers wrack my body, but I focus on the vision, on what Morcant had revealed:

That he might not be alone with his torture, which makes him all the more deadly.

19

THE GHOSTS THAT HAUNT US

WESTON'S ARMS TIGHTEN AROUND MY waist as the bike picks up speed. We pass through the town like phantoms, never stopping, leaving mist in our wake as more rain attacks Fort Caldwell.

I don't realise where I'm taking us until we're on the long stretch of abandoned road leading to the Morcant Estate.

I slow to a stop and kick up the stand. The engine rumbles beneath us since I'm too afraid to turn it off, not when the Reaper might still be out there, hunting me, watching.

"What are we doing here, Hunt?" Weston asks, voice low.

A shiver races down my spine as I lift my helmet off and take in the looming dark forest around us. Unlike previous nights, there are no spirits being led to the estate—or at least, none that I can see. I can't sense them, not when Morcant blocks their emotions.

I shake my head and get off the bike. "I don't know."

"So much for a nice, relaxing date," Weston mutters, though amusement brightens his tone. "I'm joking." He reaches for my hand, and I let him take it; the warmth of his fingers seep through my leather gloves, but my hand remains cold as I wait—wait for the Reaper to attack, wait for spirits to arrive, wait for Morcant to show himself and finally do what he's been threatening all these weeks.

"Hunt?"

I shake the thoughts from my head. "Sorry. Lost in thought."

He stands and comes around the bike, keeping hold of my hand. "Don't be sorry. Just...talk to me."

"What do you want to know?" I ask.

"Everything." His hand tightens around mine. "Why you?"

I frown. "What do you mean?"

He shrugs. "Why are you a Hunter?"

"Because my parents were. Aunt J is. Tate and Darren are. My mom's parents were. It's kind of the family job."

Somewhere in the trees, a branch cracks. I spin in the direction of the sound, tightening my grip on Weston as I do. Every instinct tells me to run, to take Weston and hide. We should—I should have turned around as soon as I realised where we are.

But I didn't.

I hope this doesn't come back to bite me in the ass.

Slowly, I turn back to him. Worry floods through him and into me. "Everything is okay," I whisper. "We're fine."

I'm not sure if I say this for his sake—or my own.

His throat bobs as he looks from me to where the Morcant house lies beyond the trees. "So, this is why you're here?" he asks, nodding in the direction of the estate. "This place?"

I release a shaky breath. "More or less. It's the job." I shrug. A chill wind picks up around us. "Morcant has been taking victims for nearly two hundred years. He's been on this plane for too long."

"How do you know?"

"All Hunters in North America know about this spot." If there were a school for Hunters, Morcant would be a whole subject on his own. "Years of remaining here has given Morcant a lot of power, and that means Hunters struggle finding ways to kill him. Too many die in the process of trying to get in and out of there."

"So, how do you plan on doing it?" Weston asks, voice low. "How do you plan on getting out?"

My breath catches in my throat. The lie is already on the tip of my tongue. "We've been studying old lore. We know what he's planning now, so we can prepare for it. Other Hunters have gone in blind. But we know what's going on now."

It's probably better not to let on that I don't expect to come out alive, that something could go terribly wrong in there.

As if sensing my thoughts, Weston frowns. "Are you sure?"

I swallow. "Why wouldn't I be?"

"Huntliegh, you said a *Reaper* or whatever tried to kill you. That seems a bit..." He stops and clenches his jaw.

"What?"

"Dangerous," he bites out, looking away.

I shake my head. "Weston...I've been in this life for as long as I can remember. I've been hunting *solo* since I was fifteen."

"Yeah, I get it. You can take care of yourself." His eyes flicker to mine, then away again. Something darkens his eyes, and his grip on my hand tightens. "I just...I don't want to see you get hurt again, Hunt. That was terrifying, getting the call from Mom. To see your Aunt and Tate in the waiting room, with cops all around... It just..."

I bite my lip. "It just what?"

"It reminded me of when my brother went missing." He

releases my hand and runs it through his messy hair. Tears glint in his eyes. "We were twelve. He ran away from home in the middle of the night. Police think he was kidnapped, but no one could know for sure."

"I'm so sorry." It explains why his family is the way it is; his parents love him, I know that for sure, but that doesn't take away the pain of losing a child. They don't have photos up because they all have his brother in them. They have a shrine in their kitchen to remember the little boy.

I don't know what to say but voicing my thoughts probably won't be a good idea.

West shakes his head and clears his throat. "I don't want to lose another person, Hunt. I don't think I can."

The soft glow of headlights breaks through the drizzling rain and darkness. I hadn't even noticed the rumble of the car engine coming towards us.

The white security car rolls to a stop. A man with dark skin and an unimpressed look on his face pokes his head out and looks between us. "Sorry to spoil your fun, kids, but this road is off limits. You better head home now before I take you in and call your parents." He looks at my bike and frowns. "That yours?"

I cross my arms. "It's mine. And we're leaving now, don't worry."

He makes a sound and waves his hand. "Make sure you do." As the window rolls up, he mutters, "Don't need no deaths tonight."

I wait until he's driven off before I turn back to Weston. "We should go home. It's getting late, and we seriously don't need to get in any trouble."

He reaches for my hand, and I let him take it. "We'll be fine," he murmurs, taking a step closer.

No matter how much I want to believe him, I can't. But I smile for him and pretend because that's all I'm good for. If

Morcant wins, I'll die anyway, and my lies won't matter.

20

THE PUMPKIN PATCH

THE CLAW MARKS WILL DEFINITELY never go away. I look at the red lines that mar my shoulder and wince at the scar tissue that looks swollen and irritated. It'll be a permanent reminder.

Sighing, I shrug my sweater on, grimacing as my shoulder strains. Despite getting the stitches out two weeks ago, and getting the sling removed last week, the skin and muscle of my arm and shoulder is still sore and tender, and I still have pain meds to take for it.

Weston's mom checks my shoulder from her house on occasion, since her son has made it very obvious that we are now dating. Thinking about it sends a shiver down my spine. *Dating.* The word is foreign on my tongue. Since my parents died, since I'd started hunting Morcant, I haven't particularly thought about *dating*, and now...

Now I have a *boyfriend*. And friends that are more than just connections. I have a life here.

But Morcant is still in the house, and that Reaper *thing* is still hunting me. And Darren... I swallow. He's out of the induced coma, but he still has a long way to go before he's up and walking again. He's lucky the Reaper didn't sever his spinal cord, apparently.

I went to see him, once. But as soon as I entered the hospital room, I ran. And I haven't been back since. Tate had looked at me and nodded, but when I'd seen Darren in that bed, almost lifeless, I just...I ran.

And I hate myself for it.

"How's the shoulder holding up?" Aunt J asks, body tense. We're one week from Halloween now, and there's still so much to do, so much still to happen. Since the attack, Aunt J has had more visions, mostly about Morcant, but she's had no luck with contacting any of the spirits from the estate. Not even little Bonnie or her friend can answer our questions about the whereabouts of the bodies.

Sighing, I hitch my bag over my shoulder and carefully stretch my bad arm out. "It's getting better," I reply, unable to meet her stare. "I'll be ready."

For the last two weeks, we've had the same fight, over and over again, about whether or not *I* would be the one going into that house. Finally, after long nights sitting around Mr Heckney's dining table, with Aunt J's amazing stress cooking, we've come up with a plan.

Aunt J, Tate, and I will go in while Mr Heckney makes sure there is enough protection around the property. Aunt J and Tate would go in during the day to fortify the house, to add more hexes and warding *against* the malevolent spirits within. Then I'll go in with them, and we'll hunt down Morcant ourselves.

It's taken a lot to even get to this point, to get Tate involved.

But we had him on our side when Aunt J explained what had really attacked Darren and who had sent it.

I just hope our half-assed plan will work.

Ghost Hunters are notoriously bad at sticking to plans.

"I've made up more protection bags," she starts, leaning against the doorframe. "Slip one into Weston's car, would you? And into your locker. That Reaper could be anywhere, and I don't want it getting to you or your friends."

I nod and take the bags she hands me, slipping them into my backpack.

"And be careful tonight, okay? I know you're excited..."

I almost forgot. Date with Weston. He said it was a surprise, something I'd love. I'm not too sure about that, but the look in his eyes when he asked me told me *he* loved it.

We've been good since our impromptu date, which still surprises me. I honestly expected him to cut me out of his life entirely after the explanation that our world isn't as black and white as it seems, that the dead still walk among us and can hurt us if they have the power to do so.

"I will," I reply, offering her a smile. "I always am."

The painful smile she gives me in return tells me she doesn't believe me. Since coming here...our relationship has changed drastically. Back when I was hunting the spirits of unruly serial killers, she had no problem with letting me go out and do as I pleased or facing off spirits on my own.

But now...the build-up and the planning has put both of us on edge. Aunt J rarely leaves the house unless she's going over to Mr Heckney's or to the hospital. She's been focused so much on this mission that she's barely slept.

Dark rings shadow her eyes, and her usually flouncy hair looks dead; she's taken to pulling it into a bun, which she rarely does, and the strands that fall through the hair-tie don't have the same curl to them.

Aunt J sighs and steps into the room, wrapping her thin arms around me in a hug. It doesn't escape my notice how much weight she's lost, or the fact that I seem only a bit better off.

"It's okay to be scared," she murmurs.

But it sounds more like a reassurance for her than for me.

I swallow, shaking my head. "If I'm scared, then something bad will happen."

She looks down at me, her eyes glassy and forlorn. "If we stick together, stick to the plan, then nothing bad will happen, ever again. Okay?"

Nodding, I suck in a breath, my eyes falling onto my alarm clock. *Almost time for school.* With the rush of planning, school is my release. Aunt J, Mr Heckney...they don't have that same reprise from the strains of the job. But I do, and although I'm grateful for it, a part of me resents *myself* because I'm leaving everything to them. Even Tate does more than me.

My stomach churns at the thought.

"I'll see you tonight." Pulling away from Aunt J, I run my hands through my hair and over my sweater and jeans. Simple, cozy, and durable, just in case Weston has something strange planned for our *date*.

God, how can I think about dating at a time like this? But my heartbeat escalates at the thought, and I feel my cheeks go warm.

Normalcy is what I'm fighting for; a chance to live a life untouched by the burdens of spirits.

Dashing down the stairs, I hit the front door before Weston can knock; his eyes widen, and his hair—messy, how surprising— falls over his forehead. He has his fist raised, and I smile as it drops back to his side.

"Good timing," he says, grinning. His eyes dart behind me and up the stairs, to where Aunt J probably stands, watching us with wary eyes. "Hey, Josephine!"

"Good morning, Weston." Her voice sounds far away, as if

she's locked in a memory or a vision. I look back over my shoulder to see her turn away and enter the office.

When I look back to Weston, his lips peel back in a frown. "Is she okay?" he asks, rubbing the back of his neck. "She didn't seem all that..."

"Happy?" I suggest. "It's not you. Just...everything with Darren and my attack has kind of taken its toll on her."

It feels...*strange*, not having to lie to him. Aunt J doesn't know he knows, so that'll be a conversation for another day. But it's the long nights of researching the gateway, circling the Morcant house in her car, practically living in the basement of Mr Heckney's house reading over every single piece of information she can that's draining her. Aunt J carries the brunt of the work and expectations on her shoulders; this is the last thing she needs to worry about.

Weston nods, offering his arm. "Shall we go?" The smile, albeit charming, doesn't reach his eyes, but I take his arm nonetheless and let him lead me to his truck.

A small spark of guilt builds in the pit of my stomach. Did I make a mistake in telling him? Is he just as worried now as we are?

We drive to school in silence, taking the time to dwell in our own thoughts. I try to think about the date, to think about school and the life that I have here, but my thoughts go to Halloween and to Morcant.

The vision of him with Delilah, the strange book on the vanity, of the body come to mind. Only this time I can see the face, the hands. I don't see the chest rise and fall.

It's me.

I push it from my mind and close my eyes; he hasn't personally attacked me since we've arrived in Fort Caldwell, and we haven't spotted the Reaper since it attacked me and Darren. But it doesn't mean he hasn't stopped *threatening me*. His visions are becoming more obscure, stranger. I don't know what to make of them, and neither do Aunt J or Mr Heckney.

I imagine Aunt Josephine, Tate, and I going into the house and being unable to find the bodies. That the protection hexes and bags that we've set up around the property falter, and we become trapped.

"You okay?" Weston asks, breaking through my thoughts. I open my eyes and notice that we're at school, the engine already off.

Blinking, I sit back and rub my eyes, trying to expel the thoughts and visions of our possible deaths. "Yeah, I'm fine."

Weston rests his hand on my thigh and squeezes. "You sure?" When I meet his stare, I nod, though it feels more forced than anything. His smile is tight, and he sighs. "Good."

If anything happens in the next week…I'm not sure what I'll do. And if I die in that house…I'm not sure what *he'll* do.

Weston grins and climbs out of the car. I blink away tears and try to smile, following him, because if I have to live, then I'd like to see that smile more.

~ ~ ~

School ends with the monotonous ring of the bell; classes empty like a wildfire is taking over the school, and the skies darken furiously with the threat of rain.

During my study period, I was roped into helping Blaire decorate the school with Halloween decorations; paper pumpkins and ghosts cover nearly all the lockers, and we managed—with Weston and Connor's help—to hang plastic bats from the ceiling. We strung cobwebs along the ceiling, too, and in all the corners.

"You did well," Weston teases, slinging his arm around my shoulder. I smile to myself and lean into him, enjoying the comfort and warmth he radiates. "You could be a cheerleader after all that work."

I snort. "Sure. Except I have little to no flexibility." I have endurance, and I can definitely run if I need to. But I can't do a cartwheel to save my life. If that's how Morcant has to go down...then we're all doomed.

"I doubt that." We walk to the car in silence, Weston opening the passenger side door for me and dropping his bag and books at my feet. "Ready?" he asks, climbing in beside me.

I shrug and sit back, closing my eyes, focusing on anything *but* my impending doom. "You still haven't told me where we're going, or what we're doing. So, no. I'm not."

He laughs as we pull out of the school's parking lot. Weston drives us in the opposite direction of our street; we continue down the road of suburbia that circles the school and down a road full of new houses, all decked out with Halloween decorations; mummies and ghosts and zombies litter the yards. Someone managed to put up a giant spider, with skeletons wrapped in its webs. Another house has a graveyard out front, with arms and legs sticking out of the ground.

"They really go all out here," I say, leaning forward to get a good look at another house. It looks like a scene out of a Tim Burton movie.

Weston laughs again, and we turn down another street, the suburbia thinning out to reveal the forest that surrounds Fort Caldwell.

Dashing between the trees, a white figure races the car. I blink, and it's gone.

I turn away and suck in a breath, forcing my heartbeat to slow down enough for me to breath.

Weston says, "Yeah. It helps that we have such a friendly community. There are a *lot* of kids in town that love the holiday."

"It surprises me," I say, voice shaking. I clear my throat and continue, "Fort Caldwell has a lot of missing persons. And with the Morcant house so close…"

He shrugs. "We don't see it that way, or well, *I* don't." He pauses and slows, stopping outside a small field. "We might have a lot of tragedy here, but I guess we can use Halloween as a beacon to those we've lost. I'd like to think that if they saw all this, they'd want to come back. And, you know, since ghosts *are* real, they can see all this."

I blink and look away. But he continues talking, getting out of the car, racing over to open the door for me. "According to the Pagans, Halloween is the night of the dead, right? They're 'closer to earth' or whatever. So, you know, even if we have lost all these people, Halloween night can be a night for them to return, and we'll be none the wiser. Except you, of course, Miss *Empath Psychic*."

I bump my shoulder into his side but can't help the smile that forms on my lips. "I'm just an empath," I reply. "Aunt J is the psychic."

The field we've stopped at is filled with pumpkins; children of all ages and their parents scuttle around in the hay, looking last minute for their pumpkins. I notice some kids playing tag, running around a scarecrow in the centre of the field. In the back, someone has built a maze out of hay and old wood panels.

"We're doing that?" I ask, pointing to it. I eye it sceptically. I love puzzles, but mostly when they have something to do with people; I like figuring out what makes them tick, or what causes them to do different things. But mazes…I hate them with a passion.

But Weston looks excited, and I can't help but match his smile. "It changes every year. Mr and Mrs Pearson, who own the farm, spend months planning it, and they've always got some kind of surprise hidden in the centre for whoever gets there first."

"You've done this before?" I ask, grinning as he grabs my hand and starts dragging me towards the hay.

He nods sheepishly. "I brought my *friend* here two years ago and she *hated* it. Complained the whole time." I turn away and clear my throat. He says, "I came here last year with Connor and Blaire, but they ditched me and made out in the pumpkin patch."

I snort. "Well, now that I'm here, we're going to have to get all the way through. I refuse to give up." When I meet his eyes, I notice a glimmer in them, a glimmer of happiness.

Suddenly, someone calls out to us, and we turn to see Connor, Blaire, and Riley walking towards us; Blaire's changed into something warmer, opting for a coat that looks softer than one of Aunt J's throw pillows, and a beanie that looks both practical and stylish. Riley, however, wears a sweater similar to mine, though without a coat, and has thrown her hair up into a bun. Connor wears his letterman jacket with pride.

Riley grins. "Funny seeing you two here." She bumps her hip with mine and takes my other arm, cuddling close to my side.

At my other side, Weston rolls his eyes. "You knew we were going to be here."

"Yeah," she says, popping her gum. "And I'm just here to make sure you don't deflower my girl in the pumpkin patch like jock-boy over there did with my sister."

Blaire's red lips thin as she glares at her twin, while Connor rubs at the back of his neck sheepishly. Weston coughs loudly, though he doesn't remove his hand from mine.

"Were there *other* plans you forgot to mention?" I ask, looking up at him.

His cheeks and ears have gone red. "Of course not! I would never." His eyes go from me to Riley, and he narrows them at her.

She releases me and crosses her arms. "Fine. Is this going to be a comp or what?"

I watch as Connor and Weston's eyes meet, and I know straight away that *this* would be a dangerous game. Two guys, both with a tendency to be overly competitive... I doubt this will end up being a date for me and West, but rather one for him and Connor.

"Oh God," Blaire says, almost like she can read her boyfriend's mind. "Please don't."

"Riley," Connor says impatiently, "pick a team."

She groans and looks between me and her sister, before picking Blaire. "I'm too young to become an aunt, sorry girl."

Blaire pushes her but doesn't complain. Instead, we walk to the maze's entrance and stand in front of it, gazing into the fields of hay.

Connor glances to us with a grin. "Let the best team win."

~ ~ ~

"Are you sure we're going the right way?" I ask, stepping carefully over piles of hay that have gone soft. I've already slipped twice, with Weston catching me both times.

He laughs, hand tightening around mine. "Don't tell me you're worried."

I raise my brow at him, slipping once again. "Oh, I'm not. I just want to make sure I can get out of here before graduation." Or before my scheduled death in one week. Either way works.

He tugs me along as we enter a different corridor, this one lined with pumpkins. Mr and Mrs Pearson have done a lot of work to make this interesting; around every bend, there is some kind of *scary* monster: scarecrows, skeletons, pumpkin men, ghosts, and more, made from costumes and decorations from the mall.

Above us, the sky starts turning pink. "We've been at this for *hours*."

"Are you, Huntliegh Parrish, *complaining*?" He glances at me sceptically and stops, crossing his arms. "I'd be very disappointed if you were. Professional ghost Hunter and all. I thought this would be easy for you."

I sigh and take a step towards him, closing the distance between us. Standing up on my tiptoes, and even with that extra height, he still has to look down at me. I glance at his lips, then his eyes; we haven't kissed since that night, even though he's pecked me on the cheek here and there, and I've done the same to him.

But I kiss him properly. I relish in the soft feeling of them, in the safety that consumes me as his lips move with mine.

"Okay," he breathes, pulling away, "that makes up for the complaining. But only a bit."

Raising my brow, I grab his hand and begin pulling him along. "I'm not joining you in the pumpkin patch, if that's what you're suggesting."

We spend another hour looking for the centre, and make it just before Connor, Blaire, and Riley do. In the end, the prize is our choice of pumpkin, which Weston carries to the truck. And because *we* won, the others have to shout pizza for our group.

This might be the happiest I've ever been since what happened to my parents. And in one week...this might just all come to an end.

21

THE REALITY OF DEATH

I BITE DOWN ON THE INSIDE OF MY cheek as Mr Heckney paces the length of the basement, wispy head bowed in concentration.

"We have two days until Halloween," Mr Heckney muses, stopping to lean over the diagram of the Morcant Estate. "Our best move is to go through the front door. Once you are in, draw *these* protection runes on the back of the door." He hands Aunt Josephine, Tate, and I a couple of pages full of large runes, some look Celtic while the others look Nordic.

"Once you've done that, you *should* be able to leave," he finishes, pointing to the door again.

I raise a brow. "Should?"

Albert Heckney waves a hand, like that's the least of our problems. "I say should because we do not know the full extent of Morcant's power. That's why I have plenty of runes there for you."

Swallowing, I look back down at the sharp lines, and the circles and spirals. *I can do this. We can do this.*

I think back to the night Weston took me to the maze; it didn't *feel* like a week ago but rather a lifetime ago. Since then, we've started *really* focusing on the job. To get myself back in 'shape'—since Tate believes I'm rusty after my injury—we've gone out and hunted down three separate spirits tormenting the living. One was a woman who died of a heart attack; unfortunately, she got to her ex-husband first and gave him one of his own. We managed to quickly burn her remains before she could hurt anyone else.

Another was that of a child from seventy years ago, forever playing in the old park out by the lake. Turns out, he drowned, and his body was never found, but he led us to where he fell in, to an old toy of his from when he'd been alive. We burned it, too, setting him free.

The last one... It sends shivers down my spine every time I think about it. A woman, lost to time. She had no malevolence, no anger or pain. She was just...*confused.* But the way she looked... It looked almost like she's been *rotting.* Some spirits resemble how they looked at the time of their death—like Bonnie and her friend—but this spirit...

It was obvious that something was changing. Whether it was because of Morcant or because of something else, I'm not sure. Mr Heckney believes wholeheartedly that it has *everything* to do with Morcant and his ever-growing power, and Aunt J seems inclined to agree. Tate and I are a little more sceptical, but I'm growing closer to the same conclusion.

My abilities, which are tied to the dead, seem to be changing too. Withering away with Morcant's growing power, Aunt J thinks. Her visions are taking greater tolls on her health—both mental and physical—but she's been forcing herself to do more, to go even further into the visions.

One day, I'm afraid she might not return from them.

Sighing, I close my eyes and rub them tiredly. When I look down at my phone, the numbers read '10PM'.

Mr Heckney continues, as if unaffected by the late hour. "We must be in there before sunset, otherwise I believe none of this will work. From my end, I will try and strengthen you and the protections while you implement them."

"And we cannot, under any circumstances, split up," Aunt J clarifies, directing her stare to me. "Even if we see your parents in there. They won't see you, Hunt."

I bite down on my bottom lip and glance down at the papers in front of me. Right. I'm going in there to free my parents from the cage Morcant has forced them into. They're still there, their bodies lost. And if I see them, they won't even recognise me as their daughter. Not if they're trapped like Heckney believes.

Every part of me knows this is what it'll be like, but it doesn't make it any easier to bear. I'll still have to face them, no matter what.

"Of course," Mr Heckney replies, obviously not sensing the palpable tension that sprung in the room. "Moving on. We all have that countdown thing Huntliegh put on our telephones?"

I nod, unlocking my phone. Less than two days until Halloween, until this all ends.

Should I say goodbye to my friends? Or should I hope for the best, even if I know it might not end that way?

Aunt J reaches under the table and takes my hand, squeezing it. I meet her stare and nod once. This is it.

"If anything happens," Tate starts, "I want you all to know that I love you, no matter what." He directs his stare to me, and I can't help it; I let go of Aunt Josephine's hand and throw my arms around him, tightening my hold on him as he falls into me.

Tears burn my eyes. I squeeze them shut because fear will do me no good against the forces of Morcant.

When Tate releases me, I breathe a sigh of relief, that our relationship hasn't been damaged beyond repair. I still don't know if he blames me for what happened to Darren—and I hope, more than anything, that he knows I blame myself more than he ever could. But we have an understanding, and for now, I'm okay with that, because I have my uncle back.

Mr Heckney snorts, ruining the moment. "Don't go saying goodbye like you expect to die. Last time I said goodbye like that, the person *did* die, and I don't want that happening again, you hear me?"

But when I look over to the old man, I can see his eyes glimmering with fear; because he knows full well what could happen if anything goes wrong in that house. He's sent so many Hunters in there, hoping that each and every one of them would walk out and the demon would be dealt with. Instead, they died, and *he* had to file the missing person's report. *He* had to live with the guilt of knowing where they really were, where they'd really died.

Swallowing, I nod to him. Mr Heckney doesn't need to hear any of this. None of us do. "We should try and get some rest. Less than two days until this is done."

The adults around me nod, but no one makes a move to leave because in reality, none of us are truly prepared to go up against Morcant and win.

22

OCTOBER 31

I CHOOSE TO RIDE TO SCHOOL alone today, since Weston has some appointment he needs to go to during first and second period, meaning he won't be back until PE. But riding in the drizzling rain gives me time to think, time to stew on everything that is about to happen.

Today is October 31st, and tonight I will probably die.

23

CALL BEYOND THE GRAVE

"ARE YOU EXCITED FOR TONIGHT?" Riley asks, popping a blueberry into her mouth. She watches me with narrowed eyes, like she already knows I'm going to lie.

I shrug. "Sure. If you're into that kind of thing." Again and again, the lies slip easily from my mouth. In truth, I'm terrified of tonight, not because I have to pretend to be normal, but because it might be my last *anything*.

Weston already knows that I'll be skipping school early, has already offered to drive me home, but I can't make him do that. I can't say goodbye or take him away from our friends. He doesn't even know it might be goodbye. If I see him alone, I know I'll crack.

Riley sighs dramatically and throws a blueberry at her sister, who looks up irritably from her textbook. "So, we're being forced by little miss popular to attend her fun little dance. And you're leaving me without a date?" she asks, looking back to me.

"Seems that way," I reply with a half-smile. Riley sighs again, while Blaire glares at the both of us.

"No one is making either of you come," she says, rolling her eyes. "Anyway, it's not like we have to stay the entire night."

I'm not, I think picking at my food. I lower my gaze to the table as the voices of my friends and other students excited for the dance, for Halloween and the parties that'll pop up throughout the night in celebration turn into a dull roar in my ears.

Connor looks up from his phone, finally, and grins. "I say we go to the old Morcant house after the dance and try to stay the night."

My heart stops in my chest; beside me, Riley agrees, while Blaire seems more reluctant than her twin. I try to suck in a breath, to tell them that it isn't a good idea, but I can't make my mouth move.

Panic slowly but surely settles in as Connor and Riley discuss their would-be plans for the night. They want to meet after the dance once it's dark and set up camp inside. Despite the obvious legends that no one could stay the night because they're either chased out of the house before midnight or are never seen again.

Connor and Riley and Blaire only think they're rumours.

But I know the truth. And so does Weston, but he's not here to back me up, to tell them their idea is stupid.

"You shouldn't," I choke out. All eyes fall on me. Connor smirks, while Riley and Blaire look at me with worry and confusion.

"You don't have to go," Connor points out, taking a bite of his lunch. "And we're not scared of some little old ghost story."

I swallow thickly. "It's just..." I trail off and try to find the words, but any explanation catches in my throat, tangling with the lies that threaten to spill from my lips.

Before I can continue, Riley has her hand on my face. "Hey,

you okay? You don't look well."

I blink rapidly, because no, I'm not. I'm not *okay*. My friends have just announced that they want to spend the night in *Morcant's house*, which is where I'm going to be tonight either getting rid of his spirit or dying in the process.

Pushing my chair out, I slip my bag over my shoulder and rush out of the cafeteria, my stomach rising in my throat as I do. I hear both Blaire and Riley call out to me, but I don't stop; I barrel through the front doors of the school and head straight to my bike, gasping for breath.

No matter how many breaths I take, I can't expel the panic, the thoughts that overtake me about what might happen if they *do* go to the house. Even if I'm inside, I can't stop them from getting trapped, can't stop Morcant from taking them too.

The drizzling rain has stopped, leaving the air cold and icy. Their plans ring in my ears, too loud for me to shake or forget.

Arms wrap around my middle, though I almost don't feel it over the dread still shuddering through me.

"Hey," Weston murmurs, voice low in my ear. "Are you okay?"

I want to say everything is fine, that there's nothing to worry about, but the words get caught in my throat. I can only nod my response, but he doesn't let go; instead, those arms wrap tighter around me, almost forming a barrier around me. The comfort could almost be enough to calm me, but it isn't.

"Connor texted me saying you ran out of there pretty quickly. Said you were freaked out."

Sucking in a shuddering breath, I lean back into him, into the strength and warmth of his body. *God*, I hope he won't join them. I hope he stays away. But I know Weston well enough now; he knows how dangerous that house is, and if his friends go in there blindly, he'll follow to keep them safe.

I shudder. "Connor suggested going to the Morcant house

after the dance," I whisper, squeezing my eyes shut. "Riley, of course, thinks it's a great idea, and I sat there and listened and couldn't tell them how dangerous it really is."

Weston's arms tighten around me. "What do you need me to do?"

I release a breath, relief flooding me. I didn't realise just how much I needed to hear those words. Him asking if I needed his help—offering it at all—means more than he probably knows.

"Keep them here, as far away from the house as possible." I push any lingering thoughts of their potential deaths aside. "Go to a party or something. Anything that'll keep them occupied. Just don't let them anywhere near me or Morcant."

I feel Weston tense behind me, but I'm not sure if it's out of fear for our friends or worry over me. It could be neither or all of the above; either way, a sliver of guilt courses through me for my part in the changes of his life.

"I think I need to go home," I finally say, pulling myself out of his arms. When I turn to face him, I notice the look of dread settling deep in his eyes.

"Are you sure you're okay?" he asks, cupping my cheek. His dark eyes trail over my face and body, as if he's searching for some kind of physical wound.

I think he knows, though, that nothing is okay.

I force myself to smile, and I grab my helmet, swinging my leg over Mom's old bike. "I'm fine," I whisper, clearing my throat. "I'll see you later."

Without waiting for a response, I rev the engine and shove my helmet over my head. I pull out of the parking lot and don't look back.

~ ~ ~

I pace up and down the living room, biting down on my

thumbnail. Aunt J groans from the couch as she slumps back against the cushions. I've told her what they want to do, and I curse myself for not even *considering* the fact that idiots like Connor and Riley and others from school will likely try and stay the night on *Halloween*.

How could I have been so stupid not to think of that?

Rubbing at my eyes, I fall to the couch beside Aunt J. "What can we do?" I ask, looking to her.

She runs a hand over her hair, eyes on the coffee table, where she made more and more protection bags. She's been experimenting, trying to find ways to boost their power. So far, she hasn't had much luck, but she's trying.

"When teenagers get it in their heads that they're going to do something, unfortunately it's quite hard to get them to reconsider," she mutters, eyes moving from the table and over to me. "I just hope we can get there *before* them and maybe lock them out."

I release a shuddering sigh. "And if that doesn't work?"

"Then if they end up in the house *with* us...you're going to have to protect them while Tate and I figure out where Morcant is keeping the bodies."

Shaking my head, I stand. "We can't split up, remember?"

"I know," Aunt J replies, sighing. She rubs irritably at her eyes. "But if it comes down to it, I want you to stay on the main floor with your friends while Tate and I try and figure everything else out."

I clench my jaw and start pacing again. "We're going in there together, and we're coming back out together."

We've had this argument before, so many times, but there is no way I'm going to stay out of the fight. Morcant attacked me, took my parents from me, and if we aren't careful, he's going to take my friends too.

"If anything," I mutter, "they probably won't be safe with me."

Aunt Josephine meets my stare with a hollow expression; eyes glazed over, she cocks her head and mouths something, lips only moving slightly, like she's a puppet, in a trance. But no sound passes through them, and a moment later, she blinks.

She shakes her head as if nothing happened. "I don't want you going into that house," she finally replies, releasing a breath. Her shoulders slump, and she rests her head in her hands. "He will come for you, Hunt."

"So, if the others end up trapped with us, they should stay with you or Tate, not *me*."

Her head shoots up. "I don't want you going *at all*."

I bite down on my lip and jut out my chin. "I'm going. The more Hunters, the better."

"You don't know that, Hunt. He's powerful. He's *old*. He probably knows everything about us too." Aunt J shakes her head in irritation and stands, smoothing down her oversized sweater. "He'll pick us all off."

My aunt doesn't even give me the chance to reply before she's reaching for her purse and keys, slamming the door on her way out. I flinch when she starts the car and pulls away from the curb, completely disappearing.

Where would she be going? Either to the hospital or to Mr Heckney's, but she's mad now, and she didn't even divulge the vision she clearly just had.

Groaning, I fall back onto the couch. My phone buzzes on the coffee table, but I don't bother checking the caller ID as I pick it up.

"Yeah?"

Hissing and crackling is the only thing audible on the other end, the disrupted signal cutting in and out.

"Hello?" I ask, ready to hang up. I don't need a prank call right now.

The hissing and crackling continues, but I can faintly make

out a voice. "Huntliegh?" the voice asks, barely audible underneath the sputtering signal.

Mom.

"Mom?" I ask. Tears sting my eyes as I lean forwards, heart racing. "Mom? Is that you?"

"Huntliegh!" her voice cuts out, and the crackling becomes louder suddenly. I think I hear something splatter, like blood on paper.

Gurgling sounds right before the call cuts off, leaving me listening to dial tone and the painful echo of my mothers' voice.

24

HALLOWEEN

SINCE ARRIVING IN FORT CALDWELL, I haven't actually *seen* the Morcant House in person; like stand in front of it and take it in properly. I've seen photographs, and I've seen the back of it obscured by trees while walking the property line. But I've never had the chance to stand in front of it.

And looking up at the imposing exterior now, I'm not sure what to think. If I should be afraid—or worse.

Tate touches my arm, and I jump, shaking away thoughts of the house. Now is *not* the time to be afraid. "You okay?" he asks quietly, while Aunt J drops protection bags around the front yard. Overgrown and desolate, the lawn looks a lot like Mr Heckney's home; trash litters what used to be the gardens, and the grass—brown, not green—reaches my thighs. Since being emptied, it looks like no one has bothered to look after the place.

I listen to Aunt Josephine whisper the protection charm and

shake my head. "I'll be fine. I just want to get this over with."

"That's the spirit!" Mr Heckney says, shoving a list of runes into my hand. "Go start drawing these on the stairs."

Biting down on my lip, I walk slowly up to the stairs. My heart leaps into my throat as I do, an image of Morcant coming to mind. I can hear the dripping of blood like a whisper in my ears, a faint giggle that could be construed as manic. If I look to the door, I know I'll see him, see what may be my possible future should tonight go awry.

I shake the can of spray-paint and carefully outline the runes; three strong, red lines, with a triangle in between. Each rune is complicated in its own way, and in the back of my head, I hear Mr Heckney warning me about getting them wrong, that their meanings can change instantly should I make any mistakes.

Aunt J bumps into me before I can do any serious damage with the paint. When I look up at her, her eyes are directed to one of the boarded windows. I haven't told her about the phantom phone call from Mom; hell, I couldn't even speak about it at all, not after hearing *blood* spattering on the other end. Reliving that particular memory keeps me from saying a word.

"You okay?" I ask. I squint up into the tree line; darkness has already settled in, casting a blue-ish hue over the forest. If we want to avoid the next round of security and idiots who want to spend the night, we might only have an hour to finish our preparations before we can enter the Morcant House.

My aunt shakes her head and steps away from me, dropping another protection bag into the garden. "I just have a very bad feeling, is all."

I swallow but push aside any negative feelings I have. "I would be worried if you didn't."

She looks up at me with sad eyes. I can't bring myself to ask why because if I do...then I know I'll hear something I don't want to. Our relationship is already rocky; she's still completely against me going in at all, but I've made it clear that I have no other choice. And since we haven't seen the Reaper since it attacked Darren and me, I can only assume Morcant is waiting to finish us—*me*—himself.

"I have hope," I say, cutting through the stretch of silence that has passed between us. I grab her hand and squeeze. Aunt J glances at our clasped fingers, then up at me. "I hope nothing happens, other than us getting out of here alive."

Aunt J offers me a soft smile. "I hope so too."

Mr Heckney clears his throat loudly from the entryway. "Can somebody give me a hand with this door?"

I glance over to Aunt J, whose gaze turns frigid as she watches the older man try to pry open the door. Her fingers go cold in mine, and her posture stiffens. I pull my hand out of hers and hurry up to where Mr Heckney strains to keep the door open.

"I'll hold it," I grunt, leaning against the door jam, "you draw."

The older man nods his agreement and begins painting on the symbols; one for protection against the dead, one for protection against the Reaper, one to amplify the ones we've already painted. He takes his time drawing, and I strain as the door pushes against me, a force unlike anything I've ever felt before.

I lean against the frame and kick my legs up to push against the door. Whatever is trying to keep this closed is *strong*, and it seems like our protection bags and hexes and runes aren't doing much to keep it at bay.

When Mr Heckney sighs, I slowly remove one leg from the door. He holds it open, with Tate on the other side, and I quickly slip out of the door jam before the door can slam shut.

"Well," I mutter, brushing my hair back out of my face, "someone isn't happy about *that*."

Tate snorts and hitches his bag further up his shoulder. "Should hope not. Josiah Morcant is about to turn to ash." He winks at me before descending the stairs. I look back to the door, and the image of Morcant hazes across my mind.

I shake my head, forcing it away. We're going to win. We are going to beat the devil.

~ ~ ~

It takes the full hour to scour the side of the house and drop protection bags around the property. The sun is definitely gone now, sending the Morcant House into an endless darkness lit only by the high beams of our cars and the floodlights used by security to watch the house.

"Do you have extra batteries?" Aunt J asks, checking her pack. I nod and pull mine from my back; I have three torches, about twenty protection bags and at least twice the amount of trapping bags for any spirit that attacks. Batteries are stored in a separate pocket, with a couple of extra little things, like crystals and bones, items that help with purification—or curse breaking, if it comes to it. Two water bottles sit in the bottom of the bag, along with gasoline—labelled as such—and salt and about four boxes of matches.

I swallow down any second thoughts. "I should be set." My stomach churns as a feeling of terror settles into my chest. *Something isn't right.* We're by the back of the house, Aunt J, Tate, and I, with Mr Heckney heading home to grab some essentials he forgot.

But as I listen, a car pulls up, and from the corner of my eye, headlights flare and shut down. Other than that, I hear nothing.

Looking back to Aunt J and Tate, I shoulder my bag. *This isn't supposed to happen.* Security shouldn't be back yet. We should be alone with the dead right now.

I start for the front of the house. I speed around the side of the building, keeping my footsteps light as I pick my way through the hip-length grass.

"Aw, c'mon Blaire! Don't tell me you're scared!" Someone—Connor, his voice slurring—laughs. *No.* I round the side of the building and pause.

Connor, Blaire, Riley, and Weston all stand by the stairs that lead towards the double French doors of the house. They all wear stupid costumes, ones I'd helped choose.

Only Weston looks mildly unimpressed, and he looks around. I'm still hidden in the shadows; one step and I enter their field of vision, but I'm rooted to the spot.

My heart drops into my stomach as I watch them go up to the doors. Connor stops and stares at the runes, lips turned down in a frown. "Some satanic shit going on here, guys," he mutters.

I swallow as he tries the door, hoping that it won't give, but watch as it opens easily.

No.

Without thinking, I run around the side of the house, jumping up the stairs. "Don't go in there!"

My friends turn to me, confusion written across their faces. Weston lets loose a sigh of relief. Behind me, I hear Aunt Josephine shout a warning.

The door is closing, about to trap my friends inside. I don't even complete the thought as I jump in the way, forcing the door to stay open. I can feel the energy of Morcant pushing against me.

I grunt as my grip slips. "You guys need to get *out*. Now!"

"What the hell, Huntliegh?" Riley comes up to me, her breath stinking of alcohol. She stumbles, punching my shoulder. "You didn't tell us you were coming! Where's your costume?"

I look between her and the others, my eyes lingering on Weston. "I'm not joking, you need to go."

Something must shake loose in Weston, and suddenly, he's pushing the others towards me.

I feel the presence of someone else behind me, helping me

keep the door open. "Okay, kids," Tate grunts, "get out of here before I call your parents about the illegal consumption of alcohol, okay?"

My heart leaps into my throat as I watch a figure appear behind Connor; a woman wearing a black dress cocks her head, blood-shot eyes glaring intently at my friend. She moves her gaze from him to me and grins.

"Behind you!" Thankfully, Connor drops out of the way, and I throw a trapping bag at the matron. I watch as it lands at her feet, directly behind him, and traps her where she stands. I repeat the incantation that's always stuck in my head:

"Hear me spirits as I speak,

Be trapped in fire,

Within the veil,

And hold until you are no more."

The matron screams as fire consumes her. It won't hold for long, but it isn't supposed to, not until I can successfully burn her body. But I can't do *that* with them here.

"Get. Out." My friends eye me warily, suddenly more aware than ever. Weston meets my glare, something like guilt filling his hazel irises.

They glance between me and Tate, who has a shotgun strapped to his back now, and he looks about ready to cock it and shoot.

"Please," I whisper, grunting as the door scrapes against my back.

Blaire and Riley hold hands, then Blaire takes Connor's. They glance down at the spirit bag, then at where the spirit was standing.

Before they can escape, another spirit appears. My friends scream and each take a collective step back as I face Bonnie, whose pale face is streaked in blood.

"Get your father," I say, grunting as the door continues to slip from my grasp. *Where the hell is Aunt J?* "Tell him to hurry. We don't have much time."

The little girl nods and fazes out, leaving my friends gaping.

"You think she'll get him?" Tate groans, pushing back against the door. But as we get closer to midnight, Morcant will only grow stronger, which means we don't have much time left.

"I hope so," I finally reply, sucking in a breath. The door moves, pushing me further into the house, cutting me off from Tate and Aunt Josephine. I turn back to my friends, hoping, *pleading* that they'll listen and *run*. "You guys need to get out before you get trapped. Just *trust me*, okay?"

The girls nod mutely; I swallow my fear as Riley gingerly steps over me, her eyes meeting mine. Tate grabs her and pulls her the rest of the way out.

In doing so, he loses his grip of the door. I scream as it shuts, locking Weston, Connor, Blaire, and me inside.

"Tate!" I yell, pushing against the old, heavy wood. I hear him swear at the other end, hear the doorhandle snap in his hand. "Get us out!" I bang my fists against the wood, which doesn't move.

This wasn't supposed to happen. This was never supposed to happen.

I take a step back and examine the chipped paint from earlier.

We're trapped.

25

TRAPPED WITH THE DEAD

THIS IS NOT THE TIME TO PANIC, I think, running my hand over my face. The silence rings loudly in my ears, time seeming to slow as I run over what has happened.

I'm trapped in the Morcant house.

Tate and Aunt J are outside.

I have three civilians trapped with me, only one who knows about this world.

And Morcant is supposed to get strong enough to leave the confines of his house *tonight*.

I close my eyes for a moment and suck in a breath. I can't leave my friends, but I can't realistically take them with me on my search for the bodies. They're liabilities, but if I even attempt to leave them alone, I know Morcant and his army of spirits will whisk them away where they'll join the dead for eternity if I don't complete the job.

No pressure.

Dropping my pack to the floor, I grab several protection bags and the remaining flashlights, shoving one into my back pocket, handing the others over. "Hands out," I snap, not waiting for a reply as I shove protection bags into hesitant palms. "Store these around your body; pockets, around a chain, wherever. They'll help stop a spirit from trying to take control of your body and protect you from immediate harm." They don't respond, but from the corner of my eye, I watch them do as they're told.

"Huntliegh!" Aunt Josephine shouts, banging her fists against the door. "Stay right here, okay? We'll get you kids out!"

I sigh, feeling my own fear shudder within me. "We won't be able to, but I'll try."

I listen as she slams her hands against the door in defeat. "You weren't supposed to go in there alone, honey."

Closing my eyes, I swallow down bile that catches in my throat. I shove my hands into my pockets, fingering the protection bags that didn't do me any good. "I know," I say quietly, sucking in a breath.

"Hunt," Weston whispers, hands on my shoulders. He forces my face close to his, and I open my eyes. "You need to tell them."

I release a shuddering breath and take a step back. I have to be calm and careful, especially now that these *civilians* are here. Morcant will use them, kill them, and it's my duty to make sure that doesn't happen.

"Everything you know about this house, about it being haunted by Josiah Morcant, about people going missing in here…it's all true," I start, meeting their stares. Blaire shudders and wraps her arms around herself. Connor looks like he's going to be sick. Weston urges me on. "We, like hundreds before us, are trapped, and Josiah Morcant is now hunting us."

Connor meets my stare. "Why?"

"Because he's spent so long on this plane of existence. His

spirit is no longer human but rather, something demonic. He needs more death in order to survive. If we're caught, he'll trap us here with him for the rest of eternity."

"How do you know all this?" Blaire snaps. A tear slips down her face, eyes shadowed with fear.

Dread and anger shudders through me, but I don't let it burrow into me. Panic is slowly wedging itself into my mind, into my thoughts. I close my eyes and force the feelings into a box in the back of my mind, where they can do no damage to me or to anyone else. Finally, I reopen my eyes and take everyone in. "I've known about this my entire life; that's what Aunt J and I do—we hunt down spirits causing problems and put an end to them."

"Is that why you're here?" Connor asks.

I nod, and the negative emotions subside. "Yes. We came here to get rid of Morcant before he could do anything else."

Blaire snorts and shakes her head, nurse's cap falling from her head. She crosses her arms over her chest and looks away, eyes narrowed as she glances around the grand entryway where we stand; a double marble staircase leads up to the second storey, and off to our right is a desolate sitting room. Two old couches are the only furniture that decorates the entrance, moth-eaten and forgotten like much of the grandeur of the house. A half-opened door across from me leads to the kitchens and staff quarters, while to our left would be the grand dining room. I've already memorised the layout, but it's different, actually being in here.

"Huntliegh?" Mr Heckney calls from the door, drawing our attention. "Can you hear me?"

"Yes!" I shout, picking up my pack. I sling it over my shoulders and beckon the others over, to make sure I can see them. "What happened, Mr Heckney? The runes are almost gone."

"Mr Heckney?" Connor whispers, face set in disgust. "The old coot?" I send him a pointed look before turning back to the door.

Mr Heckney clears his throat. "Seems like the ones we put up earlier weren't strong enough." I groan and roll my eyes. *Of course they weren't.* "But I might have a solution! Do you remember when I mentioned that book? The one Morcant used to write the names of those who joined his church?"

A shiver descends down my spine. Images from my vision, about Morcant and Delilah, and the old book in the bedroom cross my mind.

I'd seen it again in my vision from the football game. Delilah watching her father as he read through it, the anger and fear from her.

I nod slowly, and reply, "Yeah. All the people he sacrificed were written in the book."

Aunt Josephine replies, "We think *that* might be tethering the spirits and Morcant here."

I shake my head, and yet I can't ignore how it's beginning to make sense. "But how?"

They hesitate for a moment, until Aunt J finally sighs. "I found ash at the back of the house, scattered. There are no bodies here. Do you smell anything?"

I suck in a breath; if there *are* hundreds of bodies stashed in the house, then naturally, we'd smell it. But the sickly-sweet stench of festering flesh is nowhere. The air is musty, old, damp. But death doesn't linger. "They could be sealed behind a doorway," I reply, but I can't ignore the doubt wedging itself in my head. Could a book really be tethering all these spirits here?

Bonnie reappears beside me; Blaire gasps and takes a step back, eyes wide. I look down at the red-haired child and kneel so we're the same height. "Is that true?" I ask, voice soft. Her blood-soaked face turns from me to the people behind me. "Hey, Bonnie. Is your body gone?"

She quietly dips her chin before disappearing once again. I sigh and rub my face. Is that a yes? Could it be possible? *Is* Morcant disposing of all the bodies as he goes and trapping the spirits here another way?

Swallowing, I stand, heart heavy. "Any idea of where we might find the book?" I ask loudly. A part of me knows it's a bad idea to be discussing it; Morcant could move it or hide it while we're talking right now.

"I would assume the catacombs," Mr Heckney replies, voice low, "the ones below the old church."

Sighing, I eye the stairwell and the door; somewhere beyond, there should be passageways that lead beneath the house, old servant halls and crawl spaces that were overlooked during the initial raid on the house almost two hundred years ago.

"Your Aunt and Tate are going to the church itself to dig around and see if they can get below. I will stay here with my Bonnie and help as much as we can," he finishes.

I take a step away from the door and begin pacing. I can't take my friends down into the catacombs, but I can't leave them up here unprotected, either not even with Mr Heckney waiting by the door. They aren't safe either way, but if Aunt J and Mr Heckney are right about the book, then we need to find it before midnight.

Connor grabs my arm and stops me, angry fear written across his features. His fingers tighten around my bicep, and I wince. "What the hell is going on?"

"I already told you," I growl, prying his fingers from my arm. "We have a ghost—a *demonic spirit*—hunting us, while *I* hunt him. My job is to find whatever is keeping him here and burn it."

He clenches his jaw, neck going red beneath the paint. "And what are we supposed to do?"

Shaking my head, I look up at the second storey, noticing the wandering spirits that are already out to play, and curse. "You three aren't safe here. You don't know the first thing about the paranormal."

Connor cocks his head, ready to bite into me, but Weston grabs him and pulls him away, while also taking Blaire's hand in his. Protective, wary, cautious. I swallow thickly and look away.

"It's not her fault we're here, man," Weston says quietly, his eyes moving from his friend's to mine. "Teach us. Show us what we need to do."

I purse my lips and look back to the stairs, then up to the landing, meeting the savage glare of the man who has us trapped here. My heart stops in my chest as a calming energy washes over me. *Not calming, sedative.* Morcant wants us to let our guards down so he can take us, take our souls.

No.

Reaching for a trapping bag, I throw it to the stairs just as his spirit vanishes. A quiet, chilling chuckle fills the air. *He's playing with us.*

But he isn't going to win.

"Just...follow me. Stay together. And *don't* get in my way, understood?" My friends nod mutely. "Hold on to each other."

"What about you?" Blaire whispers, tucking her hand into Connor's.

I cast a quick glance around and head for the stairs, intent on going up. If we check here first, then we can rule out the house. If we go underground too early, then Morcant could trap us. Eventually, we'll lose air, die of either asphyxiation or hunger or dehydration, or by the hand of one of the many spirits residing within these walls.

"I've faced off serial killers and murderous housewives," I reply, releasing a breath. A shiver runs down my spine as I take the first step. "I think I'll be fine for the most part."

The soles of my boots are too loud in the eerie silence as I climb the stairs. Weston hooks his finger into the belt-loop of my jeans, despite me saying I'm fine. And despite myself, I appreciate it.

When we reach the landing, I pick up the trapping bag and shove it into my pocket. I bite down on my bottom lip, drawing blood. Up here, children run in playful circles, unaware of the living people who invade their home; the orphan boys who went missing years ago chase one another in a ghostly game of tag, their bodies fazing in and out of sight. They're probably running and hiding from the matron, who remains trapped below, but not for long. The bags only work for so long.

Along this corridor is supposed to be bedrooms; at one end is the master bedroom, where Morcant slept, and at the other, his daughter, Delilah's. Somewhere down an adjacent hall there's supposed to be a library and office, hidden behind a panel in the wall.

I watch as three young women, wearing nightgowns drenched in blood, float down the hallway; their hair—red, blonde, ebony— float around their heads, like they're lying in a pool water, stuck in a stasis of being forgotten. They're just as unaware as the boys, it seems, as they pass us without any recognition.

"What the hell is happening?" Weston murmurs, lips close to my ear.

I shudder and quicken my pace, leading my friends towards the master bedroom. "They're trapped in a stasis, like a reoccurring dream. Some spirits—like the matron downstairs—are powerful enough to break hold of it, while others, like Bonnie, Mr Heckney's daughter, are just free to do as they please. Others are trapped in the moments before their deaths, while others have no recollection of even dying."

Slowing, I take in the hall; wallpaper peels in the corners from water damage, leaking down the old panelling like blood. The damp, musty smell of old buildings becomes stronger the longer we walk.

"How come we can see them?" Connor asks from behind.

"Most likely because of the spiritual energy radiating from the place. Spirits thrive off death because it's like a power source for them," I reply, sidestepping a rather ominous puddle. "Normally, you wouldn't see them because they exist on another plane. Tonight, though, they're even more powerful. Partly because of Morcant, partly because it's Halloween."

Weston tugs on the back of my jeans, forcing me to pause as Bonnie's friend appears in front of us. Blaire says something, but I focus on the boy, who fazes in and out of sight.

"This little guy is going to help us," I murmur, offering him a smile.

The boy, though, isn't looking at me; his eyes are on Weston, who has gone rigid behind me. The only reason I know he's still there is the taut way he pulls on my jeans.

But an image flashes to mind; *a simple wall with peeling paint, with the word 'West' written in blood.*

I suck in a breath. "Weston, who is this boy?" When I turn around, there are tears trickling from his eyes. "West?"

He lets go of my jeans and wipes at his eyes. "My twin brother," he whispers. "Ethan."

I look down to the spirit, and my heart cracks.

I'm not the only one who lost something to this house.

I grab West's hand and squeeze it.

"Ethan?" The spirit meets my stare, bloodied face devoid of emotion. "Do you know where Morcant hides his book?" The young boy looks between me and Weston again before disappearing completely. I sigh, rubbing at my eyes. "We have to keep moving."

Behind me, West wraps his finger into the belt-loop of my jeans again, tugging once to signify that we're ready to move again.

Further down, the hall splits in two; at one end should be the master bedroom, though in the beam of light from my torch, I see only a gaping hole in the floorboards.

We probably should have brought rope. A trickle of fear begins to wedge its way inside my thoughts once more.

I stay vigilant as I search for the hidden panel that leads into the office and library. I remember it vaguely from Mr. Heckney's blueprints of the house. Josiah Morcant notoriously had secret rooms and hidden doorways throughout the house. At the time, the people of Fort Caldwell saw it as eccentricity; now, it's just terrifying.

I lead the group into the corridor. We pass the spirits of the young girls again, though this time they're joined by two more young women. All in nightgowns. All bloody. They disappear behind a wall, and I start towards it with narrowed eyes.

"We need to be extremely careful when entering a room," I say, running my hands over the walls. I bite my lip and pull on a wall sconce, but nothing happens. "If we get trapped inside then that's it. We're going to have to work together to make sure the door doesn't close on us."

"Can't we just wait for your Aunt to come get us?" Blaire asks, shoved between West and Connor. When I look back, tears are streaming down her face. "Didn't Heckney say she was going to find another way in?"

I sigh and walk up to a built-in shelf, pulling at random books. "We could, but then we'd turn into sitting ducks. The more we move, the harder it will be for Morcant to get into our heads."

"What do you mean?" Connor asks, bring up the rear of the group.

"I mean—" I trail off and smile as an urn gives way beneath my hand to reveal a hidden room. "Morcant is powerful enough to leave images inside your head. When I was in Seattle, he managed to attack me, and he did so again when I arrived in town."

The door swings open, and I motion for West to hold onto it as I step into the library. Dust rises as I step onto red carpet; every wall is covered in books, with a desk situated directly in the centre of the room. There are a couple of plush, red chairs scattered around the library, and I rush to grab one, shoving it in the way of the door.

"Someone needs to stay at the door and make sure the chair doesn't move." My heart hammers in my chest. Is there a chance that I'm wrong about this, wrong about giving any of them this task? I have to risk it, don't I? There's an angry, demonic spirit after us. I doubt we have much of a choice, but I'm still hesitant to step away.

Connor raises his hand and takes to standing against the doorframe so that he has a clear view of both the library and the hallway beyond. His jaw ticks as he does, though. Riley and I might make fun of his classic Ken-doll looks, and sometimes he isn't as perceptive as others, but he's protective of his friends.

Friends that, I don't think, include me anymore.

Blaire makes no move to remove her hand from his, and clings to his side. "I think I'll stay with Connor, if that's okay."

I nod. "Keep an eye—and ear out—both of you. We'll search the library." The pair doesn't bother looking at me; at this point, I would much rather them hate me, so long as they get out of here alive.

That's my job now, along with trying to get that damned book.

Grabbing West's hand, I drag him further into the library. When I look up at him, he doesn't meet my stare. The Hunter side of me tells me to ignore it, but the part of me that wishes for something normal pushes me to speak up.

"I get that this is a lot to take in," I murmur, squeezing his hand, "and I get that after tonight you probably won't ever want to talk or see me again, but..." I pause and swallow thickly. "Just know that you were never supposed to get involved in any of this."

Finally, West meets my eyes, his own wet with the tears he shed for his brother. "You weren't planning on coming back from this, were you?"

My stomach lurches. "No. I wanted my life with you to be

normal, to not have this hanging over me. I told you because I wanted you to understand, so that I didn't feel so alone." I wave my hands around, indicating to the room, to the house and what it all means. "And now I know how selfish that was. Maybe if I'd stayed quiet, you wouldn't have come."

"What did this guy take from you?" he asks, voice soft. "I see it now, you know. The loss. What did he take?"

I bite down on my lip; I haven't seen them, my parents. Maybe they're trapped elsewhere, or maybe Morcant is holding on to them.

"Hunt?"

"Four years ago, my parents rolled into town thinking they would be the ones to finish the job here." I shake my head, feeling tears spring to the surface. I wipe angrily at my eyes. "They thought they could do what no other Hunter could; take down Morcant, and free the spirits. But they came into the house and never left. They're still regarded as a missing person's case. Mr Heckney was the one to call it in, too."

Weston's hand tightens around mine. "Well, we better help Ethan and your parents then, yeah?" I nod and try to swallow the lump in my throat, but relief washes over me.

Releasing his hand, I walk over to the desk, pulling open one draw after another. *Empty.* The top of the desk is littered with loose papers, none of them with names or any indication of where the book might be held. I even try to see if the draws have fake bottoms, but nothing pops out.

If he's been writing names in the book for the last one-hundred and sixty-nine years, he's going to have it close to his main haunting ground.

As far as I know, he can't leave the house's boundaries, so that means it's most likely somewhere here. But the house is *huge*, meaning we'll have to keep moving, keep searching, before he traps us like the others.

"Uh…Huntliegh?" Connor points to the hallway. I run to the door as dozens of spirits fill the hallway. They turn towards where we stand in the library doorframe.

They remain unmoving, fazing in and out of existence as we watch.

"What's going on?" Weston asks from behind me, once again hooking his finger into my belt loop.

Swallowing, I watch as more and more spirits appear. "I'm not sure," I murmur, shaking my head. "But I don't think it's good."

26

WHAT LIES BENEATH

THE LAST TIME I SAW MY PARENTS, they were alive, kissing me on the forehead as they left our small three-bedroom house in Salem, Massachusetts. They said they'd be back in a week. It was only supposed to be a scouting mission, and they were supposed to return so we could all go back together.

A week turned into two, and then they were gone.

I never pictured seeing my parents again like this, though; their faces smudged with blood, clothes torn and mangled, their fingers black, like they'd been digging in the earth. My mom's red hair stands on end, one side of it matted and a much, *much* darker shade than the other. Her paper-thin white skin seems to almost glow. My dad... He doesn't look any better, his dark hair a matted mass atop his head. The cross he usually wore around his neck is gone, and so are his glasses, probably lost to the dark crevices of the house.

Swallowing, I take a step back, colliding with West's back. *Real. West is real.* My parents are dead, merely trapped spirits with no new or current thought processes. They are souls, needing to be freed.

Bile rises in my throat. *Separate yourself.* One thing I've always strived to do is separate myself emotionally from the job. And for the most part, I do a good job. I can see beyond the people they used to be and do the job.

But I curse Morcant for sending my parents to me now.

Anger boils deep in my blood.

I'd kill him if he weren't already dead.

Their eyes are on us—on me—but they are blank stares, unfocused, like they aren't comprehending what's going on around them. They're probably completely unaware of who they are and what they're doing in the house, stuck in a kind of time loop. They definitely don't recognise me, not in the way Ethan recognised West.

"Should we be running?" West asks, tugging on my jeans.

"I, uh," I trail off. Should we run? I'm not even sure what's happening. These look like spirits stuck in limbo, unaware of their surroundings, caught in an endless cycle, not like Ethan or Bonnie or the matron. They don't look dangerous.

"I don't think they want to hurt us," I reply, though uncertainty makes my blood run cold.

As the words leave my lips, the spirits appear closer, fazing in and out of existence. Behind me, West tenses, fingers tightening in the loop of my jeans.

"They're surrounding us," he whispers, keeping his voice low. I turn in a slow semi-circle to see that more spirits have appeared in the library behind us. "What do we do?"

I don't know. "Just...wait. This might just be a ploy to scare us," I murmur, reaching for a trapping bag. If any of them attack, then I'll fight. But for now, they look like chess pieces, being moved around by an unseeable hand.

Leaving the bag in hand, I wait, the incantation on the tip of my tongue. If they're encircling us for Morcant, then we need to start moving again.

Towards the back of the pack, Bonnie reappears, pointing towards the hall we came down earlier. Her lips move in a silent '*Go!*', signalling for us to leave.

Don't need to be told twice.

Around us, the spirits move again.

Pushing around Connor, I indicate for the three of them to join hands; West behind me, with Blaire in between him and Connor. "If we stay here any longer," I say, taking a step out, "then we'll be easy pickings for Morcant. We have to start moving again."

The three of them nod; I doubt they want to fight with me after all this. Though they probably won't ever want to *speak* to me after all of this is over. But I don't care, so long as they all get out of here alive. I'll accept their hatred if that means they live.

I take a timid step into the hall and wait for the spirits to move or attack. I even wait to see if Morcant appears to stop us, but nothing happens. Flashlight in hand, I motion for the others to follow, feeling West tug on my belt loop as we move, just a simple indication to let me know that he's there, that they're all there.

My parents don't move as I walk up to them, their eyes glassy and unseeing. I reach out, hand hovering over my mom's cheek, before pulling away completely.

I will fix this, I promise, biting down on my bottom lip. *I will.*

~ ~ ~

The hallways converge back into the one main hall by the stairs. Groaning, I look back the way we came, to the spirits that still wait patiently.

There are no more signs of Ethan or Bonnie.

"*You will be mine,*" a voice whispers, so close to my ear that I jump. "*You and your friends will join me.*"

A tremor dances down my spine. Swallowing thickly, I start walking again, heading in the direction of what used to be Delilah's wing; the ancient records Mr Heckney dug up—and in some of the old books I read—gave some detail as to what Delilah's role had been in her father's master plan. Some claimed she was to be the devil's new bride, in a Persephone and Hades kind of deal, while others believed she merely saw something she wasn't supposed to, leading to her untimely death.

"Do you have any idea where we're going?" Connor asks from the back. The poor guy keeps swinging his torch in every possible way, like that'll stop Morcant or any other spirit from taking him.

I eye the walls and doors; other than this once being Delilah's wing, it also housed mental patients back when the house was converted into an asylum.

Those same patients who died in the house still wander this hall.

Behind me, Blaire makes a sound. "Won't they attack us?" she whispers, her fear a bitter taste on the back of my tongue.

Shaking my head, I step around the patients. "Despite popular belief, mental patients aren't as dangerous as they're believed to be. Most, if not all the time, they're so misunderstood in life that they remain calm after death," I say, looking over my shoulder. One woman smiles broadly as we pass and waves as if to welcome us, whereas a younger man rocks an invisible child in his arms and asks if we want to hold his little sister.

These people are completely aware that we're here and are unbothered by it completely.

"What's up with that?" Blaire asks, voice soft.

I sigh. "They're the forgotten ones; luckily for us, they don't care. Most are harmless, too, so don't worry about it."

"Huh," says West. "Most horror movies…"

"Get it wrong," I interject. I wave a hand at the patients, who in return all make an attempt to wave back. "The living totally misunderstand them. If they ever attack, it's usually because they're protecting someone or something. My aunt, for instance, was chased into an old asylum when she was fifteen. She was running away from some creep. The spirits recognised her energy as good and helped her by leading the guy away." I shake my head as we turn into the next maze of halls. "Hollywood gets it wrong."

~ ~ ~

The spirits appear without so much as a whisper, their corporeal bodies fazing in and out of sight. It's a mixture of good and bad; some are spirits we've already run into, like the mindless ones outside the library, while others are new, their energies reddened with anger.

When the first one lunges, I let loose the incantation I know by heart, the spirit bag a blur as it hits the ground and erupts into flames. The spirit, now encased, lets out a roar so violent the floor shakes.

The other spirits take it as their chance to attack. I'm not sure what to expect, but they don't fight us physically.

Emotions crash into me: anger that tastes like charcoal and sour lemon, sadness that makes my bones ache, and fear so potent it brings me to my knees.

I collapse and lose the pressure of West at my back. The lights of our torches flick off; somewhere behind me, Blaire screams, loud enough to make my blood curdle. I want to stand—*I have to*—but the pressure at my chest, the wave of emotions, keep me down.

I can't scream.

A child no bigger than Bonnie breaks through the darkness, though the hallway around me is different. The wallpaper isn't bleeding or peeling in the corners. Worn carpet covers the ground.

The boys' home.

He looks at me with nothing but hatred in his eyes. His little hands are clenched into firsts so tight the knuckles are white.

Help, *I try to say, but my voice is locked away. I reach for the boy, but he steps back. His eyes go from me to the figure behind me.*

Through the pain, I turn, but the agony that's thrust at me pushes me back down into the ground. I see only feet; milky white skin, bruised and cut. The hem of a nightgown caresses the ankles. I force my gaze up to see blood spatter on the white, fresh and bright against the white fabric. A hand reaches for me, but I don't take it.

Behind me, the anger of the boy spreads into fear.

Morcant's daughter, Delilah, watches me with the steel gaze of a hawk, her plump lips parted, hair in loose curls down to her waist. Gorgeous and deadly is the only way to describe her as curiosity brightens her eyes.

Until he enters the vision.

The tick of his pocket-watch is the only sound in the vision. His footsteps make no sound, though the occasional tap of his cane makes tremors run down the length of my spine.

My muscles tense as he approaches, his coal-black eyes on me. He looks exactly like every damn depiction of him; the prim and proper man in front of me looks like he stepped straight out of a Victorian period piece, with a top hat and waistcoat. The only part of him I don't quite see clearly is his features, but that's fine by me.

I push through the pain and fear that holds me down and struggle to my knees. I move on instinct to protect the little boy behind me, though when I sneak a quick glance over my shoulder, he's gone.

Morcant stops, only one step behind his daughter. "How peculiar..." His voice is like rich honey, deep and smooth. Not what I was expecting at all.

Before he can do anything else, the vision blurs and turns to shadows. I'm swept back to the present; the floor beneath me is cold marble that's coated in a layer of dust.

Once the vision clears, I suck in a breath and search for Morcant or the other spirits, but they're already gone, having been swept away themselves, nothing more than attack dogs to keep us away.

But panic still races through me, sending shivers down my spine. "You okay?" West asks, voice low in my ear. I feel the tremor in his hands as he grips my wrists, forcing me to look at him.

But images from the spirits cling to the corners of my vision, the feeling of their pain and fear drowning me. Closing my eyes, I suck in a breath. I tamp down on their emotions and focus on my own, on remaining in control.

"Where's Blaire?" Connor asks, dragging me from my thoughts.

"She should be right here," I reply, reopening my eyes. But when I search the hallway, Blaire isn't there.

West and Connor both look around, their eyes going to their hands. She'd been *between* them.

"Guys. Where is she?" My chest tightens, my heart slowing in my chest. Oh God. Oh God. *Oh God*. We—I—lost her. How could I lose her?

I suck in a breath and cover my mouth. There are no doors in this part of the hall, no way that she could have been dragged into an adjacent room. And the floor is thick, impenetrable marble; there are no trap doors. She could have been taken up, but... I close my eyes and release a shuddering breath as the weight of what had just happened falls on me.

I lost someone.

I lost my friend.

And she could be anywhere in the house, dead or alive.

"What do we do?" Connor asks, running a hand roughly through his hair. "What the hell do we do?"

Looking up, I eye the ceiling, then the walls again. Morcant had built this house for this *precise* reason; so he could lure people in and sacrifice them like he did with the members of his church. He would have had trap doors and hidden panels around the entire house, lying in wait for someone to slip up.

But if he were to sacrifice her…then he'd take her below ground. "Get something heavy and start breaking down the walls," I state, heading towards an old table. I grab the first thing there—a bronze candelabra—and begin smashing the bottom of it into the walls.

It's cathartic in a way.

Weston uses the butt of his torch, swing it into the wall across from me. Connor, though, chooses to break the table, and begins using the leg as a bat.

We spend fifteen minutes smashing the walls open, looking for a clear path *down*. I have no luck, mostly hitting old plaster and likely breathing in asbestos. But I only get to foundation, no hidden passages.

Adrenaline burns away the panic and fear. My thoughts are only about Blaire. *We'll find her*, I want to say out loud, but not even I can make those kinds of promises.

I try not to think about how she could already be dead.

"I found something!" West shouts. He starts kicking at the wall, and soon enough, both Connor and I join in, channelling our frustrations into breaking down the wall to the passage beyond.

Coughing into the crook of my elbow, I step back and stare

into the shadowy abyss. A spiral staircase leads down into thick darkness. West flicks the flashlight on and shines it down into the hole.

I sigh as my heart hammers harder and louder in my chest. "Looks like we're falling down the rabbit hole, fellas." My heart rises in my throat as I step onto the old cement stairs. I wait for the tell-tale rumble of a bad structure, but it doesn't come.

"Wait," West says, pulling me back before I can take another step. "Maybe one of us should go first?"

I raise my brow and shake my head, scoffing. "If this were football, then I wouldn't mind. But spirits and the dead are *my* thing." I take a tentative step forwards and test the old cement to make sure it won't collapse halfway down. It doesn't move. "If anyone is going to go first, it'll be me. You two just need to keep your eyes out for manholes."

Connor makes a noise in the back of his throat before saying, "Manholes?"

"Yes, manholes. Small tunnels and holes in the walls and foundation. Places a spirit can hide and drag you away." When I glance back, Connor looks about ready to vomit or run—or both. "Look. As long as you keep you keep an eye out, then there shouldn't be any more disappearances." My friends nod, and I finally step into the hidden passage.

Unlike other passages I've been in before, this entire tunnel is made of cement, leading straight into the catacombs below. If I look closely enough at the walls, I can see black and brown stains leading all the way down.

Blood, from people trying to get away. There's no new blood, but that doesn't mean anything good. Blaire is either unconscious, or already dead. I hope more than anything that it isn't the latter.

I keep my flashlight directed to the stairwell, while West and Connor have theirs facing in every other possible direction. The space is too enclosed, but I'm thankful that we'd destroyed the entrance; it means that there's a chance we can get out again once we have Blaire without fear of being locked down here.

The lower we go, the darker and damper it becomes; moisture covers the walls further down, and the stairs become increasingly slick with the wetness that now coats the air. Moss grows over the walls, covering any other remnants of fighters trying to save themselves from being sacrificed.

"Watch out," I murmur, pointing my light to the stairs. The boys stop, giving me grunts of affirmation. Good enough. I continue at a slower pace, the stairs like ice beneath my boots. One wrong step, and I'll lose control.

I hit the landing and pause, sucking in a breath; three hallways branch off the main landing, all dark with no possibility of light, each paved in what looks like marble beneath an inch of water. No wonder Morcant is getting more desperate; this place will go under soon. The foundation is bound to give way once the water rises high enough.

Suddenly, I'm thankful for wearing boots and not Converses like the boys, who seem to hesitate before joining me in the water.

"Keep your eyes open," I murmur, handing them both trapping bags. Both look at me, then the bags, confused. "You throw, I repeat the incantation. Hopefully, it'll hold, even with the water."

Weston nods and grips the bag tight, whereas Connor pockets his, eyes bright with curiosity. "Let's just find Blaire," he says, though something in his voice has changed, hardened.

Pursing my lips, I face the three tunnels. One seems to go under the front of the house, whereas the furthest likely leads towards the hidden chamber below the church. If she's anywhere, she'll be there.

I point to the furthest one. "Let's go that way. It most likely leads towards the forest."

Connor, though, begins heading towards a different tunnel.

"I'll go this way, cover more ground."

"No." I grab his arm and pull him towards me. "If we split up—"

"We'll what?" he snaps, wrenching his arm from my grip. "Someone might get taken by the big bad spirit? Newsflash, Huntliegh, that's already happened. The love of my life is somewhere down here, and so far, you haven't been much help."

I swallow a retort and clench my jaw. "Just remember: you're the one who chose to come into the house. I told you not to, I told you to get out. You all put your lives at risk when you walked through those doors."

"What about you? Shouldn't you have followed your own advice?"

Shaking my head, I point towards the farthest tunnel. "I resigned myself to my fate weeks ago, Connor. I already knew I was either going to die down here and fail or live long enough to move on to the next job. That's what I do, what my aunt and uncles do. That's my job. But you walked in here with a cocky attitude thinking you were going to be safe, and now that your life is on the line along with mine and Blaire's and West's, you want to risk it all because you think you know better?" I push him towards the other tunnel. "Fine. Do it your way. Just don't come haunting me when you've been caught. Either of you."

Flicking on my torch, I head down the tunnel that heads towards the forest. Behind me, water splashes, and I feel a tug at my jeans. I spin around to face West. "What?"

"You can't—"

"I can't what?" I ask, throwing my hands up. "I can't say that? Should I make him feel better? Newsflash, guys, this is the world I live in. This isn't an episode of *Scooby Doo*, where we take off the bad guy's mask and reveal ropes and jump scares. Aunt Josephine has visions about spirits and the living. I'm an empath and can receive their emotions and sometimes their thoughts before they died. I can sometimes even feel the emotions of regular people. My mom was the *best* Hunter, and my dad was the brains of their operation. Tate and Darren? Just as good and have been hunting for just as long." I roll my eyes and turn away, going back into the tunnel. "I will find Blaire, with or without you guys."

I can *feel* the tension in the air, feel it flare while I walk, but quick splashes tell me they're behind me.

I'm on the ground, forced into the water by phantom hands before I can even blink. The stale water coats my face and tongue, drowning me. Bitter fury burns down my throat as I struggle to remain calm, but the spirit is forcing more than water down my throat.

"Huntliegh!" Weston shouts, and in the distance Connor shouts something in reply, but I can't breathe.

Something holds me down in the water, and whispers in my ear, "*You won't see your friend alive, little girl. None of you will be seen alive.*" The pressure intensifies on my back and neck, until darkness blurs the edges of my consciousness.

Just as quickly, the pressure is gone; I roll over and suck in a breath, hands grabbing at my arms, pulling me out.

"Are you okay?" West asks, pulling me close to his body. I close my eyes and force myself to regulate my breathing and slow down my heart rate. "Hunt?"

Clearing my throat, I nod. At my other side, Connor has his hand tucked securely into mine, almost like the fight earlier never happened. "Fine. But we need to hurry," I reply, throat burning.

When I open my eyes again, Connor and West are sharing a look.

A scream pierces through the silence of the catacomb, unsettling and sudden. We run into the corridor without hesitation, water sloshing up our legs.

The water thins out the further we go; the tunnel shifts in size, growing smaller in some sections then larger in others like a funhouse at a carnival. Dread makes my heart race.

Down here, spirits seem to be clearer, more attuned to their surroundings. We run through them without a second thought, but I can *feel* them go through me, feel their emotions from when they died; panic, anger, fear, serenity. The emotions come and go like a wave, washing away after a moment to give me a second of peace.

We're forced to stop at a crossroad. "Seriously?" I gasp, hands on my knees.

West pats my back, but he seems to be breathing just as heavily. Down here, the air is thicker and damp, heavy.

Swallowing, I straighten and eye the three possible paths; go straight ahead, go left, or go right. A counter measure, or some way to get victims confused, probably both.

I guess Morcant thought of everything while building this hell.

"Any bright ideas?" Connor asks, taking a step into the centre. He looks up, squinting at the ceiling. Stepping up beside him, I do the same. It almost looks like a latch, and some old, decaying rope.

I smile. "We're still on the grounds. If we can get up there..."

"Then we can find out where we are," West finishes.

"How good are you guys at acrobatics?" I ask, eyeing them. Weston has broader shoulders and a thicker chest, whereas Connor looks lighter and faster. Strength and agility.

West shrugs and eyes the height. "I could get you up there on my shoulders," he says, eyes moving to me. "Reckon you could handle it?"

Since there are no more screams or spirits to guide the way, I suppose we don't have much of a choice.

Weston squats and lowers his head motioning for me to step up onto his back. I look behind me at Connor, who spots for us. The blonde jock nods, and I do as I've been instructed; I carefully step up onto West's shoulders, feeling Connor's hands on my ankles as the boy beneath me shakes under my weight. He stands, though, to his full height, giving me enough leverage to push at the trap door above.

It doesn't give.

Clenching my jaw, I pull at the latch and jiggle the bolts that hold it in place, feeling something *else* push against me.

"Morcant or something else won't let this one go," I say through gritted teeth, looking down.

I meet Connor's stare, but he shrugs. "Keep trying. It probably hasn't been opened in a hundred years."

Sighing, I bend my knees slightly and tug.

Dirt falls through, followed by what looks like a set of bones. Beneath me, West steps back, leaving me unbalanced and holding onto the opening for dear life.

"West!" I shout, grunting against the sudden strain in my arms. Above me, Bonnie appears, Ethan with her. They stand, hand in hand, against the moonlight.

Not moonlight. The reflection of it. We're in the greenhouse.

Bonnie points in the direction of the old church, and I nod. "Do you know if Tate and Aunt Josephine made it there?" I ask. She nods once before taking Ethan and disappearing.

West's hands clamp around my ankles and so do Connor's. "Do you know where to go?" West asks.

"Yeah!" I reply, letting go of the hatch. I slowly bend down and reach for Connor, who grabs me under my arms and lifts me off West's back. "We go right."

The boys nod, and we take off in a jog towards the old church, leaving the set of bones behind.

27

DEAD PARENTS

A SET OF STAIRS AND CARVED, STONE DOORS give away the identity of the church's old basement; the stone doors show scenes of the devil, parading as the serpent and pressuring Eve into taking the apple. Then it shows scenes depicting a hellish landscape, all muted red and black, with creatures who resemble demons from renaissance paintings. And there are figures that have the pink flesh of humans with chains around their necks.

I shudder and creep up the stairs, pushing on the door. Surprisingly, it gives way, but I pause, holding my hand up to stop the boys from following.

"Keep an eye out," I whisper, squeezing West's hand, "while I go in. If we all enter, there's a chance we won't all make it out."

West shakes his head, ready to argue, but I kiss him lightly on the cheek. "Please, stay out here." His eyes plead with me, and my own urge to stay back rises in my throat, to let this job go, but I *know* Blaire is in there, and I can just feel Aunt Josephine and Tate trying to get to us from up above.

I let go of his hand and nod to Connor, who lowers his eyes. I suck in a breath and force my heart rate to slow, until I'm calm, until I know I can't be affected by whatever is in the room with Blaire. A strategy I learned from my mom, years ago.

The door creaks, a sound that echoes in the catacombs. I steady my hands as I enter.

The world seems to slow as a vision takes hold before my eyes.

My parents, walking through the same door, their hands clasped around Dad's cross. They have spirit bags and flashlights at the ready. Mom has her hair up in a messy-bun, though thanks to the damp air and humidity, it's sticking up every which way possible, a lot of it clinging to her face.

"Are you sure about this, Josh?" Mom asks, voice soft. She tenses and looks around at the sanctum; tapestries depicting hell and the devil adorn the stone walls, a stone slab in the centre still dark with drying blood. Mom's hand tightens around Dad's as they take a hesitant step forwards.

Behind us, the stone doors slam shut, locking into place. "Crap." Dad pulls Mom back until they're pushed up against the doors. I watch them, like a phantom in the corner of the room, forced to observe their final moments, forced to watch them die.

Stop this, *I think, trying to get myself out of the vision. I didn't come in here to see this—I don't* want *to see this, but even if I squeeze my eyes shut and reopen them after a count to ten, Mom and Dad are still here, still against the door.*

Dad pulls an iron poker from behind his back—rusty and flaking, it must have been a part of the original set in the house. Dad brandishes it in front of him like a sword, like that'll help against the two hundred year old ghost.

"There's nothing else down here, Meg," Dad whispers.

"We've checked everywhere. No bodies. No hidden crypts."

Mom shakes her head, panic filling her movements as she tears free of Dad's grasp. She walks around the room, hand on the wall, pushing down every so often, like it'll give way to some other hidden passage.

But I already know there aren't any bodies; they are just confirming Aunt Josephine and Mr Heckney's suspicions. Once killed, Morcant disposes of the bodies in a way that leaves the spirits trapped here.

Which means I need to find the book.

Mom circles the room twice with no luck; no hidden panel opens, nothing shifts, and they're still trapped.

Dad, on the other hand, approaches the stone slab in the centre. I walk up beside him and swallow down the bile that rises in my throat as I look down at the blood that has pooled in the slab.

"Honey?" Dad says, beckoning Mom over. I watch as she approaches the slab from the other side. "Blood's fresh."

"Someone recently died," she murmurs. Mom spins in a slow circle, glancing warily up at the top of the chamber. I do the same, noticing what has to be the old entrance from the church. But the whole thing looks like it's been covered in cement, to either stop anyone else from entering or trapping him in.

Dad nods sadly and dips the iron poker in the blood. The tip of the poker catches in a small hole on the side of the slab. "Well, would you look at that." Mom and I quickly turn to him. "I'd say there's enough blood down here to belong to the spirits trapped here."

"Meaning we have something to burn?"

The blood. *Why would Morcant risk keeping something like* blood *around for so long? But I lean over with Mom and Dad, and gaze down the drain. Unless...he probably had it drain straight into the earth, meaning it would be impossible to burn.*

Dad, probably thinking the same thing, shakes his head. "There must be something else. The blood is tethering the spirits to the house, no doubt, but I don't think that's what's trapping them here."

Mom sighs and a low laugh rumbles through the room. "Morcant," she says. Mom, the bravest woman I know, takes a step towards the sound and narrows her eyes at the figure that appears beside me.

My breath catches in my throat as the demon himself fazes into existence.

"Let this be a lesson to you," he says, his voice carrying like a whisper on a breeze. "You cannot stop me. No one can."

The vision ends abruptly, leaving me standing alone in the chamber, West and Connor at my back. I blink once before noticing Blaire's body on the cold slab, eyes closed.

I suck in a breath and rush over to her, feeling for a pulse. "Connor!" I cry, looking over to see him jump up the stairs with West hot on his heels. The boys gather around Blaire's unconscious body. "We need to move her *now*, before he comes back."

As I say it, the doors slam behind us, trapping us in here—with *him.*

Laughter rises from the thickening silence as the room descends into darkness, our flashlights flickering out. Cold air seeps into the room, chilling me to the bone as my heart rate quickens, my chest tightening.

Swallowing, I take Weston's hand. His fingers tighten around mine, cold and calloused.

"*Well*," the voice whispers, so close that I feel a breath on my cheek. "*What have I caught?*" Morcant's honey voice grates against the stone walls, both loud and soft in my ears. I shudder. Fingers of ice brush the back of my neck. "*Four tributes now.*" I wince as the phantom hand of ice clasps around my throat. "*I like your kind. They put up a fight, thinking they can defeat me. No one can defeat me.*"

Connor makes a sound in the back of his throat before crying out. I listen as his flashlight drops to the stone floor and rolls away, as he falls along with it. But I can't do anything to help him.

Behind me, something tugs sharply at my bag, pulling me against the stone slab Blaire still lies on. My hand is furiously ripped away from West's, cold fingers wrapping around my own instead. The tugging on my back doesn't stop until I'm pinned against a wall across the room—completely split up from my friends.

"I'm going to finish you, Morcant!" I shout, trying to pull myself away from the wall, but the grip doesn't release me. "I'll be the one to end you!"

A face, white and sunken, appears in front of my own; the man wears spectacles over his black eyes, his moustache dripping blood, like he's been drinking it.

The demonic spirit looks me over with a calculated eye, lips upturned in a sardonic smile. My breath catches in my throat as he steps closer, so close now that our noses are almost touching. "Do you really think you can take me on?"

I still can't move, can't push away from the wall, but I pull a trapping bag from my back pocket and drop it at my feet. The incantation leaves my lips, in an almost silent whisper:

"Hear me spirits as I speak,

Be trapped in fire,

Within the veil,

And hold until you are no more."

Morcant laughs as the bag catches fire, now the only light in the room; it casts the room in a soft, orange light, giving me enough time to see Connor gripping the side of the stone slab, Blaire's hand over his as she tries to sit up. West is on the floor too, hand outstretched towards me.

Swallowing, I meet Morcant's eye as his lips split into a nefarious grin. As suddenly as he appeared, he's gone, fazing out of sight. It doesn't mean he's left us, though.

Whatever force slammed me into the wall finally lets me go, and I fall heavily to my knees beside the still flaming bag.

"You okay?" Connor asks, struggling to his feet. I watch as Blaire throws her arms around him, crushing him into her. She nods furiously, smothering her face into his chest.

I release a breath of relief and turn to West, who is still on the ground.

"We need to get out of here." Climbing to my feet, I stumble to the door and push against it, my shoulder throbbing harshly against the stone. It won't give.

We're still trapped.

I slam myself against it again, listening as stone scrapes but doesn't budge.

Groaning, I pull away from the locked doors and run a hand through my hair. There *has* to be another exit out of here, *something*.

West moans from the floor, touching a hand to his forehead as he tries to push himself up into a sitting position. "What happened?" he asks, cursing softly under his breath. Thankfully, he makes no move to stand.

"Morcant trapped us in here," I reply, dropping my bag to the floor. I open the side pocket and pull out a box of matches and a metal tin of lavender, salt, before striding over to the slab.

The hole is right where Dad pointed, half-coated with old, dried blood. It has a plug, and when I lift the small stone circle, the putrid smell of festering blood hits me.

Blaire covers her nose and slowly stands from the slab, keeping one hand on Connor as she does. "The hell is that smell?"

Grimacing, I take a tentative step back from the hole and shake my head. "Blood. Lots of it." My three friends groan in unison. Slowly, I pour the mixture into the hole before pulling a match from the box. I strike it, watching as it splutters to life. Without a word, I drop the flame into the hole and watch as it falls into whatever pit that's down there.

I strike three more matches and drop them in, one by one, until smoke starts to rise and I'm sure *something* down there is burning.

"Is that what you needed to do? To get us out of here?" West asks.

As if on cue, the stone doors scrape open. Both Connor and Blaire take a step towards it, but I hold up my hand. "Mr Heckney said we need to find the book."

"I think what you did was enough," Blaire snaps, but she hesitates, Connor still by her side. Finally, they've figured out that listening to me is safer than going off on their own.

Weston grabs my hand, and we watch the doors completely slide open, giving us a perfect view of the water-logged hallway beyond. Water slides down the stone walls and drops from the ceiling, hitting the stagnant water with an echo. But there are no spirits lingering, no Morcant or my parents, no Bonnie and Ethan.

There is no one, and to me...that seems odd.

Swallowing, I pull my hand from West's and stalk towards my bag, hitching it over my shoulder. Overhead, I hear scraping, and quickly fall back into line with the others, grabbing West's hand once again.

At the very end of the hall, a spirit appears, half-hidden by a bend in the hall. *Bonnie.* I watch as she completely disappears, going back to what I hope to be the entrance.

So far, she's helped more than anyone else. If any spirit can get us out, then it'll be her. "Come on," I say, motioning towards the door.

Carefully, we check ourselves—West takes hold of the back of my jeans once again, while taking Blaire's shaking hand. Connor takes up the rear, one hand in Blaire's, the other clutching at an iron poker. *Dad.* My friend nods to me, and I turn away, blinking tears from my eyes.

Leading the way, I drag us back through the waterlogged hall, down the bend where Bonnie disappeared. She appears again, her face still half-hidden.

Not half-hidden. Half-burnt. Had setting fire to the blood in the slab been enough to untether the trapped spirits? Been enough to start the process? Or will I still need to find the book? Morcant could *easily* stop the fire should he choose to; he's done it before, countless times. Nothing is stopping him now...

Unless this is what he wanted.

My chest tightens as we come around the bend, losing sight of Bonnie. We're getting closer to the grate, to the body.

I cast a quick glance over my shoulder at the others; West meets my stare, eyes full of fear, and Blaire doesn't look up from the sloshing water. Connor looks away, the iron poker still gripped in his hand.

We pass underneath the manhole, and I pause, searching the water. "It's gone."

"What is?" West asks.

"The body." I point to the manhole, where the skeletal remains fell through. "It's gone."

The four of us move to stand in a circle underneath the manhole, and I look up into the dark square above us. There is no way the body could fully disappear; not without being physically moved.

So, where did it go? It isn't beneath the water; I kick my foot through the murky liquid and feel nothing hit the toe of my boot, and it isn't like there's a current. The water down here is stagnant, unmoving.

No, there's something else down here, playing with us. I can't be sure if it's just Morcant growing stronger or if there truly is another entity among us.

I kick the water one last and time and listen as the sloshing sound echoes throughout the tunnel. "Let's go."

28

THE DEAD DON'T CHOOSE

WE'RE BEING FOLLOWED. I sensed it almost as soon as we made our way up the hidden stairwell. But I say nothing to the others as we wind our way up and back to the second storey of the house into the halls of the dead. Waiting for us is Ethan, but Bonnie isn't at his side.

My heart skips a beat as we stop before the boy, his corporeal body fazing in and out of sight. Something about the wideness of his eyes makes him look alive again—and not in a good way. Those eyes, so similar to Weston's, are so full of human fear that it makes me pause.

From the corner of my eye, I spot a streak of white cross the hall and enter another wing of the house, disappearing almost as soon as I spot it. It reminds me of the hunt that brought me here— of Brock and his white jersey. I pause and glance between Ethan and the far wall. Beneath one of the long-forgotten paintings is a long, deep slash in the faded wallpaper. My breath catches in my throat. For the life of me, I can't remember if that was there before we went down into the catacombs.

Behind me, West tugs on my jeans, stopping me. We stand in the centre of the hall; I cast a quick glance behind me to check for the Reaper, but there's no way for me to sense it around us. It's not in the hall behind us anymore, but it's somewhere. The hall to the front of the house stands before us, completely open.

Part of me wants to turn us around and go back down into the main foyer to wait out the rest of the night, but another part of me needs to know if there's anything else here in the house with us.

If we *are* being hunted.

No spirit could leave that kind of mark in the wall, not even Morcant.

Heart thundering, I continue down the hall, *away* from the gashes. If anyone else has seen it yet, they've made no comment about it. That makes it easier to ignore.

A chill shudders through my body, and another flash of white crosses the corner of my eye. My grip tightens on one of my spirit bags, and I let the flashlight in my other dangle from my fingers in a looser grip, ready to use it as a weapon if I need to. If anything comes out at us, I'll be ready—I have to be.

Floorboards creak behind us, and I turn, flashing the light in the direction of the sound. My breath catches in my throat, and my heart drops into my stomach.

A blank, white face stares at us, long-taloned hands stretching out, as if ready to pluck Connor from the group. A growl stretches from its mouth, a dark crimson dripping from its exposed teeth.

Fresh blood.

No. Has it gotten to someone else? Someone outside?

I don't give myself the chance to think before screaming, *"RUN!"*

I push the others in front of me, giving them a head start

down into the main atrium of the house. Hesitating, I speak as calmly as I can into the trapping bag and throw it at the creature before dashing after my friends.

The creature roars, though I doubt it has anything to do with what I've done. It isn't a shriek of pain, but more like a battle cry— a *hunting* cry. It's caught our scent, and it's ready to take us— *me*—down.

Following the others, I leave the hall and take the stairs down two at a time. The wood beneath my feet shudders at the pressure and gives way, my ankle rolling under the sudden snap, but I force myself to continue. I breathe in short, painful gasps as I bound to the bottom of the stairs.

West is the first to skid to a stop, pulling Blaire between him and Connor. His dark eyes meet mine, and without thinking, I'm reaching for his hand. He pulls me into him, wrapping himself around me, and I raise the flashlight to shine over the top of the stairs.

Nothing is there.

I almost collapse, but West's arm stops me.

"The hell was that, Hunt?" he asks. He's managed to keep his voice low, but I hear the urgency behind his words. He's afraid— and he should be.

I suck in a breath, shaking. "That was what attacked Darren and me. That's why I was in the hospital." I meet his stare. West's mouth opens in both awe and fear. Blaire has started crying again, though her tears are silent, and Connor...he looks more in shock than anything, though his face hardens when I look over to him. "It's a Reaper."

"A Reaper? Like, scythe, takes you to hell, that kind of Reaper?" Connor asks.

I nod hesitantly. "It's trapped here, kind of like the spirits. Only it can be controlled. Specifically, by Morcant. Technically, from what I know, Reapers *should* be more powerful, but this one..." I shudder, thinking about how it came after Darren and me. "This one has locked onto me. My spirit. It wants to add me to the collection." As I speak the words aloud, tears well in the corner of my eyes, and my fingers tremble. I glance down at my hands—they look white in the darkness of the house, white like the Reaper. I shudder. "That thing won't stop, especially since it's in the house now with us."

"It wasn't in here before?" West asks.

Shaking my head, I quickly wipe away the tears and straighten. It isn't fair on them for me to break down. "No. I don't think it was. I mean, unless Morcant had it hidden away, but it would have been on us almost immediately." I furrow my brows and shake my head again. "Unless..."

"Unless it came in *after* us," West says. He and Connor share a look before glancing down at me. Is it possible that the Reaper came in *after* we did?

Blaire sobs and Connor wraps his arm around her tightly.

None of us say anything for a long moment, all too wrapped up in the possibility that there *is* a way out of here. We just have to figure out where.

I bite my lip. "If we find a way out, then you guys need to go. Go get my aunt and Tate, and leave me here."

West starts shaking his head, but Connor meets my gaze, eyes hardening. Gone is the Ken-doll, the boy who couldn't take anything seriously. "Okay."

"What the hell man?" West asks, turning to his friend. "You seriously want to leave Hunt here?"

Connor glances from West to me, and nods. "She knows what she needs to do, dude. We're only slowing her down."

West starts shaking his head again, but I stop him from saying anything else. "This is what I do, okay? This is *my* job. None of you should've had to witness any of this. And so you need to *leave*, let me finish this."

"Like hell!" His eyes darken, and he takes a step towards me. "Hunt, my *brother* died in here. And I'm not leaving you."

"And so did my parents," I reply, stiffening. "So did a lot of other people. West, look around you. There are *hundreds* of spirits trapped in the walls of this place—old, young, men, women. Morcant took whoever he wanted. Don't add yourselves to that list."

"You shouldn't have to do any of this alone," he replies, voice softening.

I shrug. "I won't. If you can get to Aunt Josephine and Tate..." I stop.

"Could we go back around to the front of the house? Is there a chance she's waiting?" West asks.

She'll still be trying to get to the old church. Trying to get down into the underground chamber. We've already seen it, been there, and we found nothing. If they go down there, and Morcant is waiting...

I can't finish the thought. Not because of fear, but because the Reaper is waiting for us at the top of the stairs.

West swears under his breath.

"That is one ugly motherfucker," Connor whispers. From the corner of my eye, I watch his hand curl around the iron poker. An idea starts to form in my mind, but I don't have time to contemplate it, not as the Reaper begins its descent.

We run. The Reaper clambers down the stairs after us, talons scraping against the wooden walls and marble floors. It could have caught us, but it's playing with us.

Connor leads the group this time, and he rounds a corner, guiding us into one of the old ballrooms. The high vaulted ceiling rises two storeys high and is made entirely of glass, though it looks like it was boarded once the house was left abandoned. An old grand piano sits in one of the corners, though two of the legs are broken, and the top is missing.

The doors to the ballroom slam shut, and we're encased in absolute silence. Blaire sobs quietly into Connor's back; West's hand tightens around mine. The Reaper, though, didn't get the chance to follow us.

I take another quick inventory of the room, hoping for weapons of any kind. I rush to a pile of debris in one of the corners and kick around until I find another iron poker, a solid plank of wood, and what looks like an old shotgun. I check the chamber. Two rounds are left.

Let's hope it works.

I take my findings back to the group; I hand West the plank and Blaire the iron poker. She takes it without complaint, but I think she's at the stage where she knows she has no choice.

Around us, spirits faze into solid beings; amongst them are Ethan and Bonnie, though they stand by the doors. My parents appear to my right, and the way they look at me makes my heart stop.

They recognise me.

Connor takes a step back, and we all fall in together.

At the head of the group stands Morcant; he leans against his cane, eyeing us with a threatening glare.

"It would be easier if you just *joined* me," he says. His lips don't move, though. It sounds like his voice is in my head. Blaire almost buckles, but she holds herself up. The fear she's carried with her since entering the house is gone. Now, she looks pissed. Morcant grins. "In the end, you will *all* be mine. There will be no pain, no suffering. You will join your loved ones."

I look over to Mom and Dad and notice their hands clasped. They have their heads cocked in that way that makes me feel like a child again, like I'm misbehaving, and instead of yelling, they're wielding their disappointment like a weapon to coax me into whatever Morcant wants. The last time they looked like that— *really* looked like that—it was the first day of middle school. It was just after our first move, and they were trying to get me to come out of my room.

I shake my head and avert my stare, turning back to Morcant.

Something scrapes against the doors behind us, outside. *The Reaper*. It stands guard as a warning—if Morcant can't take us, then the Reaper will.

I understand the threat.

Stepping up, I release West's hand. "Unfortunately for you, I'm getting sick of these games. I would *love* to stay and chat, but honestly, I just don't care. Your time here is over."

"Is it, though?" The demon in front of me smiles. His voice feels like nails in my head. "I have everything you want, little girl. Why not take my offer?"

"What I want," I reply, trying to keep my voice steady, "is my *living* family. Those two are only reflections of what they used to be."

Morcant drops the smile and the pretence and takes a measured step towards us. Above, the skylight rattles, and a wind howls outside. "I do not think you understand what it is I am offering you, girl. I am offering you immortality."

"We don't want that. We just want to leave and make sure you can't hurt anyone else."

His lips twist up in a sadistic smile, but he doesn't say anything.

"Huntliegh?" *Mom*. "Huntliegh, come with us. Please."

Dad. "You can do it, honey. We believe in you. We miss you."

I refuse to look at either of them, instead keeping my gaze on Morcant. "Nice try. But my parents would never want me to join them."

"Oh?" Morcant smiles. Ethan fazes into being beside him, and my parents join him. Behind me, West chokes. "But they do. They all do. They want you here, with them. And if you decide not to…"

The other spirits around us start burning, their corporeal

beings turning to ash before our eyes.

"They disappear, and not in the best way, child. Now, what do you choose?"

29

THE BOOK

A STRONG FORCE KNOCKS INTO OUR GROUP, splitting us apart. The deadlier spirits—the ones we saw in the parlour when we first came into the house—take on physical bodies. It's harder for them to do, but with their pent-up rage and the backing of Morcant, they're able to do as they please.

One man—he looks like an escaped convict, with shackles and a bloody mouth—swings at me. I duck. Rage is thrust upon me, followed by a throbbing pain in my temple. Another spirit reaches for me, and this time lands a blow.

Standing amongst the riled spirits is Morcant; his lips turn up in a mocking smile, and he tips his hat towards us before disappearing entirely, leaving the spirits around us to finish the job.

I pull three spirit bags from my pack and throw them into the crowd. Three of the dangerous looking ones succumb to the trapping spell, but others fight their way to the front.

"Got any more of those?" Connor asks.

I hand him one of the spirit bags. It falls into his palm, and he closes his fist around the velvet. He repeats after me.

"Hear me spirits as I speak,

Be trapped in fire,

Within the veil,

And hold until you are no more."

We throw the bags into the crowd, trapping another four.

West holds himself against a gnashing woman; her teeth are covered in something black, like she came straight out of a horror movie. I throw a bag in his direction and trap her before she can take a chunk out of his neck. West sends me a thankful look before using the plank of wood as a bat, swinging it in an arc to keep the spirits away.

Bonnie, still half-burnt, appears before me. She, too, has taken on a corporeal body, though instead of attacking us, she fights the other spirits. She's younger than most, that's clear, but while the rage in the older spirits—the ones who've been here longer—is wild and uncontrollable, it seems hers can be focused. I watch in awe as she fights back, controlling herself enough to inflict real damage.

Ethan does the same, as if learning from Bonnie. He uses what strength he has to stop an older spirit in its place before it can attack Blaire. They both faze out of sight.

The doors behind us creak open, and I half-expect the Reaper to appear to finish us off, but there are no flashes of white, or talons, or bloody teeth.

Bonnie appears in front of me, eyes wide as she says, *"Go!"* I look to the others, but they're fighting the spirits.

"Connor." I hand him my pack, pulling several trapping bags out as I do. I also hand him the shotgun. "In case the Reaper returns."

"What about you?" he asks. He doesn't fight me, though, and takes what I give him.

"I'll be fine," I reply, looking back to see Bonnie, but she's gone. "But be careful."

"You too." He motions for me to go, and I do.

Bonnie parts the crowd from the doorway enough for me to escape, and I run for the front of the house. I hear the fight raging on in the ballroom. A pang of regret shudders through me, but I shake my head.

They'll be fine. Bonnie and Ethan are protecting them. They'll be fine.

I look up the stairs and meet Morcant's stare. No longer does he look arrogant. Instead, he looks afraid. *Why?* Out of the corner of my eye, I see a girl—one of Delilah's friends, wearing a twisted smile on her face.

I realise then that I haven't seen Delilah since entering the house. Where is his daughter? Trapped somewhere else?

Morcant tips his hat and starts down the hall.

And like an idiot, I follow. He leads me through the house and disappears around corners before I can reach him.

The demon stops before a closed door and disappears behind it.

Should I follow? It's a suicide mission. For all I know, the Reaper could be waiting inside, ready to tear me apart before I can blink. But if that were the case, why hasn't it attacked me already? Why not rip me apart while I'm standing here, hesitating?

If Morcant *really* wants me dead, he would have done so by now, right? He wants something else from me. Something to do with that room.

I reach for the handle and twist it; it's cold to the touch, almost like ice.

The door opens slowly, and I step inside.

~ ~ ~

The bedroom looks untouched, even after years of remodelling, use, and abandonment. But it's clear this bedroom once belonged to Delilah Morcant; pink lace sheets cover the large, four-poster frame. Curtains of lace are tied back around the bed, and pillows cover the surface, surrounding a lump under the sheets.

Not a lump. I cover my mouth with my hand, noticing then the body of the girl laying in the bed.

She looks as if she merely sleeps, like she hasn't been dead for the last hundred and sixty odd years; her dark curls are neatly spread around her head, and her lips are red and plump, like she'd just applied lipstick. And her skin... It looks like porcelain, like it'll break at the touch. She wears white ribbons in her hair like an innocent child.

I don't understand why, but Morcant is gone, leaving me alone with his daughter.

I know this room...

A small altar stands by the boarded window, and the old, leather-bound book sits open on the table. Four lit candles surround it, along with a bowl of blood beside it.

It's the book from my vision.

The book.

"What the hell?" I whisper aloud. I stride over to the altar and pick up the book, flicking through the pages. It feels like any other book, and yet, I sense something different about it. Something that makes my blood turn to ice. *MEGHAN AND JOSHUA PARRISH, ETHAN MACKENZIE, BONNIE HECKNEY.* I find their names along with their date of death. Along with everyone else still trapped in the house. Morcant's name is there, too, but not Delilah's.

Why isn't her name here?

"You should not be here."

I spin, clutching the book to my chest. Delilah looks me over, her spirit as solid as Morcant's. She eyes the book before meeting my stare, but I sense the anger flaring within her. There are two of her—the one standing before me, and the other in the bed.

Without thinking, I throw the spirit bag at her feet, whispering the incantation.

But nothing happens, much like how nothing happened when I did it to Morcant. The girl in front of me laughs, though there's no amusement in her cackle. She takes a step forwards and reaches for the book. "Give it back. It does not belong to you."

"And it doesn't belong to you, either," I whisper, tightening my grip on it. She cocks her head. "Don't you want to be free? Free to cross over and be away from your father?"

The smile that twists her lips sends my heart into my stomach. "I will be free, but I need the book. Hand it over."

As she takes another step, Morcant pulls her back with gritted teeth.

Around me, the world turns black.

~ ~ ~

The old church appears first; darkness surrounds it, the moon hanging in the sky like a giant eye. It watches over the several people that wander onto the Morcant Estate, watches them enter the church, but I doubt it will watch them leave.

Standing at the door, Delilah Morcant smiles pleasantly at all who enter. She hands them brochures and bibles. She even wears a pretty dress the colour of lilacs. But there's something sinister hiding in her eyes as she greets each person; a family of five, an older man whose smile is darker than hers, two older women who fuss over how pretty Delilah looks. More and more enter the church, maybe twenty or so, before she finally walks in and closes the doors behind her.

I follow at a slower pace and walk through the walls like a spirit. Standing at the head of the church is Morcant himself. He wears black robes, like a minister, but there's no cross around his neck, no Jesus icons. There's confusion in the eyes of the people in the church. They expect to worship god on this night, but they see no god in this room.

Delilah strikes the group first, slicing open the throat of the man who had eyed her like a piece of meat earlier.

All the while, she smiles in relief. She smiles like she's at peace.

Screams erupt throughout the hall; one of the older women faints while a child starts crying. Several try to get to the doors, but one of Delilah's friends—I saw her spirit wandering the halls of the house—blocks the exit, a hammer poised in her hand, ready to strike.

The other friend stands behind Morcant, and it's then that I see the fear in his eyes.

I stumble back from the slaughter. I watch Delilah and the girls kill every single person in the church. There is no sacrificial ceremony, no drinking of blood or bathing in it, no clear worship of Satan.

It's a bloodbath, sure, but it's more like watching a slasher film.

I wince, looking back to Morcant. He watches me with fearful eyes. The other friend holds a knife to his back. He does nothing to stop his daughter from killing the churchgoers.

He does nothing to stop anything.

~ ~ ~

The scene changes, and now we're in the underground altar room. One of the friends lies atop the cold stone, grinning up at Delilah while Morcant stands back.

"You must stop this, Delilah," he says. The other friend stands beside him, the knife once more poised at his back. "This is not God's work!"

Still looking down at her friend, Delilah smiles and slits the girl's throat. I cover my mouth with my hands, determined to stay quiet; I'm sure she'll hear me if I make a sound.

Delilah sighs, and with her bloody knife, she turns around. She eyes the blade, then looks over to her father. "How would you know anything about God's work? You claim to worship him, but you killed my mother in cold blood. That was not God's work." Morcant purses his lips. "You were also able to fuck the maid under the watchful eye of God without repercussions, and then you killed her too, to keep her quiet. Why are my actions judged more than yours, Father? Is it because I am a girl?" He remains silent, watchful. She laughs that bitter laugh of hers before turning back to her now dead friend. She stopped sputtering blood only moments before. "With her sacrifice, I will live again. With all their sacrifices, my Lord Satan will give me life in another time to do his bidding."

Morcant starts shaking his head again. "And I will stop you."

Her smile disappears. "You will do no such thing."

A flash of grey appears in the corner of my eye. This time I make a sound as I stumble back.

The Reaper looks different here, less terrifying-alien and more human. It has the features of a man, with a straight nose and wide lips. Robes of grey cover its body. Red eyes focus on Morcant.

The Reaper doesn't answer to Morcant.

It answers to Delilah. And he, too, is afraid of it.

Morcant's face turns white as the blood rushes from his head. He begins to shake. He is no longer the feared man he once was. No. He created the monster that is Delilah, and he regrets everything.

The Reaper attacks, and the vision disappears.

~ ~ ~

I take a step back, away from Delilah and Morcant. *This was all her.* Delilah Morcant, who has been mourned as another victim of her Father's ruthless murders, is really the mastermind behind everything. She was the one trapping the spirits in this house, was the one who committed the murders that closed this house down originally. She sacrificed her *friends* for her own gain.

Taking another step back, I almost drop the book.

Delilah smiles ruefully and takes a threatening step towards me. "You should not have seen that."

Before she can take another step, two spirits appear, fazing into reality.

My parents. "Mom." Hesitation sweeps through me. If I burn the book, then they'll be gone. And standing in front of me now, I'm not sure if I can do that, not when she looks so normal, so alive.

My mom has always been beautiful, just like Aunt Josephine, and I remember Dad mentioning how he always wondered why she chose him. Mom is beauty-pageant gorgeous, with the personality of a Nobel-peace-prize winner. Her smile can light up a room, and her wrath can start a war.

And the way she smiles at me now, I see that piece of life, the piece that told me she is really my mom and not the shadow of her. "Mom..."

She steps forward and hushes me, lifting her hand as if to touch me. Behind her, Morcant holds onto Delilah, but I can't be sure how long it'll last, if it will at all.

I turn back to Mom and then see Dad. "Daddy...what do I do?"

Dad has always looked like a nerd, with his glasses and freckled face. His thick mass of dark waves are always messy, and he could never quite get around without stumbling over something. But when he's with Mom, I can see why they love each other; apart, they're opposites—Mom with her fiery attitude and Dad with his cautionary manner—but together, they fit.

Even in death, they fit.

I sniff. Dad tries to smile, but it comes off pained. "Burn the book, sweetie. Get rid of it."

I look between them. "What about you?"

Mom speaks this time, her voice cracking. "Our time is up. It's time for you to release us, like you do with all the other spirits. It's time for all of us to go."

Behind her, Delilah screams, the sound echoing in my ears.

"Quick," Mom says, motioning towards a pack of matches. "You don't have much time."

I suck in a breath as a tear slips down my cheek. They're right, I have to set them free, have to burn the book and release the other spirits, but the thought sends my stomach roiling, because this will be it. This will be the last time I see them until death comes to collect me.

Dad looks behind him, then back at me. "Now, Hunt, do it now."

Delilah breaks free of Morcant's grasp; she roars and thrashes, and somewhere in the house, her cry is met. The ground shakes beneath my feet, and the chandelier above us breaks, smashing at her feet. When I look over to her, the whites of her eyes have taken on a red tinge.

Working for the devil, definitely, I think, and grab the matches.

The book falls from my hand as I strike the match. I let it fall and pull a small canister from my back pocket. *Gasoline.* My other pocket has the salt and herbs. The match hits the open book, and I pour the liquid over the pages. I drop the cleansing mix next.

Fire reaches for the ceiling, and Delilah screams in agony.

Backing away from the book, I cough as the smell of smoke reaches my nostrils. My parents watch me from behind the fire, and I watch them burn, too, as the flames eat at their names scribed in their own blood.

Morcant and Delilah burn slower, though. She watches, horrified, as she slowly turns to ash. The body in the bed disintegrates, too, as if following her lead.

Josiah Morcant smiles happily for the first time since I met him, before the fire finally takes him too.

Delilah stumbles two steps towards me, the snarl on her face enough to make me back up further. But she screams one last time before the book burns her with it.

"Huntliegh!"

I collapse as the door to the bedroom is wrenched open. West stands in the doorway, face covered in sweat. Blood wells under his nose, and a bruise covers his cheekbone, but he looks otherwise unhurt. I notice Connor and Blaire behind him, too, but I can only meet West's stare as the room catches fire.

Part of me wants to stay, to join my parents as they cross over. It would have been easier, right? To let myself succumb to the flames, like I imagined I would.

But another part of me recoils from the idea, especially with West and Connor and Blaire watching me. The doors should have finally unlocked. Why didn't they get out? Aunt Josephine will surely walk in now with Tate and Mr Heckney at her side.

You need to get up, Mom's voice says in my head. *You need to get up and live.*

A flash of white—*no*, I realise, *grey*—catches my eye as the Reaper streaks across the bedroom. The creature stills as the flames reach it. It's no longer tethered to Delilah. It looks like the creature from my vision, the Reaper it had been before.

Relief hits me and so does gratitude.

The Reaper is finally free.

It takes me a moment to find my footing, but when I do, I clamber over the bed, narrowly avoiding the ashes of Delilah's new body. West reaches for me and grabs my hand, pulling me into his chest.

"The fire..."

"Leave it," I croak, coughing. "It's time this place burns."

I meet his stare, and he nods. Blaire grabs my other hand as we start back towards the front entrance. Behind us, the fire licks at the rest of the house.

The main doors to the once great fortress slam open; Aunt Josephine's red hair looks as wild as the fire, pulled back from her face in a blue bandana. Then I see Mr Heckney with a handkerchief covering his nose. Tate and Riley follow. Their eyes are on us as we race down the grand stairs of the Morcant Estate and exit the house.

Blaire pulls away and throws her arms around her sister. Aunt Josephine reaches for me, and I let West go, allowing her to engulf me in her arms. The fire starts to consume the back of the house, creating a warmth at our backs.

Aunt Josephine coughs and meets my eye. "What happened? What's burning?"

"The house," I say. "I'm burning the house."

Her brows lift, but she says nothing more about it. She barks orders for everyone to leave.

The house is finally burning, and there's no one left to stop it.

30

THE BURNING TRUTH

WE WAIT UNTIL THE HOUSE IS WELL and truly burning before reporting anything, though I have no doubt someone has already called in the pluming smoke to 9-1-1. It takes them roughly ten minutes to get here, and by then the fire's high enough to engulf the house and bring it to the ground.

In the strangely quiet moments before the sound of sirens reach us, there are thoughts so clear and yet so terrifying that it would have been easier to just...toss them into the fire as well. And yet I don't. I let the thoughts burn like the embers and ash that rain down on us.

The firefighters hesitate before putting out the fire. We stand back and watch them, all silent. "Good riddance," one says.

"I knew people who went in there and never came out. The place needed to go down," says another.

Connor's and Weston's parents arrive not long after, and by

then we've corroborated a story good enough for the officials to believe. *We went in because it's Halloween, and that's what stupid kids do. Someone saw our flashlights and called our parents. We got locked in, and there was someone else in the house with us, following us. By the time we made it back to the front doors, our parents and Mr Heckney kicked in the door. We don't know where the other person is.*

It's believable because that's what the police have feared; that someone has been squatting in the house, taking out any who trespass. *A copy-cat killer*, the deputy calls the lunatic. *He deserves to burn.*

The paramedics arrive not long after, mostly to check on Blaire. We told them she was grabbed by the guy and dragged down into the cellar where she was knocked out. The paramedics determine that she has a concussion and will need further medical attention. The boys only have minor scrapes and bruises, and I'm lucky enough to only have bruising on my arms, one paramedic says.

It doesn't feel that way, but I smile nonetheless and thank him.

Aunt Josephine and Tate lead me over to her car and make me sit down on the old leather seat. West follows and so does Connor. Riley wanders over while paramedics tend to Blaire, giving me a little shake of her head. Hopefully, someone explained to her what's going on.

"What really happened in there, Hunt?" Tate asks, leaning against the side of the car.

I sigh and rub my eyes. Every breath burns with the smoke from the house. "Morcant *wasn't* behind any of the murders, or the trappings, or any of it."

"What?" Aunt Josephine kneels down in front of me. I meet her stare. "What do you mean?"

I release a breath. "It was all Delilah."

Aunt J frowns. "Morcant's daughter?"

I nod. "She was the one who massacred the church. She and her friends. It was in rebellion to what her father did to her mother." I recount what Morcant showed me in her bedroom, detailing how the spirits were tethered to the book, rather than to their bodies. When I burned the book, I was able to set their spirits free. I told Aunt J about Mom and Dad, and how the little boy who trailed Bonnie was really West's twin brother.

Aunt J rocks back on her heels when I finish, rubbing a hand over her face. "Unbelievable. But they're gone, right? No more evil spirits?"

"I watched them burn," I say slowly. "I think they're really gone."

My aunt releases a breath, and a tear slides down her face. The lines of stress that once marred her face seem to visibly ease. "I never thought I'd see the day."

"What I don't understand completely is why," Riley says, wrapping her arms around herself. "Why you guys? I mean, I get that your parents were killed by the crazy ghosts that actually *attacked* us, but what I don't understand is why he handed himself and his daughter over now."

I shrug. "I don't either, and I'm not sure if we ever will."

Riley looks less than pleased with that answer, but she doesn't say anything else. And to be honest, I don't care anymore.

The thoughts that were burning along with the house come tumbling from my lips. "I don't think we were alone with the spirits the entire time."

Aunt J pauses. "What do you mean?"

I bite my lip and look to my friends. "When Connor and West and I went down to look for Blaire, we found what looked like a manhole, so we opened it. There was a body. When we came back through later, it was gone."

"That could have been a spirit," Tate says, rubbing his cheek.

I shrug. "You're right, but I dropped a match down into where they drained the blood. It didn't do much, but it weakened the spirits—the ones allowed down in the catacombs."

"And the only spirit we saw down there was Bonnie," West says, shoulders tensing.

I purse my lips and force my gaze back to Aunt J. "Where is Mr Heckney?"

~ ~ ~

Aunt J and I find the old man sitting alone in his living room. The scene would have been amusing: the fire crackling in the hearth illuminating his side-profile, the glass of amber liquid in one hand, while the other grips a faded photograph of his daughter.

Very sad.

I step into his line of sight and cross my arms. "Want to explain what the hell you did back there?"

Heckney's lips pull down into a frown, disgust igniting in his eyes. "Those aren't very nice words."

"You almost got us killed," I snap. "The *actions* I'm about to take won't be pretty either. I don't think the police will care if you're handed over to them with a black eye."

Heckney's gaze meets mine. "What do you want me to say?"

"Admit you sold us out—all of us. Me, Aunt J, my *parents*. Admit you *fed* Delilah Morcant victims and hand yourself over." I take a step forwards.

"I might as well kill myself." He chuckles humourlessly, fingers tightening around the objects in his hands. His eyes drift away from mine, and he goes back to staring into the fire. "I have nothing else to live for."

My hands are trembling, the breath in my tightening lungs sharp, agonising with every breath. "You have taken everything from me."

"It was nothing personal." Heckney doesn't meet my eye. "But I never intended for you or your friends to be caught in the house. I thought you would be safe from them."

I shake my head. Behind Heckney, my aunt shifts uncomfortably. "You were going to sacrifice what was left of my family?" I ask.

"You're a strong girl," he replies quietly. "You would have found a way to survive."

Any words get caught in my throat as I stare down at him. I didn't want to believe it, but I can't deny how it all makes sense. Heckney was in the middle of it all, and I didn't see it—none of us did. He was the architect of our failure.

But I succeeded.

We escaped. We survived.

"Blaire will name you as her kidnapper," I say quietly, his gaze drifting back to mine. There's nothing within his once familiar eyes. "The police are on their way. You'd do best not to fight the arrest. We're all going to testify against you, and you'll be locked up for the rest of your miserable life."

For the first time since arriving, Heckney downs the amber liquid in his glass in one gulp. He drops the empty glass to the floor, and it hits the carpeted ground in a muffled *bang* and rolls towards the fireplace. I flinch as he sets the photo frame on his lap.

When he makes no other move, I contemplate forcing him to stand but I sneak a look at Aunt J, who shakes her head. She reaches out a hand towards me, and for the first time tonight, I see her exhaustion; her shoulders slumping forwards, her skin pale, the hems of her jeans and long coat wet with mud.

Our eyes meet. "Let's go home. We'll let the authorities handle him, Huntliegh."

My breath escapes me. I've been wound so tight since leaving the burning ruins of the Morcant house that I haven't taken the chance to breathe.

I hesitate before returning to Aunt J's side. I bite the inside of my cheek as I spare Heckney one last glance. "I thought you were our friend. Someone who wanted an *end* to all the death. I thought you were on our side."

"Perhaps I might have been, once," he replies. "But no. I was never a friend, Huntliegh Parrish."

I close my eyes and fight back tears as I step away from him. Aunt J's hand catches mine, and she pulls me close, wrapping an arm around my shoulders.

I don't fight her or the exhaustion as we make our way to the car. Tate waits for us, leaning against the driver's side door. Otherwise, we're alone in the night.

Tate asks Aunt J about what happened, and she explains that Heckney confessed. I don't listen as Tate makes a quick phone call—probably to Mr Contreras, who'll tell the police.

Instead, I close my eyes and let the night carry me away into a restless sleep.

~ ~ ~

In the coming days, news outlets flood Fort Caldwell, clamouring for an inside scoop into the *Morcant Copycat Killer*. The story going around town is this:

Four local teens thought they could stay the night in the old Morcant house, a feat no other has accomplished. But once their friend went missing within the walls, they tracked her down and uncovered one of Fort Caldwell's deepest and darkest secrets. That same night, they named Albert Heckney as the one responsible for locking them in the house and hunting them. The girl who was taken confirmed she saw the older man.

After years of not knowing anything, the town quickly jumped to believe this story.

Heckney was arrested that same night. I don't remember anything else about what happened once we left his house, or how I ended up in my room. But I haven't left the house since, content in staying within the safety net that surrounds it.

Even if I wanted to leave, it'd be difficult. Reporters have been lurking outside for days. Not even Weston and his family have left their house.

My phone is heavy and cold in my hands, silent since Halloween. I don't blame my friends for not wanting to talk to me. I inevitably put their lives at risk.

I blow out a heavy breath and drop the phone onto my comforter. I close my eyes as a shiver racks my body.

I was supposed to die October 31st, but despite the odds, I lived. I freed my parents' souls. I stopped an evil spirit before she could take over an entire living town. And I saved my friends.

I completed the mission.

But somehow, I still lost.

EPILOGUE

"IT'S NO BIG DEAL," I SAY, STEPPING OFF the curb, hazy sunlight glaring down at me. The landscape that surrounds the prison is dry, a far cry from Fort Caldwell and the lush forest enveloping the town. "Aunt J, I need to do this."

On the other end of the phone, my aunt is quiet, which isn't one of her usual traits, but I also don't recognize the painful *silence of disapproval* I usually face. "*It's a school night,*" she replies quietly on the other end of the phone.

I crack a smile, but my heart races even harder in my chest. "I'll be back at a reasonable hour."

"*I don't like the idea of you being in the city alone.*"

My only other option would have been to bring Tate, but he dislikes the city more than Aunt J, and I doubt he would have come quietly knowing where I'm going.

Darren has finally recovered, and I think he and Tate are ready to pack up and leave Fort Caldwell. Darren doesn't blame me for what happened, either, but I still blame myself. Part of me wants him to stick around, him *and* Tate, but I can't ask them to do that. There are still things they have to do without me and Aunt J.

"I'll be fine." I try to say it with enough conviction that she has no other choice to believe me, but even I hear the slight tremor in my voice.

Aunt J sighs. *"Be careful in there, Hunt."*

"I will."

"Love you."

"I love you too." The call ends, leaving me alone on the sidewalk with only my own thoughts to keep me company. There are others here—adults, a couple of moms with children—though they primarily keep to themselves. An older woman approached me earlier to ask me why I'm here, but otherwise, no one cares about me.

My stomach squeezes as I approach the prison. Everything is a blur of bright, buzzing lights and blue uniforms, steel-grey walls and the smell of metal. The guards don't look twice at me until I'm inside the visitor's room; a short line of desks with thick, bullet-proof glass separating me from the dangerous criminals. I pass three men with shaved heads who are too focused on their visitors to meet my stare.

There's an empty space between the third man and Heckney. A part of me is grateful for the potential privacy, but my heart rate speeds up as I take a seat, feeling like I'm too far away from anyone who could potentially help me.

Fear, icy and sudden, spears through me as I take in my first glimpse of Heckney in months.

"Hello, kid," he says after I sit and pick up the phone. I tighten my grip around the thick black plastic.

"Hello, old man."

A bitter smile cracks across his dry lips. "When they told me I had a visitor, the last person I expected was you."

Leaning back in my chair, I watch him for a moment. His hair is shorter, more grey than white, and there is a peppering of stubble lining his chin and cheeks. But he's thinner now, gaunt, the bones of his face and hands protruding against the skin.

But looking at him now, I see a man who had a hand in ruining my life and killing my parents, who helped trap my friends with a psycho ghost who wanted to give herself a new body and live again.

"Why'd you do it?" I ask finally. "Really? Why side with the psycho who killed your daughter?"

This time, Heckney lets the silence linger. We only have an hour, and yet even that feels too long. The silence drags, droning out the conversations at the other end of the table. Heckney and I watch each other until I can't take the silence any longer.

"Well?" I ask, drumming my fingers on the metal table.

The corners of his lips lift up in a mocking smile. "Desperation, my girl."

I can't help but scoff. "Seriously? You led Hunters to their deaths because of...*desperation*? Your *desperation* killed my parents?"

For a moment, Heckney looks away. Anger burns in the pit of my stomach. I hope he feels shame and guilt. I hope it's eating away at him like it eats away at me. I hope he's suffering with the truth, that it keeps him awake at night. I hope he doesn't feel any peace.

I bite the inside of my cheek as my cheeks flush.

"When Bonnie died, I lost everything. My wife was dead, my brother a right old jerk, and I had nothing." Through the thick plastic window separating us, I catch the blur of tears in his old eyes, but he blinks them away. "I went into that house, you know. To find her. The police could give me nothing, and I thought they were full of shit. So, I walked in there thinking I would not return."

"That was like, forty years ago," I reply. "Did you ever regret what you did?"

"Of course." He releases a heavy breath. "Every time. But you must understand, I saw what my life could be, if I did what they wanted."

"Morcant and Delilah?"

He nodded. "It was around this time that they added security to the house. There were no longer enough spirits to sustain them. They needed more and they were not getting any. So, they made a deal with me."

My shoulders tense. "You get to have Bonnie in your house, so long as you send in Hunters."

Again, Heckney nodded. "It was not ideal. Throughout the years, I sent many souls into the house. There was always a part of me that hoped they would succeed, but I never gave them what they needed to do so."

"The book? You knew about it?"

"Indeed." His posture changes, and he leans forwards. "I only ever caught glimpses of it in dreams. I've always been susceptible to the supernatural, you know. I didn't think much about it until a Hunter said she saw something similar in a vision. She told me about how Morcant and his daughter would write the names of their parishioners in a book of theirs. It fit the story in my head. But it was Bonnie and Ethan who confirmed it for me."

I wanted to say something about Ethan and how he should have done something then to stop Morcant, but one look at the old man, and the biting comment dies on my tongue.

"After that, I sat on the information. A couple of years later, your parents roll into town." His eyes meet mine. "I almost told them, the day they came to me."

I stiffen. "Why didn't you?" Part of me doesn't want to know, but I need answers. "You could have stopped it all back then."

"Desperation and cowardice. I did not want to lose my Bonnie, and I was afraid of what might happen should your parents fail."

"But you told me."

Heckney's gaze softens as he releases a breath. "We were running out of time."

I lower the phone and sit back, mind a whirlwind of information. Tears burn behind my eyelids, threatening to spill while another part of me wants to throw up. I'm not sure what I expected, but knowing he had a way to end this all *before* makes me sick.

Slowly, I pick up the phone again and watch him.

"You have allowed the life of hunting to consume you, as it consumed me," he says, voice low.

"I am nothing like you, Heckney. I never sacrificed innocents for my own selfishness."

Heckney narrows his eyes. "Haven't you?" he asks, leaning forwards.

On instinct, I lean back, pulling the cord of the phone taut. The words strike something inside me; would I have turned into Heckney, if given the chance? If I was with my parents when they were taken, if I didn't have Aunt J or Darren and Tate, would I have regressed and chosen to sacrifice others to see them again?

I don't want to tempt the idea, but it burns deep in my gut.

Heckney makes a sound and sits back in the metal chair. "Thought so."

I scowl. "You implied I already have."

"Did you not risk your family by going to Fort Caldwell to avenge your parents? Did you not then risk the lives of your friends to finish the mission?"

"Because you put us in that situation!" I hiss, fully aware that guards can, in fact, hear us, and probably think we're insane. It's probably assumed for Heckney, but I want to escape here in one piece. "And I didn't just *go* to Fort Caldwell, I was led there. That wasn't on me."

I suck in a breath and release it slowly. "If it weren't for you, we would never have been in that house. But Delilah would have *won* if it weren't for us. She would have gotten herself a new body. *You* were aiding a literal *demon*."

"I only did what I had to do to make sure I could be reunited with my child. Like you made sure you could be reunited with your parents."

"But we are *not* the same, Heckney. What you did... You took Weston's twin *brother* away from him. You took my parents. You almost killed Blaire." I remember the fear and guilt that pulsed through me when we realised she was gone. Morcant—or Delilah—sending so many spirits to confuse us, their emotions sent to torture me.

It sends an ache through me. I should have done better.

I purse my lips as he speaks again. "We are not very different, you and I. The life we were thrust into consumed us, but you chose a path of righteousness and revenge, while I chose to simply survive. You Hunters live like the spirits you hunt; you protect the living right under their noses, but you are never seen, never make an impact in the lives of those who cannot see beyond the veil. But you, Huntliegh Parrish..." He pauses and cocks his head. "I watched you grow in those weeks. I watched you change. But your nature... That is something you will never escape."

I bite the inside of my cheek to stave off a stupid retort. No matter what I say, he'll always think the same. He doesn't see what he did as wrong. I can't be surprised.

But I hoped that maybe he changed.

I was wrong.

"Don't let the spirits fool you, Huntliegh Parrish." His gaze turns watery as he stares down at me. "Death comes to all those who walk the line of darkness. Only we know to fear it."

I shake my head. "I don't fear death."

"Perhaps you should."

To that I hang up the phone, but my gaze never leaves his. An alarm sounds above my head, so loud it makes my ears ring, but I try not to let it distract me from the man being escorted from the glass.

His words are an echoing whisper in my ears as I follow security guards and weeping, angry women out of the visitor's room. My heart thumps to the beat of my footsteps, hurried and loud, as I retrace my steps through the prison. Once again, everything is a blur of grey, dark shadows dancing in the corner of my vision.

I slip through the guards and people like a ghost, a ripple in the everyday workings of their lives.

Maybe, like Heckney said, I'm not built for normalcy.

~ ~ ~

Warm rain brings me to the present, where I wait for a Greyhound bus.

I don't know what awaits me back in Fort Caldwell, besides the life I worked so hard to maintain. Certainly nothing normal, not anymore.

Blaire and Riley are gone; they weren't able to take the constant coverage, so Mr Contreras packed them up and moved to the other side of the country, where they can have a fresh start away from the *Morcant Killer*. I can't blame them, not after what they were forced to witness. I wanted to protect them from it, but instead they were dragged into the middle of it all against their will.

But I still speak to Riley on the off chance she has a question about spirits at midnight or wants to send me pics of her new cat, Auggie. She doesn't blame me, but I can hear the uncertainty in her voice sometimes when she tells me how Blaire still wakes up with nightmares. I might not have been the direct cause of her suffering, but if it wasn't for me, there's a chance her sister wouldn't be in this kind of pain.

Unfortunately, I don't think losing my friends is something I can blame on Heckney. I did that to myself.

A group of older women in knitted cardigans wielding canes and umbrellas make for an approaching bus. I look up in time to see that it isn't mine before directing my stare down at the grey sidewalk. Spots of rain darken the cement.

I pull my phone from my pocket and see two texts. The first is from Aunt Josephine, just to tell me we're having family dinner tonight, that I should try and get home before sundown.

The second is from Connor.

We still hang out, strangely enough. More than I thought we would. We've gotten closer since our night in the Morcant House, the night that led Connor to figure out what he wants to do with his life. I've tried to talk him out of it, but there's a determination in the way he studies the occult that even I admire.

I never would have taken Connor as the type to hunt ghosts, but he slid into the role so smoothly I might have thought that he's been doing this for years. The ability to see them hasn't stopped him; enough work and training can give someone the sight, especially after a night in the Morcant Estate.

The text, like most between us these days, is a screenshot of an article from at least twenty years ago, and a single question: *is this ghost related?* Sometimes it's a simple yes or a no, depending on whether or not I ask Aunt J to check.

I don't respond straight away and instead pocket my phone. I'll leave it for the two-hour trip back to Fort Caldwell as something to occupy my mind.

But my mind is a traitor, and so is my heart.

My thoughts stray to the prison and the night that changed

everything. I got my revenge and set my parents free. I should be moving on, and yet I can't. Heckney is in my head and I can't shake him.

After three days of solitude, locked inside my bedroom, I came to a decision about my life: I don't have one, and I never will. Paired with sobbing, reruns of *Supernatural* where I skip any and all episodes that have anything to do with spirits, and maybe enough ice cream to make me lactose intolerant, wasn't sure what to do.

In the span of one night, I lost two friends, a man I thought was on our side, and my entire understanding of the spirit world.

What was always simple now made less sense; spirits *rebuilding* their bodies, books written in blood to trap the dead, demons...

I release a heavy breath as I wait, heart aching.

I didn't lose Weston straight away...

He tried, but things were changing. His parents considered moving, but he was adamant on staying. For me.

They still packed him up and left.

These last couple of months have been tiring. I try not to think too hard about everything that happened. I'm lucky enough to still have my family, to have Connor. School is almost over, and then I'll figure out what to do.

I don't want to run anymore, to go job to job without having a real life.

More than anything, I want to *live*.

The rain steadily grows heavier, so I slip beneath a shelter and fit myself between a pregnant woman and her wide-eyed toddler and an older gentleman who smells like tobacco and spearmint.

Through the haze, I try to keep an eye on the buses coming and going, but there are so many people constantly crossing my path that I'm not sure which bus is mine anymore.

And then I see him. The busy streets don't take away from the soft, boyish charm that radiates from him; the way his hair falls over his forehead, dark and wet, or the plain sweater half-tucked into his jeans. A backpack slung over his shoulder drips.

I haven't seen him in over a month now. We've texted but I've kept my space. Heckney's words continue to ring in my head as the sky fully opens, drowning the city in a torrential downpour.

I try to turn, but his eye catches mine, and I pause. My heart turns to thunder in my chest as Weston stumbles to a stop in the middle of the sidewalk.

I suck in a breath, but I don't hide. I don't run.

Entering the miserable rain, I shove my hands into my pockets and rush to Weston's side. He doesn't seem too bothered by the downpour, but I can feel droplets running down my spine like the cold touch of a spirit, which is enough to have me grabbing his arm and pulling him towards shelter beneath a shop's awning.

"Hey," I say once we're finally free from the rain, but I don't look him in the eye. Shame curdles deep in my gut.

"Hey."

Hearing his voice sends a tremor through me, one filled with longing and hope. Missing him has felt like a deep ache in my chest, and no matter what I do, I can't get rid of it. Weston was the first person to show me that life—a normal, mundane life—is worth living, that not everything has to be about the job.

I clear my throat as a beat of awkward silence passes between us. "You live here now?"

West releases a heavy breath. "Hunt, please."

I purse my lips. "What?" Before I can stop them, tears burn my eyes. Weston doesn't sound the same.

"Look," I start, as he says, "Hunt."

Fear grips my heart as I finally look up and meet his gaze. "You first," I whisper, unable to trust my voice.

West hesitates and drops his hand. "You have no idea how terrified I was that night, Hunt. To see you fighting *ghosts* and then to see you want to give up." The slight tremble in his voice almost breaks me. "Why did you want to give up?"

"Because I thought it would be easier," I whisper, mouth dry. "Because I thought it would be better for you all if I just...died with my parents. That was my plan originally. Sacrifice myself for the overall good of the people, make sure Morcant couldn't hurt anyone else." My head spins as his gaze bores into mine. The truth is like a faucet I can't turn off.

"Would you have still done it?" he asks. "If I weren't there, would you have sacrificed yourself?"

"Yes. Like I said in the tunnels, I wasn't prepared to get out of there alive," I answer him honestly, and watch as his heart breaks when I do.

A tear, or maybe it's a runaway raindrop, slips down his face. He hastily wipes it away. Tears sting my own eyes, but I push the feeling away.

"So, that's it?" he asks. "You wanted to die. Is there anything worth living for, in your eyes?"

"I chose life." He meets my stare, and another tear slips down his cheek. "I chose life, because in the time I spent with you, with Connor and Blaire and Riley, I realised that I *liked* living. And I..." I shake my head. "I wanted to at least try for more."

"You were still ready to walk away though." He glances towards an oncoming bus. The pregnant woman and her toddler rush towards it, the child with their hand held tightly against the onslaught of rain; I wish I was with them, escaping this. "I still lost you in the end. You disappeared after that night."

I bite my tongue. "I didn't mean to."

"But you did." The steady pounding of the rain grows lighter around us. Through the angry grey clouds, the sun threatens to break through.

Weston releases a heavy breath and scrubs a hand over his face. "But I was no better."

"You didn't have a choice, your parents—" But I stop when I see the look in his eyes. A fear so vulnerable it makes my heart quake.

I let him down in Delilah's bedroom. I was prepared to give up when he believed in me so fiercely.

"You wanted to leave?" I whisper through the loud pounding of my heart.

Shame and guilt turn his cheeks a dark red as his eyes flicker from mine. "I wasn't sure what I was fighting for anymore, Hunt. Mom and Dad wanted out of town because of Ethan, but I..."

"What did you want?" I ask.

West looks away, jaw clenched. "I wanted to try *us*. I wanted *us* to work, because almost losing you that night *hurt*."

My heart stops in my chest as our eyes meet, and I can't help the tears that drip down my face. A sob lodges in my throat, and although I try to wipe away the tears and the effect he has on me, I can't. Because I want that too. I want *us* to work, to be real and not some kind of last-minute death wish of mine.

Can I do this? Can I finally move on from Morcant and my parents' death and embrace this new life? This life of not chasing death and expecting it to find me around every corner?

I have to try, not only for myself, but for West and Aunt Josephine, and everyone else in my life. I owe it to them and me.

"I almost lost you," he murmurs, taking a step closer. "I almost lost all my friends. But you...you're the strongest out of all of us. Seeing you almost *give up* after everything? And then the radio silence. I lost you all over again. Blaire and Riley were gone and you and Connor..."

I swallow as he backs me against the exposed brick behind us. He reaches one hand up to tuck a stray lock of hair behind my ear before resting his warm palm against my cheek.

"I don't want to lose anyone else," he whispers finally, dark gaze boring into mine.

My heart flutters, and for a moment, I forget where we are, who we are, and only see a flash of what life can be; college in a town not overrun by ghosts, where my only worries are projects and whether or not I'll see Aunt J on the weekend, where I don't have to *pretend* to be normal anymore.

I don't think I'll ever escape the spirits that still roam this world, and one day I will want to go back to hunting. It's the one thing I know I'm good at, the one thing I know will help people.

But I'll fight a little harder and, hopefully, longer.

Smiling, I take Weston's hand under the lights of the city street where we stand forgotten in the shadows of an awning. Here, nothing can get to us.

Not even the ghosts that haunt us.

THE END

SIGN UP TO STEPHANIE ANNE'S
NEWSLETTER FOR MORE
INFORMATION ABOUT UPCOMING
RELEASES, FREEBIES, AND MORE!

SIGN UP NOW TO GET AN
EXCLUSIVE LOOK AT
"THE UNHEARD STORY OF
DELILAH MORCANT"
A SHORT STORY

ABOUT THE AUTHOR

Stephanie Anne grew up in different parts of Australia before her parents settled down in a small beachside town in northern New South Wales when she was twelve.

There, she developed her love of reading, and began penning *The Lost Prince Of Cadira*, amongst other books.

Currently, she is in her third year of Griffith University, completing her Bachelor of Arts in Creative Writing and Literary Studies.

https://www.stephanieanneauthor.com/

Acknowledgments

I need to thank you, the reader, first of all. *The Haunting Life of Huntliegh Parrish* was a dream, a need for something like *Supernatural,* but more ghosts. I loved *Ghost Whisperer,* and I loved *Supernatural,* but I wanted to see something that combined the two concepts.

That's where this story came from, that need for more female led stories, where friendship and love save the day. I grew up on shows like this, so I thought it was time to write about it.

I wouldn't have been able to do this without the support of my family: Emily, my sister, who this book is dedicated to, and my mum, Jenny. I also want to dedicate this book to Klaus, a man who watched me grow up, who supported me and my writing, who recently passed away.

I also want to thank my Alpha readers Dee and Taylor, who read the very first draft of this book for me. They were instrumental in the development of this story, and their help meant so, so much to me.

To Celin, my cover designer. Once again, she exceeded my expectations with this cover, giving me more than I ever expected. Thank you for working with me again, and thank you for creating such an amazing cover!

To my editor, Camilla, thank you for looking after my book. We had some problems, but you were amazing, and you truly kept the essence of the story in mind while editing. Working with you has been amazing, and I'm excited for us to work together again.

Lastly, to the beta readers: Leeva, Kassi, Jenny, Meghan, Abbey, Celia, Zoe, Shana, Jorgia, Christina, Hope. Thank you for reading the first half of this book: your feedback was everything I needed. Thank you.

CONTINUE READING FOR A LOOK INTO STEPHANIE ANNE'S SHADOWLAND SAGA

STEPHANIE ANNE

1

NEW ORLEANS

The hairs on the back of Eliza's neck bristled as she crept through the night. Barbs of ancient magic prickled her skin; it danced across the night with the power of a thousand stars, pulsing throughout the New Orleans cemetery like a dazzling conduit of enchantments and curses. The whispers of the dead were carried on the chilling autumn breeze, brushing over her skin like phantom fingers, sending a course of shivers up her spine.

The prickling sensation did not cease as her own magic formed a living barrier around her. It speared out into the night like creeping vines, connecting her with the essence of New Orleans and its dead, who lay in the maze of stone tombs around her.

Eyes followed her, their gaze watchful. Keys clutched between her steady fingers, Eliza stepped around cement blocks and withered flower bouquets, stopping before a towering white mausoleum, heart pounding in her chest.

In the branches, she heard the screeching caw of crows. They sat perched in the skeletal limbs of the dilapidated tree to her right, their beady eyes as bright as the stars that glared down at her from the sky. They continued their dangerous song, even as she glared from the shadows, but they were the only thing she could hear in the endless night.

She still felt it, though, that sense of not quite being alone. Despite the precautions she had taken to protect herself—charms sewn into the hems of her jeans, the iron ring on her pinkie finger—it did not stop the shiver of doubt that coursed down her spine. The sensation of being followed had sent her careening into the cemetery. The familiarity of the cemetery steadied her racing heart, but not by much.

Eliza's green eyes flickered over the shadows, searching the cracks in the mausoleums. They darted down the small alleys between the white stone structures that usually housed spirits who had been forgotten, bound to the land and not their resting places. Despite that knowledge, she let herself imagine she was completely alone with the dead. But even the dead weren't that quiet.

As if summoned by the deep entanglement of power, Eliza's magic rose and swelled until it surrounded her like a protective shield. A flash of silver caught her eye, and drawing in a shuddering breath, Eliza looked up to the space above the white marble mausoleum.

The air continued to pulse with that strange and dangerous magic; its ancient thrum drew her out of the darkness, sent her own magic spiralling back to her out of fear. In the back of her mind, she felt that ageless power whisper to her, a tangle of raw energy. The iron on her finger heated. Something told her to run.

Her blood ran cold, fear rearing its head. She wanted to turn around and run, but she was caught between terror and stupid curiosity.

Silver moonlight reflected off a drawn sword; Eliza's gaze travelled up the shining blade to the armoured hand that held it. Even in the dark, with the dim light of the city illuminating the cemetery, she couldn't mistake what she saw as she continued eyeing him—pointed ears and piercing green eyes. *Faery*. Lithe and tall, his silhouette stood out against the blankets of light that made up the New Orleans skyline. Only one thought entered her head as she took him in: *I am in deep, deep shit.*

Sitting on his shoulder, with irises of molten gold, was a raven with the darkest feathers. The ancient power she had sensed thrummed from that being, Eliza realised, as she took a hesitant step back. *A Changed One.* That deceptive power of Shifting radiated from the gold-eyed raven.

They were not of the mortal realm, where magic was squashed, and darkness lay in the hands of humans with power. Nothing as ancient as the Changed One, with its immeasurable power and immortal status, would be caught dead wandering through the mortal realm, or following Eliza through a New Orleans cemetery. And she knew they had not been banished to this world, either. Not in the same way she had, not like Kay.

They were something else entirely. They did not belong here.

Eliza ran.

Mausoleums and graves stretched out around her, filling her senses and her vision, until all she could see was death—perhaps even her death, too.

A Faery Knight and a Changed One. She snorted, even with the fear drumming deep in her bones. Never in her life had she felt such power, and never before had she imagined it would be directed at *her*. It both terrified her and excited her. But she knew to run first and ask questions later.

I'm terrified of a freaking bird, she thought. Eliza skidded to a halt and swore. Standing by the exit, the Knight waited, his ancient sword still drawn. His back was to her, and despite her situation, Eliza poked out her tongue before turning away. She eyed the mausoleums with frustration before running once again.

She knew the place better than the Reapers who guarded it. And she should have been able to get herself out. Overhead, the caw of crows signalled her appearance. But her gut told her it wasn't the mortal creatures who dwelled in New Orleans who gave her away.

Twigs snapped beneath her feet, and though she stayed upright, every so often her feet would snag on a piece of loose rubble or slip on stray flowers that had blown off the mausoleum doors. Eliza's breath turned to ice in her lungs as she continued her sprint through the darkness, only stopping when she slammed into the side of a soot-stained mausoleum, shaking free the dried flowers and layer of wet leaves that cascaded down her back.

"Shit." She hated the feeling of wet leaves clinging to her neck. They reminded her too much of slimy bugs.

Swinging around, she ploughed straight through the half-visible silhouette of a spirit.

Walking through a spirit was not like walking through air, especially when she—and she alone—could see them. For a regular mortal, or her grandfather or Kay, a spirit felt like a cold patch of air. For Eliza, it felt like stepping through a wall of jelly and coming out the other side unscathed.

The spirit in question took a dignified step away, her loud, "Excuse you!" filling the air. Eliza flinched and stepped into the safety of the darkness behind a mausoleum, though for the most part, she knew the Faery Knight and his raven could not possibly be able to hear the two-hundred-year-old ghost standing in the light of the waning moon.

"Hush up," Eliza said, forced to keep her voice low. They might not be able to hear Miranda, but they certainly could hear *her*. "Something is following me, and I need you to be *quiet*."

Eliza had met Miranda years ago by chance—the spirit had

been newly awakened in modern day New Orleans after being dug up in light of an old murder investigation… Or so Eliza had been informed by the young woman's spirit. Miranda had been shot in the chest, the bullet recovered—and matching that of a recent murder victim. It had been Eliza's first—and only—attempt in helping the spirits. At the time, it had been exciting, but Eliza had quickly learned how dangerous her magic could be in the eyes of mortals. It had been enough for her to be discrete with the power that came so naturally to her.

The spirit's gaze followed Eliza's; together, they half-heartedly searched the darkness between the mausoleums, even the rooves, but everywhere Eliza looked, she could not spot that flash of silver or the golden glare of the raven. That ageless magic still thrummed through her, though she couldn't feel the full extent of it anymore.

"Ahem." Miranda coughed, drawing Eliza's attention back to where they stood, back to the soot-covered mausoleum and the fences to her right. "What is following you? And will it cause *me* any harm?"

Eliza rolled her eyes, though her heart still raced in her chest—from the sprint and from fear. "I thought I was being followed by something…" *By a Faery Knight and a creature changed by ancient magic. Because, yeah, that'll go over well with the traditionalist.* She grimaced. Miranda knew nothing of the magical realm and its otherworldly occupants. Eliza wanted to keep it that way.

"Looked like a Knight," Eliza continued. "Maybe." She felt a pang of guilt lying to Miranda, but Eliza doubted she'd handle questions about her world, even if the questions came from a curious spirit.

Miranda followed at a distance as Eliza walked up to the fence and checked both avenues before setting herself up to climb.

"I do not believe I have ever seen a Knight here before," the ghost mused, her gloved hands resting over the top of her bloodied chest. "Was he handsome, like the Knights in Momma's fairy-tales?"

Eliza hesitated halfway over the top of the crumbling wall surrounding the cemetery. Below her, on the other side, the streets were nearly empty, as if the people of New Orleans knew to fear the cemeteries at night. She grunted, swinging her other leg over. "I was a little distracted," she said, sparing the spirit one last look. "I'll see you tomorrow, Miranda."

The spirit merely looked up at the wall indignantly, arms crossed tightly over her bloodied chest. "Good night, Miss Elizabeth. I do hope the bed bugs eat you."

Eliza laughed. Jumping from the top of the fence, she landed silently on the balls of her feet, and rose.

Just as quickly as she appeared, Eliza made sure she disappeared. Knowing that she wasn't alone, that she was being followed, only made her move faster. Even in the swallowing quiet of the street and the enveloping darkness, Eliza felt eyes on her; eyes that did not belong to anything from this world.

Eliza shoved her hands into the pockets of her hoody and started for the road home.

Despite the darkness—the shadows that seemed to devour the light and feast on the stars—Eliza could find her way. Ever since she could remember, the streets of New Orleans' French Quarter was her backyard. The metropolis of light and colour, of people and customs, had swaddled the scared five-year-old when she had first appeared in the mortal world. And since then, she had sworn to care for them in the way they had her.

The old building Eliza called home appeared before her, sitting between two larger, modern blocks of wrought iron and red bricks. It had two storeys with a red-brick exterior and wraparound balconies, with rooms that held artefacts from another world and a courtyard filled to the brim with magic. Eliza couldn't imagine herself living anywhere else. Not in the mortal world, and certainly not in the world she had been born in.

Sometimes, she forgot that she was not entirely from Earth.

Sometimes, she wished forgetting were the easy part.

Standing across from the house, Eliza hesitated. Still, that feeling of being followed did not leave her. Had she been wrong to come straight home? *No,* she thought. Her grandfather would know what to do, surely.

She bit her lip and looked back down the street towards the cemetery. She thought the Knight would be there, watching her from the other side of the road. But there was nothing.

A light flickered on in one of the front rooms, then another in the courtyard. Pursing her lips, Eliza already knew what trouble would be coming for her, especially if her grandfather *and* Kay had sensed her arrival, and knew that midnight had already clicked over without so much as a word from her.

With a sigh, Eliza crossed the street, shoulders hunched. She stopped at the dotted line in the centre of the road, brows furrowed. The hairs on the back of her neck prickled once again, and her gaze darted behind her shoulder. She searched the dimly lit street for that flash of silver or the golden irises of the raven but found nothing. Not even a blip on her radar.

Nevertheless, she sprinted the rest of the way, skidding to a stop once inside of the wrought iron doors, then slammed them shut.

If they followed her home, they'd be pissed to know how fortified the house was. Magic protected them there, though it was only a whisper of what belonged in the other world. It was that sense of safety that calmed her racing heart.

Swallowing the lump in her throat, Eliza slowly uncoiled herself.

"Elizabeth." The darkness that surrounded the entryway receded as the courtyard lit up, revealing not only herself, but her grandfather, who stood in the doorway with his arms crossed. At his side, their flat-nosed cat, Odin, paced, copper tail twitching, one blue-green eye blinking up at her. Both, unsurprisingly, looked disappointed.

She stood at her full height—nearly as tall as her grandfather—and spoke. "I can explain, please."

Fortunately, her grandfather, Davis, was a forgiving man, but with his arms crossed and thin lips pursed, Eliza could not help but wonder if perhaps she was slowly destroying that trust he had in her. She had promised to be home by eleven, and yet the large grandfather clock in the courtyard continued to tick past midnight, until it was closer to the witching hour than her curfew.

"Something was following me," she said, releasing a heavy breath.

Almost like breaking a trance, her grandfather sighed and shook his head, silver hair mussed. Odin ran into the courtyard situated at the centre of their house and beckoned them to follow. At a distance, Eliza walked behind her grandfather as he said, "Something is always following you." His voice was soft, not reprimanding, but not forgiving either. Tired. "What was it today?"

At seven, she had constructed an elaborate story about how she had become friends with the gnome who walked her to the babysitter's on Fridays, and at age ten, Eliza had claimed an ogre had been following her home from the park one day. Saying something was following her wasn't a surprise, and she knew that. It didn't stop her heart from dropping; the lack of faith she felt from her grandfather stung.

But Eliza hesitated nonetheless, biting down on her bottom lip. It wasn't that he would not *believe* her, but Eliza knew the story of the boy who cried wolf too many times. But still, she tried. "I'm not lying," she said, following him into the courtyard. Sitting at a wrought iron table and chairs, Kay poured three cups of tea.

"Or joking. Something is *out there,* and it was following me."

Kay, who had been in her life since Eliza first entered New Orleans, sat with her thin arms crossed over her chest. Eliza's first memory of her was bright and magical; the New Orleans city park and the Botanical Gardens; willow trees with limbs reaching for the grass, children running through the gardens. Eliza had been five. Kay had told Eliza about her own world, of a girl lost to her people for a crime she did not commit.

Eliza's grandfather did not turn around as he said, "I did not say that you were." His voice took on a softer tenor as he pointed to one of the faded, paint-chipped chairs. "Sit."

The inner courtyard of their home was decorated like that of a movie set, Eliza thought, like something a Hollywood director imagined up about how Witches or faeries lived in their enchanted homes. Creeping vines dressed in white, black, and red roses climbed up the walls and over into the balconies, creating a wall of flowers. It was like nature was slowly reclaiming the foundations of her home. Taking up one side of the courtyard was a garden, tended to by Kay, and in it grew plants that would not usually survive the New Orleans climate, or the mortal world's limited magic.

At the other end of the yard was the grand, mahogany grandfather clock her grandfather had brought from their world, and it, too, had been overtaken by the creeping vines that filled their home.

Kay slid her the cup of steaming peppermint tea with a tight-lipped smile; the older woman withheld her disappointment, but Eliza could see it sparking in her violet eyes. "Took you long enough to get home," she said.

Eliza merely shook her head, exasperated. "Like I said, I can explain." Her guardians remained silent as they watched her. Davis had finally taken his seat at the table and sipped slowly at the cooling tea in his withered hands, while Kay stretched her arms out. Odin, too, joined them, sitting at his own place on the fourth chair.

A strange sense of foreboding settled over her, like the other shoe was about to drop. Almost like a snap, and it was gone. It left her feeling somewhat apprehensive, anxious as she stared down at the swirling mint tea. But she could not shake that feeling of being watched, of being observed by the raven and the Knight.

Fae, she reminded herself, rolling her eyes. *Fae were following me.* She couldn't be sure if that had anything to do with the blood-relation she had with the immortal creatures, but she wasn't entirely sure if she wanted to find out. Eliza knew little of her heritage, other than that her parents had been close with Kay and Davis, and that any blood relations she had were long dead by the time she had stumbled out of the portal and onto the streets of New Orleans.

Some nights, that lack of knowledge—the unanswered questions and the forgotten memories—left her feeling hollow, like a large part of herself was missing.

For the most part, she played it off. Her family—the only one she had and the only one that cared—were in New Orleans, in the world she'd been exiled to. But she feared asking questions would separate her from the only family she had.

In the twelve years she had lived here, Eliza had never felt so alone as she did when trying to explain herself to her guardians. It twisted in her gut as she looked at them, and she knew it didn't really have anything to do with the fact that she claimed to have been followed—it had everything to do with how she didn't belong to the world she loved.

Eliza met Kay's stare, then Davis's, and cleared her throat. "The museum had some late visitors, out-of-towners who clearly could not read our closing times. There was a creep who wouldn't leave too." Her boss had let her leave through the back, but she didn't mention that, nor that the creep had made more eye-contact than Eliza deemed appropriate. "I got out at about eleven, and I felt *something* following me. I decided to cut through the cemetery, and I saw them."

Kay's brows shot up, but those violet eyes of hers remained unworried. "Who?"

"Ghosts follow you all the time, dear," her grandfather reasoned, reaching a weathered hand towards her. Something in his eyes darkened, and for a moment she thought she saw recognition flare in his silver eyes. "Most of the time, you do not notice them. Perhaps these ones realised you could sense them and took to following you to get your attention."

Heat flooded her cheeks, but she shook her head. "It wasn't spirits! I can tell the difference," she said, a bit indignantly. "Anyway, I doubt *Fae* spirits wander around New Orleans like a bad smell."

If she had wanted a reaction from her guardians, Eliza did not get it. Kay's eyes darkened, while Davis's lips thinned, but neither of them said a word.

Eliza looked between them. "I'm not making this up," she said, slumping in her seat. In the chair beside hers, Odin meowed loudly. She ignored him with a twist of her lips. "There is a Faery in New Orleans, or is that something you won't believe?" Despite herself, anger thrummed deep in Eliza's bones, making her fingers clench and her heart beat erratically in her chest.

The grandfather clock struck one, and the courtyard filled with a twinkling faery song to announce the hour, almost like it was mocking Eliza and her fear. But fear of what? The truth of it brought her stomach into her throat.

Faeries are tricksters, Kay had told her once, years ago. *But they are ancient, and they are deadly.*

Eliza wasn't even sure *where* she fit on the mortal spectrum, what with the traces of Faery blood and magic pumping through her veins. That uncertainty left her feeling alone, *different*. Would she master immortality like Kay and Davis? Or would she wither and die while her family lived on?

Davis cleared his throat and pushed his tea aside. Her grandfather locked eyes with her, a white envelope now tucked into his hands. "I cannot believe that you are almost ready."

Curiosity swelled within her, despite the anger and indignation she'd been feeling moments before. Almost like a switch had been flipped, Eliza focused on him rather than the Fae. "Ready for what?" she asked quizzically. Her eyes dropped down to the envelope.

Davis slid the paper to her, though did not release his grip. His fingers shook. "There is much that you have not been allowed to know up until this point. What I am about to give you will change your life, but it does not have to change you."

Eliza cocked a brow; her whole life, she had known there was something more to her training, more to the reasons why she was forced from her home world of Cadira and into the throng of the mortal realm. Though she dreamt of the life she could have had in Cadira, she had grown to love New Orleans, for the city and its people had raised her as one of their own. Perhaps she was going back—back to the world that had thrown her away, back to the world she had no memory of, other than the copper scent of blood mixed with crisp air and death. Perhaps her grandfather was ready to send her away, or at least tell her *why* she was even in New Orleans in the first place.

But... Eliza shook her head, something deep within her revolting at the idea of going back. A sudden seed of fear wedged itself in her gut at the thought. *No,* she thought, swallowing thickly, *I'll never go back. Not if I have anything to do with it.* She wanted to know about her past, about her life before New Orleans, but not at the expense of losing everything she already had and loved.

As if sensing the fear Eliza tried to withhold, her two

guardians shared a look of despair and worry.

Eliza clenched her teeth and slowly dragged the envelope towards herself. "Is it from Cadira?"

"Yes, it is," Davis said quietly, folding his hands together. Eliza noticed the small tremor in his fingers. Did he know? Was he aware of what was written within the letter? "I never thought it would come this soon. I honestly thought there would be more time."

Her heart pounded as she slid her nail beneath the envelope's seal. With every movement, her hands shook from trepidation. What was it? She wondered if the letters contents would change everything.

First, she noticed the smell of ink that bled through the parchment, strong and sharp against the perfumed smell of roses that wafted from the paper. Roses made her think of a woman, perhaps a relative of hers, but she couldn't dredge up a memory. Was one of them contacting her at long last? Eliza tried to think of the possibility, and realised if it were a Cadiran relative, then they had probably learnt of Eliza's upcoming eighteenth birthday, though it was still at least five months away. Based on what she'd learnt of Cadiran politics and customs, Eliza would be preparing for her entrance into society, if she still lived there, that was.

No, she thought, with an inner shake of her head. Her hands shook as she held the letter, unable to open it. Maybe she was to be drafted in some war for the king; she was technically still a citizen of Cadira, and there were whispers that a war was brewing on the horizon. Perhaps she was to fight with her magic.

Or...

Eliza slammed down those thoughts and pulled the parchment apart to read the bleeding, inked words:

Elizabeth Kindall, daughter of the mountain tribes,

apprentice of Portal Keeper Davis Kindall.

By request of King Bastian III, you are hereby invited to the Winter Palace to stand before His Majesty to honour the agreement held between your guardian, Keeper Davis, and His Majesty, the king. For reasons best kept secret for your safety and the kingdom's, you will be expected by the entrance of the closest wards by sunrise, one week from receiving this letter in your realm.

In the name of the King and his followers,

His Royal Attendant.

A breath escaped her dry lips as confusion swelled within her. *An audience with the king?* Either she royally screwed up or there was more to her past than she expected. Best case scenario, it could be a royal pardon for whatever crime had sent her to Cadira. She wasn't sure, not when she had no memories of her time in Cadira. Worst case, a claiming or an arranged marriage. *Don't rule out the possibilities yet*, she thought, biting her lip, *the king could want anything.*

The only thing she cared about, however, was if she'd be back in New Orleans by the end of that day.

The king... It had to be a joke. Eliza searched her guardians' faces for an answer, but they were closed off from her.

Catching her stare, Kay sighed. "Kid..."

That fear she had almost forgotten gripped her tightly as she gazed upon her two guardians. Even her grandfather had tears pooling in his dark eyes. Their pale faces seemed to crumple at the sight of the letter.

Eliza knew little about her king. The line of Cadiran royals ended with him, though there were rumours of an illegitimate child hidden somewhere and a hope that the son stolen from him, his true heir, was still alive.

The first time Eliza had heard about the legendary attack on the king, she'd been twelve. Kay had described the brutality of the event; the dead queen and princess, the prince stolen from his crib, the mass murder of every soldier and staff member who happened to get in the way of the intruders.

A shiver danced down Eliza's spine.

"What does this mean?" she asked, pushing back a tangle of hair that had fallen over her face. Only moments ago, she had been worrying about a *Faery* in New Orleans following her. "Do the Fae have anything to do with this?" She *was* distantly related to the immortal creatures that dwelled beyond the Willican Forest, and they were following her.

Davis frowned, shaking his head, but Eliza saw something flash in his eyes. "Let King Bastian explain it all to you."

Outside their home, Eliza could hear the distinct song that was New Orleans; late night jazz music drifting up from Bourbon Street, muffled rumbles of traffic, the occasional wail of a siren, and the cheers that sporadically arose down the street.

Everything that made New Orleans home, she realised, would be taken from her. The king wanted her to go to Cadira for an audience. Would she ever return?

Eliza tried not to let *that* fear shine too brightly in her eyes.

"Let the king explain," Kay said finally, eyes still glistening with tears. "Out of respect to him, let him explain."

Eliza shook her head, clenching her trembling hands into fists, feeling the sharpness of her nails bite into the soft flesh of her palms. "Fine." She slid out of her chair, sighing deeply.

Kay reached out a hand but stopped. "Eliza…"

Eliza merely shook her head. "I'm going to bed." A single tear slipped down her flushed cheek. "I'll talk to you in the morning."

Without another thought about the king's mysterious summons, Eliza shuffled into the parlour of the house and up the heavy wood stairs towards her bedroom. She passed collections of odds and ends, things that made her home magical and brilliant and exciting, things she knew would not go with her to Cadira.

Would she have to pack? Eliza considered the old, worn duffel she had shoved under her bed, the one with the hole in the side that Kay had patched with pretty satin from Cadira. She thought about her *Game of Thrones* t-shirts and *Marvel* socks and realised that none of those things had any place in that world.

To go to Cadira, she realised she would have to give up a critical part of herself; the normal, home schooled, museum worker, who listened to indie jazz bands in her spare time and had too many piercings in her ears.

The things she cared about... they didn't belong in Cadira; her smart-mouth and ripped jeans certainly didn't belong amongst the ruffles and tiaras of court. *She* didn't belong amongst the dazzling creatures of her birth world, no matter how much she'd once tried. She'd given up when she realised the reality of her situation—she wasn't sure if she fit there, and now she didn't fit in New Orleans either.

She released a breath; she was *meeting* with the king in his Winter Palace. That did not mean she had to stay there, right?

Eliza flipped the light-switch of her room; above her, constellations appeared so bright they lit up the ceiling; a legendary queen pointing towards the west, her crown pointing north, and in the other corner of her room, the Goddess Azula looking over her. Eliza's room was her only true connection to her birthplace, the closest she had ever let herself get.

The open window across from Eliza revealed the eeriness of the streets of New Orleans; the streetlights flickered on and off, and the buzz of electricity echoed in Eliza's ears.

Suddenly, underneath the floodlight, a form shrouded in shadows, appeared, his silver armour reflecting the light at odd angles.

Eliza took a hesitant step forward.

The Knight raised his head and met Eliza's stare. The gold-eyed raven, perched on his shoulder, cawed, as if calling for her to join them.

For some reason, Eliza deeply considered jumping from her window and disappearing into the night, leaving behind the worries of a desperate king and the expectations that were suddenly thrust upon her.

Before she could take another step, the light flickered again, and they were gone.

<u>WANT MORE?</u>
THE **FIRST 3 CHAPTERS** ARE AVAILABLE **FREE** IN STEPHANIE ANNE'S NEWSLETTER!

HEAD ON OVER TO *STEPHANIEANNEAUTHOR.COM* AND SIGN UP NOW!

THE LOST PRINCE OF CADIRA IS ALSO **FREE** ON KINDLE UNLIMITED.